# THREE BRAVE WOMEN

Linked through marriage to three brothers, the Underwood women prove time and again that they are a force to be reckoned with.

Jodie has travelled a hard road to reach prosperity, despite her husband's constant unreliability. Yet she can't sever ties with John.

Widowed at a young age, Laraine believes her marriage to Rick was perfect. Will another man ever be good enough to fill Rick's shoes?

Dee has everything she ever wanted: a husband she adores and a beautiful little girl. But she knows that her family's happiness is founded on half-truths.

# THREE BRAVE WOMEN

# THREE BRAVE WOMEN

*by*

Elizabeth Waite

**Magna Large Print Books**
Long Preston, North Yorkshire,
BD23 4ND, England.

British Library Cataloguing in Publication Data.

Waite, Elizabeth
Three brave women.

A catalogue record of this book is
available from the British Library

ISBN 978-0-7505-3981-4

First published in Great Britain in 2014 by Sphere

Published in Large Print 2014 by arrangement with
Little, Brown Book Group

Magna Large Print is an imprint of Library Magna Books Ltd.

Printed and bound in Great Britain by
T.J. (International) Ltd., Cornwall, PL28 8RW

# Chapter 1

## 1986

The huge iron gates of Lewes Prison slammed to with a loud clang, but John Underwood didn't look back. He kept his eyes to the front and did his best to put a spring in his step. He was dressed this morning in a pair of beige trousers, a fawn shirt with a brown tie, open-toed sandals and a navy blue blazer, the same clothing he had worn last May. Six months ago these clothes had fitted him. This bitterly cold November morning the blazer hung loosely on his much thinner frame and his trousers only stayed up because a prison officer had given him a safety pin to secure the waist-band.

John knew he had lost a lot of weight during his stay in prison, but he had also lost his pride. He still couldn't come to terms with the fact that he'd got nine months for not having a road tax disc. His own fault: he'd been given two warnings. It was laughable really when he thought of some of the madcap schemes he'd got away with. At least he'd had three months knocked off his sentence for good behaviour.

How he wished he had his heavy Crombie overcoat. Ten to one his mum had sold it or, more than likely, given it away. It was a shame but true: you wore the same outfit coming out of jail that you'd worn when entering that huge morbid-looking penal institution. What he did have was fifty pounds in notes and three pounds and fifty pence in change that had been in his wallet and his pocket on the lovely spring morning he'd been sent to jail. He also had a set of keys that would open many doors and some secure boxes in which he had stored documents out of harm's way, together with a few items which, when sold, would ensure he didn't starve in the near future.

His elderly mother smiled as she heard his key in the front door. She had just been on the phone to Jodie, her daughter-in-law. She loved that girl dearly, as indeed she did all three of the girls that her sons had married. Pity about John, the lovable scoundrel of the trio. He had joined the Royal Navy as a nipper and for many years he hadn't done too badly, considering the scrapes he'd got himself into. Within two years of him having married Jodie, and her still only eighteen years old, they had had two sons, and by God their mother had done her best for them from the day they were born. It was certainly no thanks to their father that both

Reg and Lenny had turned out to be good-looking and hard-working young men. What did still amaze Marian Underwood was the fact that Jodie had never sought to obtain a divorce from John, even though he had certainly given her grounds enough. It was also a fact that Jodie had been going with Philip Conti on a steady basis for years now.

John bounded into the room as if he'd only been away on holiday, threw his arms around his mother and held her close. During this spell in prison he'd come to realise that he missed his family. What had surprised him was that his wife had bothered to keep in touch, writing him newsy letters and telling him about the funny things that little Ann, the newest member of the family, was getting up to. Thinking of Jodie had kept him sane. Remembering the smell of her, and how lovely she always looked. He wasn't daft; he knew only too well how he had messed up with her over the years, and now he didn't stand even a remote chance of winning her back. At least they had remained good friends. Jodie had always been self-reliant, even in the early days when he had been in the Royal Navy and their two young sons had been little more than babies, and in spite of some of the dirty tricks he'd played on her, she had become a successful businesswoman. He hadn't heard a word from either of his sons during his spell in prison, but he knew he had no right to expect anything different. He had never been there for them and it was far too late now for him to attempt to be a good father. Smothering a deep sigh, he sniffed the air. 'Now why am I surprised that my dear old mum is cooking me a real fry-up for me breakfast?' he said, laughing loudly.

'Well, I might be dithery on me feet, but I can still cook, and it will be a pleasure to see you eat the plateful I'm about to set in front of you. I hate to admit it, John, but believe it or not, I've damn well missed you popping in and out.'

Marian Underwood was well into her eighties, yet there wasn't much that went on around her that she didn't know about, and she was not shy at expressing her opinion. As she watched her eldest son tuck into his eggs and bacon, she sipped at the cup of strong tea she had poured out for herself.

Her other two sons had taken after their father; their love of the sea had often made her think that salt water ran in their veins, and they were never really happy when on dry land. Both Derrick and Richard had aimed high and had achieved great things at a very early stage in their lives. Each had joined the Merchant Navy, studied hard and eventually gained enough credentials to become a Master Mariner. By the time they had met the young ladies they wanted to marry, they were in a wonderful position to offer their brides not only an unusual life but an exciting way of seeing the world.

Poor Jodie, she hardly ever complained, yet she must have felt at times that she had drawn the short straw with John. Whilst receiving mail from her sisters-in-law sent from all ports of call, describing their exciting lives with people to wait on them, Jodie had been left behind with two baby boys born within a year of each other. Time had flown by, and Reg, Marian's eldest grandson, was now twenty-eight years old and his brother Lenny twenty-seven. Both young men were a credit to their mother.

The morning was almost gone. John had spent more than an hour upstairs sorting out his clothes and deciding what he was going to wear. When he finally breezed back into his mother's kitchen, he certainly looked an entirely different man to the one who had left prison that morning.

'And where would you be off to now?' Marian asked as she set out her ironing blanket on the table. Without waiting for an answer she continued, 'I suppose you'll be wanting to stay here with me until you decide whose table you're going to set your feet under.'

John was grinning broadly as he answered. 'Mother, I have noticed how nicely you've set out my bedroom – new curtains and bedspread. Don't tell me you're not looking forward to having a bit of company.'

'I'm saying nothing, but it would be nice to know whether I can lock my front door before I go to bed of a night.'

For a moment John had the grace to look ashamed. 'If it's all right by you, Mum, I would like to stay here with you for a while, but say so now if you'd rather I moved on.'

'I don't want to hear any of that old blarney. Of course you can stay – you know you can always call this house yer home if needs be – but I don't want to be awake at night wondering if you're coming in or not.'

'That's fair enough. As far as possible I will keep you posted as to my comings and goings. Meanwhile, give us a kiss an' I'll be off, but I'll be back in time to have dinner with you. Shall we say half past six?'

This time when John took his mother into his arms, he was more aware of just how frail she was. If he could only finalise a couple of deals he'd had on the back burner before he'd been sent away, he would really put himself out to take care of her.

'Thanks, Mum,' he murmured as he released his hold on her. 'You've given me a great welcome home; you almost killed the fatted calf for your wayward son.'

Marian grinned as he brought her hand to his lips. The kiss was light and confident, full of promises that at this moment he had every intention of keeping. But would he be able to?

'Get away with you,' she said as she shooed him towards the door. She sometimes wondered if her firstborn son had Irish blood in his veins. Never mind the Blarney Stone; he could wheedle the hind legs off a donkey.

Later, having finished her ironing, Marian was folding away the blanket when she heard the front door open and two voices calling out, 'It's only us, Mum.'

Jodie, John's wife, and Laraine, who had been Richard's wife, were totally different in looks, yet as they came into her warm kitchen, their faces wreathed in smiles, they certainly complemented each other. Jodie, the elder by three years, was an inch or so shorter than her two sisters-in-law, with a slim figure and a truly beautiful face. She had dark brown eyes, and as with all three of Marian's daughters-in-law, her hair was her crowning glory. This was only to be expected, since all three of them had been in the hairdressing business almost from the day they'd left school. Jodie's hair was thick and dark, almost jet black, with a sheen of red in it, and it was always stylishly set. Looking at her now, it was hard to believe that she had two grown-up sons. Thank God they had turned out so different from their father. Reg and Lenny owned a building business, and according to the time and tide, they also went fishing. Huge great boat they owned, moored very conveniently on the foreshore of the beautiful house owned by their uncle Derrick and his wife Delia.

Laraine was the exact opposite to Jodie, since she was tall and slim, blue-eyed, with silky blonde hair that hung halfway down her back. All heads turned when Laraine entered a room, for she really was a stunning beauty. The way she dressed went back to her early days when she had worked on a fashion magazine. Jodie and Dee, her sisters-in-law, would tease her that she could be wearing sackcloth and ashes and still every man would watch her as she walked down the street.

Laraine's husband, Richard, had suffered a heart attack and died on board ship at the age of just forty-four, leaving Laraine with their very young twin girls, Adele and Annabel. On the death of her husband Laraine had gone to pieces, becoming very fragile, but with loving care and a whole lot of encouragement from her two sisters-in-law, she had pulled herself together and at least outwardly was a self-assured, successful businesswoman. Of course she missed Richard, and sometimes, when she was alone, her heart would start pounding as she yearned for what might have been. His death still seemed so unfair, and she had become aware of just how much the depth of loneliness could hurt.

'And where's Dee?' asked Marian as she stood at the sink filling the kettle before putting it on to boil.

'She's here,' Jodie said quickly. 'She's just popped in to see her mum and dad. She's done quite a bit of baking over the weekend and she's brought a nice fruit cake for them. She won't be long.'

Marian Underwood laughed to herself. It was nice that Mary and Jack Hartfield Delia's parents, lived next door to her. They were, and always had been, good neighbours and exceptionally kind friends. One way and another they were tied up with the whole of the Underwood family, and there wasn't a single member who didn't love them to bits and know they could always turn to them if in trouble.

Their daughter Delia, known to everyone as Dee, was a fairly tall, slim woman, with green eyes and a gorgeous head of dark blonde hair that had a distinctive shade of bronze running through it. Well, some weeks that was an accurate description, though with Dee one could never really tell, because she changed the colour of her hair as often as most women changed their bedlinen.

Once more the front door opened and another chorus of voices called out. This time an additional three adults came into Marian's kitchen.

'Good morning, Mum,' Dee said, as she planted a kiss on the cheek of her mother-in-law. 'I've baked you some shortbread and an apple pie. I'm glad to see you've just put the kettle on.'

'Don't know where she finds the time to do all this baking,' Jack Hartfield remarked to his wife.

Delia Underwood was as dependable as the sunrise. She watched out for everyone, and each person who came to her large, beautiful house on the seafront in Newhaven was sure of a true welcome. Unlike Jodie, Dee never seemed to acquire a suntan. She had a creamy complexion that defied the sun. There were lines on it, but they were so soft, so natural, you didn't even notice them. Instead you saw in Dee a good person who smiled often, a genuinely warm-hearted woman.

Delia was still blissfully married to Derrick, despite the fact that he had fathered a baby with a prostitute while he was a patient at a burns unit in Belgium. Caught up in an explosion on an oil tanker, Derrick had suffered horrific burns, leaving him appallingly disfigured and with the loss of his left arm. For almost a year Dee had had no knowledge of her husband's accident nor of his whereabouts. Derrick had been adamant that she was not to be informed. During that long, hellish period, he did make sure through the shipping line and the insurers that his wife and twin sons, Michael and Martin, were more than adequately provided for. Now, with hindsight, Delia often pondered on whether, before Derrick had left England to go on that fateful trip, he had had a premonition that his luck might run out.

It wasn't such a bizarre thought, because before leaving he had certainly set his affairs in good order, even making sure that his wife and sons had a lovely house in which to live. He'd paid the full asking price and seen that the purchase was speeded up and finalised before he sailed.

During many horrendous operations, Derrick had been given the best medical treatment available. As far as his personal needs went, he had been cared for and attended to by an orderly, Bob Patterson. There had been many days, however, when he had almost given up, and the doctors had feared not only for his bodily wounds but also for his state of mind. It had been Bob who had realised that Derrick was still a red-blooded man, and thinking that he was doing him a huge favour, he had brought a prostitute called Chloe Warburg into the burns unit. In Belgium, prostitution was legal. Providing the female was checked over and passed by the authorities, she was given a licence. At the time it had seemed a very good idea, and Bob had felt that the time Derrick had spent with the young lady had been of great benefit to him, helping him to regain much of his self-confidence.

However, Chloe had become pregnant, though not one person other than the mother-to-be had been aware of this fact. Nine months later she had travelled from Belgium to England, taken a taxi to Hammersmith Hospital and given birth to a baby girl. Twenty-four hours later she had disappeared, leaving the baby behind with a slip of paper attached to its shawl on which was written Derrick's name and part of the address of the house he had bought for Delia.

The time following that birth had been heartbreaking.

Derrick, that tall handsome, beautiful man whose looks drew women to him, had been horrifically burned and was still having to endure more surgery. There had also been fears that he was suffering mental illness. Yet the decision had been made to inform him of the birth of this baby. Straight away he gave orders to his bank to pay for the baby girl to be cared for.

It was through Social Services that Delia had discovered the bare facts. Needless to say, she was shocked and alarmed. She just did not want to believe that her darling Derrick had slept with another woman and made her pregnant.

For once, it had been John, Derrick's elder brother, who had come to the rescue. Over the lengthy period since Derrick's accident he had been the only one to visit him, and though fully aware of just how awkward it was going to be, he had made the decision that Delia had to be told the full truth.

'You're not only telling me that Derrick has been severely injured in an explosion on board his ship, but that for all these months you've known of his whereabouts and have also been his sole visitor. And now you've got the gall to go further and inform me that my husband has been sleeping with another woman!'

By the time Dee had finished ranting and raving at John she had been in a terrible state. Her hair was in a mess from where she had tugged at it, her face was red and the terrible sobs that were coming from her throat were almost choking her.

It had taken John a couple of hours to calm his sister-in-law down. Explaining time and time again that Derrick had only slept with the prostitute on one occasion, and that it had simply been sex. An arrangement made on a business footing.

'Please, Delia, try to understand. Derrick didn't want to see anyone, least of all you. He was afraid you would feel sorry for him, and felt that that would be the worst thing that could happen.'

Realising that John was being utterly honest with her, Delia had had no choice but to sit quietly and examine her own conscience.

Two days later she had forced herself to visit the baby in Hammersmith Hospital. She had been terrified as she stood at the side of the cot and wrestled with her own emotions. Staring down at this tiny scrap of a baby, her eyes had stung with unshed tears.

What a situation!

Could she just walk away? Wouldn't she be forever wondering if the baby had been sent to an orphanage? She would have dearly loved to discuss this dilemma with Jodie and Laraine, but it wasn't their problem; it was between her and her husband. Yet it wasn't right to burden Derrick with the details either. He had already made financial arrangements for the baby's well-being, but health-wise he was in no fit state to do more.

The surgeons at the burns unit of East Grinstead Hospital had solved the problem for her. In their wisdom they had declared that two days and two nights at home with his family for the festive season would do Derrick a great deal of good. Two medical orderlies had accompanied him to the house by ambulance on Christmas Eve and had seen him settled in safely. His face was still badly scarred, but a new ear and two new lips had been formed and stitched into place.

The whole of his chest, neck, jaw and mouth, right up to his cheeks, were still badly affected.

Everything was going to take time, and many more operations would be needed. It would be a long while before a false arm could even be thought about. What upset Delia most was that Derrick was very much aware of what had happened, particularly to his dear face.

That first night she and Derrick had slept separately, twin beds in the same room, and Martin, the elder of their sons by about five minutes, had come in to help bath and dress his father the next morning.

Christmas Day had been wonderful. The whole family, including all the in-laws, had been present and many loyal friends had popped in. The only topic of conversation that had been intentionally avoided had been the plight of the baby girl still lying in a London hospital.

At nine o'clock in the evening everyone had tactfully made ready to depart to their own homes. Martin and Michael between them had got their father up the stairs, undressed him, put him in his pyjamas and helped him into bed.

When the boys had come back downstairs, Delia had stood up, only to find that her legs were shaking. 'Mum, you're not afraid of being on your own with Dad, are you?' Martin had asked.

Not wanting to be a nuisance or to spoil their evening, she had assured them that she would be fine. 'You two get yourselves off to wherever it is you're going and I'll see you in the morning. Thank you both for today.' Her boys hugged her lovingly before they parted.

It had been a good half an hour before Delia had felt she could climb the stairs to spend the night with her husband. With lights in the lounge turned low the Christmas decorations and the tree looked so beautiful. Derrick had now spent his first night and one day in this lovely home that he had bought for them. She told herself she had nothing to fear, that he would recover and that they had a good life ahead of them.

Yet it was weird the way she felt about her own husband. During those long lonely nights when she hadn't been aware of where Derrick was, she would have readily admitted that she longed for him to be in bed with her, to feel his arms around her, and yes, to enjoy the fulfilment of the satisfying sex they had always had together. Now the thought of it didn't seem right. It was different. It had been such a long time since she had even been able to touch him.

Earlier in the evening he had grinned at

24

her over the rim of his glass, and it had been the same wicked devil of a grin he'd used from the day she had first met him. That was many years ago!

Would it be different now? She'd asked herself the question over and over again. It would surely be difficult.

She had known full well that Derrick wanted her, needed her, and the truth had been that she too had a need, even a longing for her husband to make love to her. But how would it work? She hadn't had the faintest idea. Just a fearful dread that one or other of them might get badly hurt.

When at last she had been allowed to visit her husband in the burns unit, it had been a terrific shock to see just how badly he had been injured. For ages she had had night-mares, waking up in a cold sweat with her heart pounding against her ribs and a scream caught in her throat.

She had to keep telling herself she had no reason to feel guilty. She hadn't caused the accident. His disfigured face had been heart-breaking to look at, but she'd told herself that she was his wife and if he had the desire to have sex with her, she would manage some-how. She had no option but to try.

All those thoughts had in no way prepared her for what had taken place on that Christmas night over five years ago.

Even now she could recall how agitated

she had felt as she dimmed the rest of the downstairs lights and made her way upstairs. Still afraid that she might make a fool of herself, she had taken off her dressing gown and lain down beside Derrick. His eyes had been glistening with tears as he raised his head to look at her, and when the fingers of his right hand brushed across along her cheek, her heart had turned over. From that very moment everything had been all right.

Those lips the doctors had worked so hard to repair, to make remarkably whole again, suddenly felt so warm, so welcoming, so unexpectedly real, and she had forgotten all the worry and heartache of the past months as they'd come together. She had been nervous as she warned Derrick he shouldn't be disappointed if it didn't go well this first time; after all, it was a long time since they had made love and he had been so very ill.

She had laughed when he had become all masterful.

'You, Dee, are my wife. I have loved you since you were sixteen years old. Now, after a very long time, we are going to make love. It maybe a bit awkward but I'm damn sure we'll manage, and loving you as I do, how could that possibly go wrong?'

She had slipped the pyjama top off his shoulders and for a moment had held it bundled up close to her breasts. She had thought at the time she would always remember this night. And she had. True, their lovemaking had not been as frantic or as energetic as it used to be, but for Dee it had been heavenly. She'd adored the slow, tender way he had explored her body, the endearments he'd muttered, the moans of pleasure. She had relished every minute of him being inside her, and when it was over, the tenderness with which he had held her within his one good arm, keeping her close to his side. Contented and sleepy, she had traced the scars across his chest with her fingers and thanked God that her husband had survived.

Now, five years later, her life was so secure. Two grown-up sons, a sweet little daughter and a husband who would always be there for her. No matter what.

To have a man who thought of you first, and last. That was more than security.

It was absolute love.

# Chapter 2

Whenever possible, the three sisters-in-law met up on Wednesday evenings. This particular evening they were all seated in the lounge of Jodie's house in Epsom. It was smaller than Dee and Derrick's house but nevertheless it was still a beautiful home set in the glorious Surrey countryside. The large, comfortable lounge had big deep armchairs and a long cream-coloured settee. The material for the curtains and cushions had been carefully chosen and they'd been made up by Jodie herself. No one could deny that she was a woman of many talents.

'More wine?' Jodie asked as she held the bottle over the glasses set on the coffee table in front of Laraine and Dee.

'Cheers,' they both replied.

Jodie left the room for a few minutes and came back with a heavily laden tray. She dumped serviettes and a handful of knives and forks on the table before handing out plates holding smoked salmon, king prawns and salad. In the centre of the table she placed a bowl of tiny buttered potatoes and a platter of warm brown rolls. 'Eat up,' she said, 'then we can get down to the week's gossip.'

'Is Derrick on his own with Ann this evening?' Jodie asked Dee as she broke open a crusty roll and spread it with butter.

'As if,' Dee grinned. 'No, Michael and Danny arrived before I left.' Michael Connelly and Danny Spencer were old family friends. The two men had lived together for a number of years. Both were very successful businessmen, and they had been instrumental in the success of the businesses of the three Underwood women too.

'You're quiet, Laraine, is something bothering you?' Dee asked.

'Not really, and I am far more relaxed now that I've had a glass of wine.'

'Well, if you needed a drink before you could unwind, there has to be something on your mind.' Jodie laughed, then quickly added, 'Come on, tell all.'

It was almost a year since Laraine had met Alan Morris, and he'd begun to play a big part in her life. She was still young, and although Richard's death had been a terrible shock, she could not mourn him for ever. Remember him, yes, of course, and love him always, but the girls were forever urging her to move on.

She had met Alan when she had been having lunch with Simon Boardman in the

House of Commons. Simon was one of the directors at Shepperton Studios, where Laraine did much of her work. It had become a source of much amusement within the family that her new male companion had been educated at Cambridge and now had a respectable position in the House of Commons. On the whole, they had all taken to Alan and longed to see him and Laraine settle down together.

Alan had been married before, and Laraine knew that the divorce had been bitter, spiteful and sad. Yet she found him fascinating, and his skill at making her feel wanted, even truly loved, was a bonus. He had travelled extensively, and had been to most of the places where Laraine had lived with Richard, which gave them some common ground. She was coming to believe that with Alan she had not only a satisfying relationship but also a lovely affectionate friendship.

So much trash was written in women's magazines about falling in love, and when Richard had died no one had been able to convince her that given time she would experience it all over again for a second time. But now? The days were brighter, the air sweeter and the sun shone more brilliantly for her. Once again life was offering her so much. It all seemed wonderful, but at the same time terrifying. Such mixed feelings. Some days she knew she was acting daft, passionate and giddy, as though she was a young schoolgirl.

Could it really be true love?

Whether the answer was yes or no, there was one fly in the ointment. Alan was possessive. Never wanted her to be out of his sight, and if they were out for the evening she wouldn't dare dance more than one dance with the same fellow, otherwise she would have to put up with Alan's murderous looks and sulky moods. Some friends told her she should feel honoured that he loved her so much. Laraine didn't see it that way. She wanted to be loved but not possessed. And she was still seething over what had taken place a few days ago.

They had enjoyed a glorious session of sex. So good, it was almost unbelievable. Alan's body was hard and firm, with muscles like iron, and as he had made love to her, powerful was the word that had come to her mind.

Later, as they were getting dressed, he had said to her, 'We'll get married as soon as you like.'

It had come to her like a bolt out of the blue!

'Will we?' she had asked, keeping her voice calm, spacing the two words.

'Of course we will.' It wasn't precisely how he'd meant to put his suggestion, but it was too late now. 'We need each other, Laraine. We suit each other well enough, don't we?

31

And I want you with me every hour of every day.'

'I see,' she'd murmured, but the truth was she didn't see. It was too one-sided. All about what *he* wanted. 'So would you have me give up my job and my various business concerns with Dee and Jodie?' she had asked him.

His reply hadn't helped.

'Surely you'd love to be at home all day? You said you adore my house; you'd be able to keep it looking nice. I wouldn't mind if you felt you wanted to change a few things. You'd have no money worries, so there would be no need for you to be earning. You would be able to buy yourself good clothes, because we'll be entertaining quite a lot. You've already proved you are a very good cook.'

Laraine had had to take a minute to draw a couple of deep breaths before she had been able to form a reply, and when she did speak her voice was far from steady.

'Sounds to me like you think you badly need a wife, but Alan, let me tell you here and now, it isn't gonna be me. I need a *life*, and I have one, a really good one as it happens, thanks in part to Jodie and Dee, who since Richard died have always been there for me.'

That statement had really rattled Alan, but his pride wouldn't let him admit it. He knew he'd phrased his proposal all wrong, but he was too angry to backtrack, and so he blustered on.

'I'm saying I could support you really well, and I thought you'd rather work at making us a nice home instead of hurrying off in your car every morning here, there and everywhere. Together we'd manage everything fine.'

'You think so?' Laraine had said sarcastically. 'You support me, while I potter around keeping house for you. Seems to me you need to advertise for a housekeeper rather than a wife.'

'Look.' He hadn't had the sense to keep quiet. 'You lead a busy life, a hard life. What I'm saying is you could have a better, easier one with me.'

'Could I?' Laraine had felt she had to turn away, get him out of her house as quickly as possible. She felt used, bruised and badly hurt. In that moment she hadn't been able to recognise just what had changed, wasn't sure she wanted to, but she had sensed that they were on dangerous ground, about to say things now they might later regret. In that instant it seemed the only reason Alan needed a wife was to keep his house in good order, help cement his position at work and act as hostess when he invited friends and colleagues to his house. And he thought she would fit the bill.

The way he'd put it was as if he was doing her one big favour.

Well, he'd been barking up the wrong bloody tree!

She had a good house and a good income and what was more she enjoyed the work she did. She'd had a fabulous life with Richard that had been cruelly cut short. But there was more to her now. More than she had realised. She had made something of her life, seen that her twin girls had been well educated and wanted for nothing, and by God, she wasn't going to give it all up to become a flipping housekeeper.

She had finished dressing, told Alan that the bathroom was free and gone downstairs to make a pot of coffee. He'd come sheepishly into the kitchen, smelling fresh, his thick dark hair neatly combed, and stood, silent, as he watched her pour coffee until his cup was half filled, then top it to the rim with boiling milk and add three sugar lumps. She knew, exactly the way he liked it. He'd smiled his thanks and Laraine's temper had subsided a little. He certainly, was a good-looking man, tall and distinguished, and most of the time he had a good sense of humour.

It was he who had broken the silence. 'You care for me, don't you, Laraine?'

'You know I do.' Somehow she'd managed to keep her voice pleasant as she said it, even though her thoughts had still been bubbling away. 'Marriage is a serious business, Alan. I've been there and I know how wonderful it can be. I still wish to God that Richard hadn't died. With your marriage things were vastly different. From what you've told me, you and your wife ended up hating each other. I'm sorry, but it isn't a risk I am about to take.'

Alan slapped his cup down on to the saucer spilling some of the hot coffee over on to the table. 'That is ridiculous,' he had stormed. 'You can't compare yourself with my ex-wife.'

'I haven't finished yet.' Laraine had known her voice was still chilly, but she was past caring. 'Until I truly believe that I can trust someone, and that the marriage would be on a firm basis of love and respect, it isn't a commitment I intend to make. I have to believe it would be a loving union for ever. Not end up in the divorce court.'

For a moment she had been really afraid. Alan's face had turned red and his hands were clenched into tight fists as he came around the table. Standing directly in front of her he had gripped her arms so tightly it had hurt. 'Laraine, it isn't fair to compare my first marriage with what you and I have now. Let's settle this once and for all.' With his face within inches of her own, he was almost hissing at her through clenched teeth.

Trying not to show her fear, Laraine had shoved his hands away and in a voice that was far from steady said, 'If I haven't made myself clear, I'll say it again. No, Alan, I won't marry you, but thank you for asking. Now I don't think you should stay here with me tonight, we both need to calm down.'

He had found it hard to believe that she meant what she said. However, she'd walked out into the hall, taken his overcoat down from the coat rack and stood there with it over her arm with his briefcase in one hand as she unlocked the front door and opened it wide.

Alan hadn't known what had hit him. Laraine had said no to his proposal. He hadn't been prepared for that possibility. He had stood at the door and reminded her that he had a good steady job with the government. Even went as far as to say that for the time being he would take on Adele and Annabel, pointing out that very soon the time would come when they would both be leaving the nest and she would really know what loneliness was like. He'd also mentioned that neither of them were spring chickens, and that hadn't gone down at all well with Laraine. She was thirty-seven years old and he was forty-five.

He went on. 'I'm sorry that I've taken you by surprise, but now that you know my intentions are good, I'm sure you'll grow used to them.'

She had held out his coat and his brief-case, but his face had been stony as she pecked his cheek and said, 'Good night, Alan.'

'Good night, Laraine,' was all he had muttered before striding off down her garden path.

She had stood there, her long blonde hair shining in the overhead lighting as a single tear slid down her cheek. After all this time he needed her as a housekeeper. At best someone well dressed to present to his colleagues. With all the suggestions he had put forward, there had never been one word of love mentioned.

Silence had reigned while the girls had been eating but neither Jodie nor Dee was in any doubt that Laraine had been lost in un-happy thoughts. They had to find out what was wrong. Make sure she snapped out of it. Not let her sink into depression again, as she had after Richard's death.

Jodie suddenly tapped the table with her fork and said, 'Laraine, why don't you tell us what has gone wrong between you and Alan Morris?'

'Who said anything had gone wrong?'

'Oh come on, love, it's us you are talking to. Neither of us has to be psychic to be able to tell you that all is not well in your world.'

Jodie knew that Laraine was always going to remember her marriage to Richard as being absolutely perfect. Yet the fact was, her husband had died so very young that she would never be able to claim that their marriage had stood the test of time. Was she ruining her chances of ever marrying again by looking for perfection? Would she ever come to love another man unconditionally?

'OK, he asked me to marry him,' Laraine suddenly blurted out.

Her two sisters-in-law looked at each other with a wry smile, and it was Dee who said, 'Well it obviously didn't please you. Why don't you tell us what happened?'

Laraine looked slowly from Dee to Jodie, thinking what dear, loving, loyal friends they both were. 'He said he needed a wife, that's about the long and short of it, and he said he was sure that I would fit the bill.'

'And what was your answer?' Jodie asked quietly.

'I told him no in no uncertain terms.'

'But why?' Dee cried out. 'We all thought you were made for each other.'

'Because having listened to all he had to say, that was my choice.'

'Do you love him?' Dee felt she had to ask.

Laraine hesitated, and Jodie threw up her hands and groaned.

'All right! Yes, I love him, or at least I thought I did. Richard and I were love's young dream and we had a wonderful privileged life together, albeit a short one. Alan is totally different, but I thought that was a good thing and that maybe we could make a go of it second time around.'

'Then why not?' Dee and Jodie asked in unison.

'Just because I have feelings for Alan, just because we became lovers, it doesn't mean I'm going to jump at the chance to be his wife. Not when he made it clear that he needs someone to keep his big house clean and tidy, and a well-dressed hostess to be there when he entertains or gives dinner parties. Oh, and he mentioned that he thought I was a good cook, but he didn't divulge whether or not he loved me. In fact there was no mention of love. He did offer to house both Adele and Annabel, with the reminder that very soon they would be leaving home and if I didn't accept his offer of marriage I would end up being very lonely. I made it perfectly clear to him that I will learn to be on my own and that I am quite capable of earning a good living for myself and my daughters until such time as they do decide to leave home.'

Both Jodie and Dee sighed heavily.

It was Dee who asked, 'So the fact that you can manage on your own, does that mean you want to be alone?'

'No, of course not.' It was Laraine's turn to throw up her hands, and as she did so she began to pace the floor.

Her two sisters-in-law got to their feet and came to stand one each side of her. All three women put their arms out wide and within a moment they were all wrapped in a tight embrace. Suddenly three voices blended as each muttered one word: 'Men!'

After which their laughter was loud and uncontrollable for some time to come.

The girls might never know it but Alan was no less frustrated than Laraine.

He had been so certain that he understood what Laraine wanted. It was puzzling to realise he'd gone wrong somewhere. For Christ's sake! He'd proposed marriage to her and she'd been right annoyed. Turned him down flat! It didn't make sense when everyone knew they had practically lived together for ages.

'Women!' he snapped, but *he* wasn't laughing.

# Chapter 3

Judith was the eldest of the three girls that the three Underwood brothers had chosen for their brides. Known to friends and family as Jodie, she had been on the scene long before the other two girls had come along. She had first met John Underwood when he was on leave from the Royal Navy, a few years after he'd signed on at the age of fifteen. When he had returned to his ship they had begun to correspond, even though John was five years older than Jodie was.

The weekend of John's twenty-first birthday, a huge party was held in Camber Sands, where most of his family lived. Jodie had been thrilled to be invited, and from that day forth her relationship with John had moved on rapidly. Before she was seventeen years old she had become pregnant. By the time she was eighteen she was married and had two sons.

Jodie had come from a well-to-do family. Her father was a director of a firm that supplied liaison officers between large post offices and buildings going up on new sites in the north of the country. Her parents had disapproved so much of Jodie being pregnant and planning to get married when she was still only sixteen years old that they hadn't felt able to attend the wedding. After a year, however, and with the knowledge that they now had two grandsons, they had made the journey down from Westmorland to see her.

They had been appalled at the situation in which their only child was living.

Just days after their visit, Jodie had received a letter from her father in which he had enclosed a cheque for the sum of ten thousand pounds. Neither he nor her mother could understand the grotty life, as they had put it, that she was living, but they couldn't bring themselves to become involved. That money had been the backbone of Jodie's successful business life. Sadly, though, it had not mended bridges between her and her parents. When the time had come for her father to retire, he and her mother had sold up and gone to live in Spain, thus depriving Jodie's two boys of their grandparents. That fact had hurt Jodie more than she would ever admit, though she had been left feeling so very thankful that her mother-in-law – and her father-in-law too before he had died – had shown great love for her boys, as had Mr and Mrs Hartfield, Delia's parents. All four had made up for so much that might otherwise have been missing in the lives of her children.

At the beginning of her married life Jodie had been so impressed with her husband, so proud to be seen out with him in his uniform when he took her dancing, and to theatres and the cinema. Regrettably it hadn't taken her long to realise that John was an out-and-out philanderer, a liar, and even, as time went on, not above stealing from her.

Poor Marian worried more over Jodie than she did about the other two put together. Jodie was a good mother who also found time to pursue a career and earn her own living. She deserved far better treatment than she got from John. It was almost unbelievable the way that girl had pulled herself up by her boot straps. When the lads were still small babies she worked four days a week for Michael Connelly in one or other of his posh hairdressing salons. On the other days she paid for the boys to be minded in a nursery, trudging through all kinds of weather with her case containing everything she needed to wash and set ladies' hair. She had saved hard to buy all the best equipment. Some of the clients she visited lived in horrible conditions without a bathroom or running hot water, and many a time she had to make do with pouring a kettle of warm water over a dear old soul's head which was bent over a narrow stone sink. Jodie's visit to these old ladies was often the highlight of their week, and it had made her many good friends. Other customers lived in posh areas, some even in residential hotels, and these ladies could afford to pay her much more for her services.

With the help of loyal friends, goodwill and a great deal of determination, Jodie had certainly prospered. Now, with her two sons grown up, both happily married with homes of their own, she owned two hairdressing salons, one in Epsom, the town in which she lived, and another in Kensington, in London. Both salons were run by staff, for Jodie now had a well-paid advisory position at Shepperton Studios. It was at Shepperton that she had met Philip Conti, who had made such a difference to her life. Now, she couldn't bear even to think about a world that didn't have her dear, wonderful Philip in it.

Philip had been born in Italy and had always been a good-looking young man, and often when working together Jodie would look over to where he was standing and notice just how handsome he still was: tall, lean, fit, with sharp features and a permanent tan. She had been in love with him from the moment he had walked into her life. More so as the years had gone by, in fact. She knew how lucky she was. With both her sons now living their own lives, she would be very lonely were it not for Philip, but she hadn't even made the effort to visit a lawyer about divorcing John.

She was well aware that the day might come when Philip would decide he had had enough of the situation, and the fact that John seemed to pop up on a regular basis like the inevitable bad penny.

Philip himself had never married. He was a very successful businessman, he had a fantastic house in Eastbourne and owned a restaurant and a nightclub in London, the running of which he left to his staff. He was also in a position of authority at Shepperton Studios. There was no doubt that he was a gentleman, out of an Italian top drawer, though he had lived in England for many years, with his mother and her sister Sylvia, a famous big-band singer.

Jodie often sighed as she told herself what a gorgeous man her Philip was, in his beautiful hand-tailored suits and Italian leather shoes, his dark hair always superbly cut. It frightened her to look into the future, or to have too much hope that what they had together would endure. Philip often declared it was the same for him. Where they were heading and how long it was going to last were questions to which they had no answers. For now the situation suited them both and was all they ever seemed to want. Sex between them was terrific. Each had had enough experience to make sure that the other was satisfied. Nothing in their relationship had ever been selfish. Each of them enjoyed making the other happy, whether it was in or out of bed. After having suffered a few disappointments along the way, they were both wise and well seasoned.

Philip would often say they were like a fine champagne that had ripened with age. Not too old yet, and still young enough to remain sparkling.

When Philip had first set eyes on Jodie at Shepperton Studios he had been stunned not only by her looks but by the accomplished way in which she carried out any request that the casting director saw fit to throw at her. Whether it was an advertisement in the making or a period film, she would immediately grasp the context and know exactly how to alter any wig or dress the hair of any female to the director's satisfaction. But her appearance also drew his attention. Small in stature, she had beautiful features, glowing skin and hair that was very similar in colour and texture to his own: thick and almost jet black. He had been devastated to learn that she was married and had two young sons, though he soon realised that it was Reg and Lenny, and not John, who constituted the biggest stumbling block to him ever being able to declare his love for her and take her for his own.

Over the years he had made an extra special effort to get close to the boys even though sometimes it made his heart ache after they had all spent a day together. Often he would have loved to stay the night with Jodie in her lovely home, or take her back to his place, but always Reg and Lenny were her first consideration. He had tried hard to win their affection, and for the most part he thought he had succeeded. He would buy them the latest toy or gadget, and would never be offended when Jodie asked if she might bring the boys on an outing with them.

It hadn't always been smooth sailing between them, though. Some time ago a crisis had arisen.

Philip had been given tickets for a new, show that was due to open in the West End of London. Jodie hadn't been overenthusiastic; she preferred to wait until the reviews were out rather than attend an opening performance. However, she thought she had hidden her reluctance well, and arrangements had been made for them to meet up at Victoria station.

Half an hour after their agreed time of meeting Philip was on the telephone. He was shouting. 'If you had no intention of meeting me, why the hell couldn't you have said so?'

'Please, Philip, calm down and give me a chance to explain. Both the boys have been struck down with some kind of tummy bug. I did try to reach you at your office, but your secretary said you had already left.'

'What the hell's the matter with them that you couldn't leave them for a few hours?

Anyone would think they were still babies,' he had yelled, his voice still far too loud.

Jodie couldn't believe he was being so unreasonable. Her anger had shown in her answer. 'How the hell do I know what's the matter with them? Even the doctor doesn't know. Anyway, what do you care?' She had brushed hard at the tears that were running down her cheeks and replaced the receiver without waiting for Philip to say anything else.

The ambulance had arrived and Jodie had travelled with her sons to Epsom Hospital. During that long night she had sunk into a swamp of sheer exhaustion and several hours later had opened her eyes to see Philip sitting in the corner of the room.

Neither of them had said anything until he spoke softly. 'I am so sorry for what I said, Jodie. Do you think you can forgive me and tell me how Reg and Lenny are doing?'

She had braced herself then, not wanting to upset him, but knowing she had to make her point.

'I do understand how you feel, Philip, but you also must know by now that when it comes to my sons, there is no choice. I do love you dearly, but for the time being at least they will always have to be my first priority.'

'Of course,' he'd quickly agreed. 'Now will you tell me what the doctors have said?'

'Oh Philip, how long have you been sitting

there?' she murmured, feeling that she was being torn in two.

'Never mind all that, just tell me.'

'Nowhere near as bad as they suspected at first. It is a nasty case of food poisoning. Seems they bought beefburgers from a stall outside the market, something I've always told them to avoid. Since they've both had drips put into their arms, they've stopped vomiting and have been in a deep sleep.'

'Thank God for that,' Philip declared, pausing a moment before he said more.

'Jodie, I know it is no excuse, but yesterday was a hell of a day for me at work and I had been so looking forward to taking you to the theatre. Forgive me? Please.' Before she had time to form an answer, he had got to his feet and come to stand in front of her. His big brown eyes were full of love as he said, 'Let me take you for a nice hot cup of coffee. We'll tell the nurses where we are and if the boys do stir they can come and find us.'

It was soon after that incident that Jodie had come to realise that the road she and Philip had travelled for so long had suddenly changed its direction. She was aware that she couldn't dither for much longer. She had to make up her mind where she was heading and also decide whether she was going to allow Philip to play an even bigger part in her life.

# Chapter 4

Dee was standing at the gates of the private school that her daughter Ann attended. She gave a sigh of sheer contentment as Ann reached the main entrance, then stopped, turned around and waved to her mother.

Wasn't it strange, Dee often asked herself, how good could come from something that in the beginning was really bad? Ann was now five years old, a real little beauty, boisterous at times, but always funny and full of enthusiasm for everything, from ball games to swimming and dancing, and never happier than when on board her big brothers' boat. Like all members of the Underwood family, she loved the sea. She was a loving and demonstrative child, still happy to be cuddled by her many aunts and uncles. She really was a joy to have around.

Most days Dee was thrilled and contented with what she would describe as her safe, loving, wholesome life and found it impossible to cast her mind back to the days before Ann had become her daughter and part of their large extended family. But still there was that rare day when she found herself mentally in the past, standing at the side of that cot in Hammersmith Hospital staring down at the wee scrap folded in a white shawl. At that moment she had made an unshakeable decision. No way was she going to allow the authorities to shut this baby away in an institution. At that point not one person had seemed to care in the slightest about what would happen to the child. Only a few days old and nobody wanted her. What a way to start one's life.

Delia knew she could have walked away there and then. Washed her hands of the whole affair. But she hadn't. She couldn't cast that baby into a life of knowing that nobody had wanted her, growing up lonely and unloved. That was when she had made her decision. To stop worrying about how the child had been conceived and do her best to see that she would be safe and happy within a real family. Even at that early stage she had been fully aware that she would be taking on a stiff fight if she was going to be able to obtain authorisation for herself and her husband to become the child's legal guardians.

The doors to the school were closed now and Ann was out of sight until three thirty this afternoon. Dee could afford to smile. Everything had turned out so very happily. The mother who had given birth to Ann had never been heard of from that day to this. Derrick Underwood was Ann's natural father

51

and his wife had become her mother from the very first time she had set eyes on her. God had been good. Ann Underwood was now surrounded with love in a big extended family.

Maybe the day would come when she might question how and where she had been born. No, Delia sternly told herself, there would be no maybe about it. Without a doubt as Ann grew older she would need answers to some big questions, and Derrick and Delia had agreed that they would tell her the truth.

There were never enough hours in the day for all the things Dee wanted to do. Her big house, situated on the seafront at New-haven, was still her pride and joy. Derrick would often laugh at her as she continually moaned about the amount of sand that found its way into the house. He would tease her by suggesting they move to London and see how well she coped with the dirt and grime of the city.

Grinning widely, Delia thought about the number of friends and family who dropped in at every hour of the day, even if only for a cup of coffee. If the forecast told of good weather for the approaching weekend, she knew to get in loads of salad, cold meats and savoury dips, besides chicken and steaks for the barbecue, so certain was she that many friends and most of their relations would turn up. Though in fact the weather didn't make all that much difference to the number of people who arrived at Marine House. Even when it was bitterly cold, with the sea rough and the high waves rolling in, they still came, with the boys and men lighting bonfires on the beach and Dee serving bowls of hot soup and hot dogs instead of salads. This was a happy house, and neither she nor Derrick ever complained at the number of visitors they had.

This great family of theirs had started off with Jodie, Laraine and Delia herself each marrying one of the three Underwood brothers. Dee loved both her sisters-in-law and in turn was greatly loved by them. She was well aware of how each of them had used their talents and their gritty determination to enable them to succeed in life, and the very thought made her swell with pride. It did make her sad to think that Laraine had lost her husband so tragically without any warning, and that John was still playing the field where women were concerned when he'd had such a good wife in Jodie. Still, he might one day wake up to the fact that Jodie and Philip Conti were an item, but by then it would be too late.

Stop daydreaming, Dee told herself as she turned away from the school and began the walk home. But once again she found herself

53

marvelling, as she so often did, at the fact that five and a half years ago she had thought the birth of this little girl had been nothing short of a disaster. With two grown sons she had thought her days of having more children were long gone. Taking charge of Ann had been a demanding task from the very start. Now, though, she always defined herself as a mother of three, and she wouldn't trade that label for all the tea in China.

She had devoted these past few years to making sure that Ann knew she was wanted and loved dearly, not only by her close family but also by her large extended family. The one thing Dee did dread was the day when she and Derrick would have to explain every detail of how Ann had been born and how Delia had become her mother.

Meanwhile, she adored her daughter. Ann always looked gorgeous when she was asleep, with one hand curled under her chin and the other wrapped tightly around her favourite teddy bear. Dee also loved the way the little girl would curl up on her lap for cuddles. Bathtime was great too, the smell of the child as she lifted her out of the warm water, wrapped her in a big fluffy towel and patted her beautiful soft skin with talcum powder. Playing with her on the beach, dressed like a boy to make it easier for her to scramble on and off of the boats. Taking her to tea parties, wearing frilly knickers that showed beneath her pretty party frock, little white ankle socks and soft leather sandals on her tiny feet. On occasions such as this her big brothers teased her unmercifully, and so for her fifth birthday party, held at Marine House, Dee had dressed her darling little girl as a pirate. Ann had loved it, telling her friends she had been shipwrecked.

Later that day Ann had jumped from the top of the stairs, pretending she was walking the plank. She had broken her arm and Delia had been at the hospital as the bone was set and put into a cast. Ann had been so brave, but with her free hand she had held on to her mummy so tightly that her fingernails had left marks on the palm of Dee's hand.

Afterwards Dee had told Derrick that she would have gladly broken her own arm if it meant their daughter wouldn't have had to suffer.

Back home, Delia was pleased to see that Derrick's car was still in the drive, and as she walked in through the front door he came down the stairs, smiling broadly at her. Having kissed her, he placed his right hand on her shoulder and stood staring down at her. Dee was thinking how much she had loved his hands; huge as they had been, he would use them so gently to touch her body when making love to her. Now he only had one, yet it was powerful enough to hold her close. The left hand was artificial; it was useful, but had no feeling.

'You've something to tell me, haven't you?' she murmured.

Derrick faked a heavy sigh before saying, 'Dee, you really do have a sixth sense where I'm concerned. Well, as usual you're right. I've had the shipping line on to me while you were out. Bit hard to grasp, but they are offering me a job.'

'Oh Derrick, don't! Please don't tell me they want you to take command of another ship.'

Derrick hesitated, and Dee drew back and stood a little way from him, but near enough for her to be able to see his face. Her thoughts were running wild. She had spent nearly six years lying next to him in bed each night. At the beginning he'd relived the horrors of the explosion in his sleep, causing regular nightmares. She had so much love for this man and also a great deal of admiration. He had suffered so much, undergone so many rounds of reconstructive surgery. It was astounding that he had got his life back together again after what had been an absolute catastrophe that could so easily have killed him.

Time had eased some of the horror of that disaster, and Dee had told herself over and over again that he would never have to go back to sea for months on end and leave her on her own. And now what?

She felt his lips brush the top of her head.

'I have to go out now. I've barely had time to grasp exactly what the firm is offering, but I promise I won't make any decision until you and I have thoroughly discussed what is involved.'

Derrick released his hold on her and walked towards the door, and as Dee watched she was struck by the breadth of his shoulders, the tilt of his head and the way his grin was spreading from ear to ear. As the door closed behind him she murmured, 'I love you so much it hurts at times.'

Derrick had been gone all day. It was a little after six when he walked through the door, a huge bunch of flowers in one hand and a small parcel wrapped in pretty pink paper in the other. Ann, who had been seated at the table, jumped down and flew to her father. 'Daddy!' she cried.

Derrick put his gifts down, then spread his arms wide and gathered his daughter close to his chest. 'And how is my bestest girl this evening?' he asked as he sat down and pulled her on to his lap, burying his face against her hair.

'I got a silver star for writing at school today and Miss Clarke said I'm getting better at my sums,' Ann stated proudly, then quickl added, 'But I did get a black mark for turning round and talking to Jenny who sits behind me.'

'Will you two please stop cuddling each other and sit up at the table properly. I am waiting to dish up the dinner.' Dee was flustered. She badly wanted to know where Derrick had been and what the outcome was. On the other hand, she knew she had to be patient, Derrick would only tell her when he was good and ready.

Derrick stood up and flipped Ann upside down, so she was still giggling when he sat her down on her own chair. He gave her the present to open – a pretty little handbag – then, straightening up, he took a deep breath and guided Dee over to the other side of the room.

'Darling, we'll talk later, but I have to say I never in my wildest dreams thought a chance like this would ever again come my way. I honestly thought my days of being a Master Mariner were truly over.'

'So you will take the job?'

Derrick looked down at the floor between his shoes and took a deep breath. 'With your blessing, I hope.'

'Oh Derrick.'

With great tenderness he kissed her forehead. 'We'll work it out. Talk later on, I promise. But now that casserole I can smell is making me feel very hungry.'

It was as if Ann sensed that something serious was going on between her parents. She was very quiet during their meal, but that didn't stop her from clearing her dinner plate and then tucking into a slice of apple pie covered with creamy custard.

# Chapter 5

Two days had passed since Derrick had dropped the bombshell: the offer to once more take up the post of Master Mariner. No doubt it had been very good for his ego, and Dee felt she would never knock that, but so many fears had crept back into her mind right from the moment he had mentioned the subject. Later he had told her that he would be completely in charge, because he was one of the few men qualified to captain a great iron supertanker.

Poor Derrick! Of course he was flattered, made to feel he was a real man once again, and one had only to look into his eyes to know how badly he was yearning to take on this job.

Not so Delia. She still loved him to bits, but that didn't stop her being afraid. And he was still in love with her. He was always saying so. Telling her that he couldn't remember ever being so happy, or that it was unbelievable to him that she had stuck by him and nursed him through his nightmares, never recoiling from his hideous scars even when he had been difficult and thoroughly bad-tempered.

Sometimes he could be absurdly romantic. She would wake in the morning to find him missing, and he would come into the bedroom smiling, holding out a great bunch of wild flowers he had just picked. How could she not love him?

'So you don't want me to take this job, even though it will only be a one-off?' he asked, tension tight in his voice.

'You've already said it will be an enormous task and a very long journey; six months, didn't you say? Can you live without me for that length of time?'

Derrick evaded that question.

'I will agree that the task is enormous, but I will be the one in charge, advising others what to do. There will be a great crew. Myself as captain, a first and a second mate, cooks and kitchen hands, engineers and approximately five or six regular seamen.'

'Good God! How big is this tanker?'

Derrick burst out laughing at the look on Dee's face. 'It's a supertanker that the Russians have sold to an Indian firm situated in Murmansk. It's three to four times the length of a football pitch, and the crew will use motorbikes to get from one end to the other.' The look on Derrick's face changed, as did the tone of his voice. 'But Dee, I do understand your apprehension and am fully aware of the many reasons you have to discourage me from accepting this job. On the other hand, the Apex shipping line would not have offered me the job if they hadn't thought I had the capability to carry it through. According to them, I came through the medical extremely well.'

'I know it's what you want,' said Dee bravely.

Martin and Michael had come in just as their father was giving a description of the iron tanker and details of what the job would entail.

'You lucky old beggar,' Michael cried.

'Talk about getting jam on yer bread,' Martin agreed.

Their twin sons had phoned earlier on to say that they had got quite a good catch that morning: loads of fish, and the lobster pots had done well.

Delia, as always, had cauldrons of boiling salted water on the go. Having boiled the lobsters, she would leave them for a few hours to cool, and then she would dress them ready to be delivered to the hotels, while the smaller ones would be sold in their local shop. Most of the fish would have been gutted by the boys whilst at sea, but it was their mum who cleaned, skinned and dressed it ready for sale.

Sensing the strain between their parents, Martin quickly suggested, 'Dad, why can't you take Mum with you?'

'Oh that's a really good idea,' said Derrick, his voice heavily sarcastic. 'And who is going to take care of Ann?'

'There's enough family around who would be more than delighted to have her. That certainly wouldn't be a problem,' Martin protested.

'The question won't arise.' Dee was quick to voice her own opinion. 'Your father knows it will be a six-month trip, and I can assure you, whether he takes on this job or not, neither Ann nor I will be going anywhere.'

'Life has suddenly become very complicated, hasn't it?' Derrick remarked sadly as he closed the front door later that evening having said good night to their two sons. He drew his wife into his arms, angry with himself because once again his beloved Delia was suffering and it was all his fault.

However, he was loath to even consider turning down this opportunity. It had come as a bolt out of the blue, a once-in-a-lifetime chance. For months after he had been so horribly injured he had felt so bad he would have welcomed death. He had dreaded seeing his wife for the first time after that explosion. He was only too aware that he looked nothing like the man she had married. One arm and half of his face blown away. His torso riddled with deep scars.

Now this job was being offered to him, and by God it meant so much. He would be his own man again. Not a wreck left to get on with life as best he could. He would be on board a ship, his feet would walk the decks and the rolling sea would be there beneath him, awake or asleep. And he would be in charge. Christ almighty, it was more than he could ever have hoped for; a remarkable chance. There would be crew to do his bidding. He would be a man again. The man in charge.

Dee had seen Ann settled into her bed, had read her a story, kissed her and given her a cuddle before tucking the eiderdown up around her dear little face. 'Good night, sweetheart, sleep tight,' she whispered. Once the bedroom door was closed behind her, she stood with her hands pressed tightly against it for a moment, then hurried back downstairs.

As she came into the lounge, Derrick turned slowly. They stood apart for a moment, then, going to him, she reached up and put her hand on his good shoulder. 'I've been acting very selfishly haven't I? I've suddenly realised how much taking on this job will mean to you. It will give you back your self-esteem, and besides, the long sea journey won't do you any harm.'

She watched him slowly close his eyes, then moisten his lips. He looked at her again before saying, 'I don't deserve you, Dee. You are a wife in a million.' Then he drew her close with his good arm and gazed into her eyes. 'Are you sure? You really are giving me your consent to take this tanker to India?'

Dee couldn't help herself: she burst out laughing. 'Like I had any choice, Derrick. What if I had tried to stop you and you had given in? Can you begin to imagine what our lives would have been like? It might even have become a toss-up as to who killed who first.'

He drew her close, his lips on hers, and when that long kiss was over he said, 'Oh my love. You put up with so much trouble from me, and yet you still go on loving me. You must know just how deep my love for you is, and always has been since you were sixteen years old.'

'Yes, I rather fancy that over the years I have got that message. I think that's enough of arguing the point for one day. As your going back to sea is going to be such an occasion, I think a drink is in order. Sorry we haven't got any rum – you'll have to wait until you are back on board for that – but we do still have a bottle of whisky.' Dee paused now and her look held such devotion Derrick couldn't fail to be moved. He held out his right arm and pulled her close. The drink was forgotten for the moment as they clung to each other, and both of them were counting their many blessings.

The following Friday, Derrick took his wife to London with him, Ann safe and happily settled with her aunt Jodie for the day. One of the men he had to see was Jack Fenwick, who dealt in scrap iron. As the day went on and place names unknown to Dee were tossed back and forth, she found herself getting very tired. It was three o'clock before Derrick told her he was finished. Holding out a black leather briefcase, he smiled at her and said, 'Everything I need to know is in here. Sometime soon I shall fly to Russia and take command of this supertanker, but for now, my darling, we are going to have tea at Lyons Corner House and then I shall take you to Regent Street and let you loose in one of the most famous toyshops in the world. No doubt you will find something there that you think will delight our daughter.'

Once Dee had had a cup of tea, she felt much better and was now busily buttering a scone. Derrick moved closer to her. He waited until he was able to take her hand, then, his voice surprisingly steady, he said, 'Actually I shall be flying to Russia in two days' time.'

Derrick's voice seemed to be coming from far away. It was a long time since Dee had felt like this. Her head was swimming and her hands were shaking, and she was having a job to focus.

'Dee, are you all right?' asked Derrick with concern.

'Yes,' she said, 'yes, I'll be fine in a moment. It was such a shock. Two days! One minute we were only talking about you going away and then suddenly you will be gone.'

They managed to buy a doll's house before leaving London, but the best of the day had long gone. All Dee could think about was how much she would miss Derrick. It had been unnerving, him springing it on her like that.

The next morning he was up bright and early and had his charts laid out on the dining room table. It was unbelievable the number of people who had got wind of this trip and were coming to the house to view the maps that set out the route the tanker would be taking: Sweden, Norway, down through the North Sea, through the English Channel past the south of England, then the Atlantic Ocean, passing Africa, round to the Indian Ocean before finally arriving in Bombay.

Derrick had been gone for seven weeks when Dee received a telegram suggesting that on the coming Thursday she should be up at Beachy Head near Eastbourne. They weren't the only ones. The news had spread fast. Crowds had gathered on this warm day in June to watch the great iron beast steer around the point.

Dee was faced with a problem. How to explain to a little girl that her daddy was out there at sea and could probably see her with the aid of a strong pair of binoculars, but that she wasn't able to see him.

Life had to go on. The whole family made sure that Delia and her young daughter were never on their own for long periods of time. Weekends still drew friends and relations to Marine House, where good food and good company were always to be found. It worked the other way round, too. Dee and her little daughter knew only too well that they had open invitations to visit and stay with any of their numerous family and friends.

Time was slipping by. It would soon be the end of July, and the schools would be breaking up for the children to have their six-week summer holiday. One bright Tuesday morning Dee was walking Ann to school. The little girl was carrying her school case while her mother held on to a few sheets of brown paper and a ball of string. At the end of term all books had to be covered and names clearly printed on each and every one.

'I'll be here this afternoon when you come out from school. You'll have a lot to carry today, won't you?' Dee had to bend her head to talk to Ann, who was still quite tiny.

'We shall probably be a bit late. Miss Whitehead said lessons are going to finish at two o'clock and we are having a tea party.'

'Oh Ann! I wish you had said before. Your auntie Jodie and I would have made some nice cakes and even a trifle.'

'No, the headmistress said she didn't want that. This year the school is providing everything.'

'Oh, very well, but I'll still be here about four. I won't mind if I have to wait. I'll stay here to see you go in now.'

'Look, there's Peggy and Lucy Ludlow coming. I'll walk in with them.'

Dee stayed where she was, not really expecting Ann to turn around today, but the minute she reached the main door she stopped and waved to her mother as usual.

Dee was lost in thought as she let herself back into the house, but her heart felt light when Jodie's voice rang out from the kitchen. 'I guessed you had taken Ann to school, so I let myself in. I have the kettle on and I've also brought some cranberry tarts that I made last night.'

'Then you, my dearest friend, are more than a welcome sight for this lonely old woman.'

'Get on with you, Dee. If anyone else dared to call you an old woman you would go ballistic.'

'Too right I would, but truthfully, Jodie, I

am so pleased to see you. There are too many hours in the day when Derrick is away.'

'I don't know what you're on about. There's hardly a day that you don't see me or Laraine, but if you are that bored, come and do a few stints in any one of our salons. I know for a fact that Michael could use another pair of hands.'

'Don't mind me, Jodie. It's just funny the way things have turned out. Derrick on the other side of the world and me feeling misty-eyed when I should be counting my blessings that he is fit enough to be working again.'

Jodie poured coffee into two cups, set them down on saucers and fetched a saucepan of boiling milk, which she then poured into a pretty milk jug. They each topped their coffee up with hot milk and smiled as they tapped their cups together. 'We've both got so much to be grateful for,' Jodie said, smiling.

'I'll drink to that,' murmured Dee as she sipped her coffee.

'Any plans for today?' Jodie asked later, as she picked up her handbag and prepared to leave.

'Not really. I'm open to suggestions, just so long as I'm back at the school by four o'clock to pick up Ann.'

'Well you may be pleased to hear that I have offered to do a charity thing at a war-den-assisted care home this afternoon. We'll have time to call in to see Michael first, and then you can come and put a few rollers into the old dears' white heads. They will be ever so pleased to see you.'

'How can I refuse when you put the offer so charmingly?' Dee laughed. 'Your car or mine?'

'Might as well take mine, it's nearer the gates,' said Jodie.

Two minutes later they were settled in the car and making tracks for Brighton, where Michael had one of the most successful hairdressing salons outside of the London area.

It had been a great morning. Michael had treated them to an early pub lunch, and by one o'clock both Dee and Jodie were working away like beavers on a line of elderly women.

'It was a pleasure,' Dee found herself saying as she held up a hand mirror for a customer to see what she had done to the back of her hair. And she meant it. While the old ladies were waiting their turn, they had begun to sing – all the old Vera Lynn wartime songs – and almost every one of them had produced a bag of boiled sweets, insisting that both Jodie and Dee suck one as they worked.

The church clock was striking four as Jodie pulled up outside Ann's school in Newhaven. 'You needn't wait if you want to get off,' Dee said. 'I expect you're going out with Philip tonight.'

'Philip is away in town all this week. He'll be back for the weekend. No, I thought you and Ann could come home with me now. I'll cook dinner and you can stay the night and make your way home when you're ready in the morning.'

'Oh Dee, that sounds wonderful, and I know what Ann will say. You know how she loves to visit your house.'

'All settled then. Do you have to go into the school to fetch Ann, or will she come out when she's ready?'

'Oh, she'll be out, though she did say they might be a little later today because they were having a tea party.'

It was a while before parents started to get out of their cars and go forward to meet their children. Lingering goodbyes were being said because it would be six weeks before the children met up again.

Dee caught sight of the Ludlow sisters and got out of the car. 'Is Ann not ready yet?' she called to the girls. 'Should I go into the school and see if she needs any help?'

Peggy and Lucy looked away and said something to their mother, who had come to meet them.

Dee bent her head to the level of the car window and said to Jodie, 'I'm just going to find out what is keeping Ann. I won't be long.'

She strode across the grass to where Mrs Ludlow was talking to her two daughters, but as she approached, they all turned their heads to look at her, and at that moment Dee had the feeling that something was wrong.

Hastily she asked, 'Why hasn't Ann come out of school with you? She is all right, isn't she?'

It was the girl's mother who answered. 'I don't quite understand, Mrs Underwood, but my girls are saying that your Ann went home at break time, just after they had their lunch.'

'She can't have!' Ann gasped, already breaking into a run towards the school entrance. Jodie had got the gist of what had happened and by now she too was out of the car and only a few feet behind Dee.

A lot of activity was still going on in the main hall. A few older children lingered, and several members of staff were busy clearing the tables.

Dee spotted Mrs Morley, the headmistress, and made a beeline for her. 'Please, please tell me where my daughter is.' There was an unmistakable sob in her voice, and try as she might she couldn't stop it. She kept telling herself not to be so ridiculous, that Ann had to be here, but her heart was thumping nineteen to the dozen and the palms of her hands were clammy.

Mrs Morley's face had turned pale, which didn't help matters. 'I had a phone call at lunchtime from a lady who said she was Mrs Underwood, Ann's mother. I had no reason to be suspicious. I didn't recognise your voice, but then I don't think we have ever spoken on the telephone. The lady said that you were going away on holiday and wanted to leave early, and that a relative would be picking Ann up at two thirty.'

'And you let her go?' Dee shot the words out.

'Did you see the person who came to collect Ann?' It was Jodie who asked this down-to-earth question. It didn't seem that Dee was capable of much speech at this moment.

'Unfortunately I have to say no. I helped Ann to gather her belongings together and I fetched her hat and blazer from the cloak-room and saw that she was tidily dressed. Then I was called away for a moment and when I came back into the main entrance hall, all her belongings had gone and so had she. I presumed she had been collected by this relative of yours. I am so sorry.'

'Not half as sorry as I am.' Dee spat the words out through almost clenched teeth. 'There was no relative to pick my daughter up and I certainly did not make any tele-

74

phone call to you. Did you bother to ring back to see if the call was genuine?'

'Again, I am so sorry, the thought never entered my head.'

'May I suggest that you get straight on to the police,' Jodie said, but it was a direct instruction rather than a suggestion.

'Do you really think that is necessary? Ann may be quite safe at home by the time you get there.' Mrs Morley was clutching at straws, more worried about the good name of the school than the fact that a small child, a pupil who had been left in her care, might have been abducted.

'Yes, I do think a call to the police is vital,' said Dee with as much dignity as she could muster. 'We must go, and we shall also ring the station the minute we get home.'

Mrs Morley put out a restraining hand, which stopped Dee in her tracks while Jodie went ahead to start the car.

'Perhaps we shouldn't be too surprised at this turn of events, taking into consideration Ann's particular circumstances.' The headmistress was on the defensive.

'Would you mind explaining what you mean by that?' Dee's tone was as sharp as a razor.

'Well, it was a long time ago, but folk will remember how you came to adopt Ann as a baby.'

Dee clenched her fists to stop herself from

striking this woman, then turned and walked slightly unsteadily to the car.

'Oh my God!' she said as she fastened her seat belt. 'That bloody woman brought up the fact that I wasn't Ann's real mother. She must have a long memory.'

Mrs Morley had shaken Delia more than she would care to admit. But thoughts of the headmistress were thrust into the background as they approached Marine House, because already there was a police car drawn up on the drive close to the front door. It was then that Dee realised that whatever was happening now, it was going to get a whole lot worse as the day went on. It was a sheer nightmare and it had only just begun.

Jodie took charge, telephoning members of the family while Dee spoke with the two police officers. Later, handing a sheet of notepaper to one of the officers, Jodie said, 'This is my name and address. Mrs Underwood will be coming home with me now and she will be staying the night.'

'Are you both Mrs Underwood?' The policeman smiled his question.

'Yes, we are sisters-in-law.'

'Very well, ma'am, I'll phone these details in, and by the time you get home there will be a couple of detectives waiting to take a statement from you both. Can you take a couple of photographs of the little girl with you, and they will want a detailed description of what the child was wearing.'

Dee, literally speechless with rage, was pacing up and down the kitchen, pausing occasionally to bang her fist on the worktop. She was feeling so helpless as she thought about the horror that was unfolding. It was too shocking and frightening for her to be able to think straight.

When the two police constables finally left, Jodie practically pushed Dee through the front door and into the passenger seat of her car. She had made enough phone calls for word of what had happened to reach every member of the family and also their closest friends. By the time they arrived at her house, almost everyone was there. They were all saying how useless they felt and bemoaning the fact that Derrick was miles away at sea when this dreadful drama had started to unfold.

Derrick was the one person who might have been able to make some sense of what was going on. He was always great in a crisis. For heaven's sake why wasn't he here? Dee asked herself over and over again.

The two plain-clothes officers and a female social worker were kindness itself. Everyone agreed that Dee shouldn't be left on her own.

'I'll stay here with my sister-in-law tonight, but I have to go home in the morning,' she insisted. 'I have to be near my phone.'

'Mrs Underwood, I'm so very sorry,' the

older detective said as he took hold of Dee's hand. His voice was gentle and almost hesitant as he added, 'We'll get everyone on to this straight away. The photographs of Ann will help. Try not to worry too much.'

Dee was tempted to tell him it was much too late for that. Images of where their little girl might have been taken and how frightened she must be were already rolling around in her head.

'Please, please, God, keep my baby safe,' she was silently praying. Yet in her mind she couldn't help but fear that her prayers were hopeless.

One way or another it was going to be a very long night. It had turned midnight and they were both ready for bed when Jodie produced two goblets and a bottle of brandy.

'Drink this,' she said, pouring a good measure into Dee's glass. 'You're going to need it. I really think you are.'

# Chapter 6

'Oh no,' whispered Jodie as she opened her front door to pick up her bottles of milk. Three reporters, one with a camera slung round his neck, were grouped together on her driveway. Where the hell was Dee? And where was the morning paper?

When Jodie found Dee, she was sitting on a bench at the bottom of the garden, looking dreadful, holding the newspaper close to her chest. Clearly she was shocked and very frightened.

ABANDONED AT BIRTH; KIDNAPPED AT THE AGE OF FIVE, read the front page of *Sussex News*. How long before the dailies got hold of the story? wondered Jodie.

'Can I persuade you to come into the house and talk about this?' she asked.

'I suppose so,' Dee whispered. Her face was swollen with crying. 'How the hell did they get on to it so quickly?'

'The reporters would tell you they're just doing their job.'

'But why do they have to rake up all the business about Ann being abandoned at birth?' asked Dee, before starting to cry again. 'It is so cruel. And where would they

79

have taken her? She will be so frightened. How long do you think before the police find her?'

Jodie found she couldn't form an answer to these questions. Instead she took the newspaper from Dee and began to read the story.

Dee herself had read the article over and over. She wondered where the press had got all the pictures from. She had almost convinced herself that it had to be the Belgian woman who had given birth to Ann who had now decided to kidnap her. But why? After all this time and when everything had been done according to the very letter of the law. Nearly six years and not one word. It hardly seemed plausible, but who else on God's earth could it be? There was no way she was going to get away with it, Dee declared to herself.

No way in the world.

By mid morning, the two detectives, Arthur Fowler and Jane Goodwin, were back. Their manner as they listened to Dee was concerned and interested.

'I'll be able to keep the press at bay,' Arthur Fowler promised, 'and what's more, you can call me any hour of the day or night.' He also said he was sorry but they needed both Dee and Jodie to appear on television. 'If you make a plea for the safety of little Ann, it may well go a long way to helping us locate her.'

'Oh, that's a really good idea,' said Dee, her voice heavy with sarcasm. 'Let the whole world know that the woman who gave birth to her and then abandoned her on the same day has now decided to reclaim her.'

'At this stage, Mrs Underwood, you shouldn't be making that statement,' the detective quietly rebuked her. 'You have no proof one way or the other that it is her birth mother who has taken her away.'

Until somebody came up with a cast-iron alternative, however, Dee was clinging to her belief. Partly because she told herself that if it was Ann's birth mother who had abducted her, then the chances were that she wouldn't hurt her. It was no real consolation, but it was better than the alternative scenarios.

When the officers finally left, Dee remained sitting at the kitchen table staring into space. There didn't seem to be anything else she could do. More than anything she wanted to speak to Derrick. She so badly needed to hear his voice assuring her that he would make everything all right. It might be possible on a two-way radio, but would it be fair to burden him with this huge problem? What could he do? Please, please, God, let Ann be found before they had to inform Derrick. She missed that man so much. Loved him. Longed to see him.

By midday, Dee was back in her own home.

The shock of losing Ann had hit her hard and she was devastated that the past was being dragged up in the newspapers and was now going to be on TV. The subject would be on everyone's lips: the fact that the child who had been abducted from her school was the same one who nearly six years ago had been abandoned by her mother less than twenty-four hours after her birth. It was appalling to think that Ann might find all this out now, when she wasn't even six years old. How would she cope? She probably wouldn't be able to. And how could she possibly understand that the only mummy and daddy she had ever known weren't going to be around any longer?

Thank God for the family and for their many friends. Everyone was rallying round, yet they were all at a loss as to how they might help. Trouble was, Dee was frightened, terrified of her own thoughts, still convinced that it was Ann's birth mother, Chloe Warburg, who had had a hand in whisking her away. And though Chloe would surely treat Ann kindly, the little girl wouldn't have the slightest idea who she was. As far as Dee could remember, Chloe spoke very little English. Poor Ann would be so bewildered.

Not being able to do anything about this wretched situation was driving Dee mad. During the long hours of the night, unable to sleep, she had tried hard to put herself in

Chloe's position, even going so far as attempting to feel sorry for her. However, the fact remained that it had been the Belgian woman's decision to abandon her baby. Why would she suddenly want to reverse that decision after all this time? It was too late. Too many lives were involved. The woman was being utterly selfish. No one should be allowed to take happiness at the expense of others.

Although Dee had not been there when Ann had been born, she could recall almost every day since she had first taken her into her arms. She had been made fully aware that nobody wanted this baby, no one would take on the responsibility, but she herself had been quick to react. Lifting the wee mite from her cot, she had vowed there and then that this baby would never feel unwanted. It had been a tough decision but one she had lived by ever since. On that day she had become Ann's mother in every sense of the word.

It was she who had held her as she fretted when cutting her first tooth, who had walked the floor with her when she'd had a nasty chesty cold. She who had heard her first words, da-da-da, and then mumma – oh how that one now rang through her mind. She who had clapped her hands as she watched Ann take her first steps.

This couldn't be happening. It wasn't fair.

What would life have to offer if their daughter was never found? That thought was driving her mad; she couldn't stay indoors any longer. She let herself out the back way and onto the beach. The sun was glinting on the water as she walked along the sand, and as she gazed out to sea, she thought about her husband. Apex Shipping had been informed of what had taken place regarding Ann, but she didn't know whether Derrick had yet been told.

From the very moment that she and Derrick had decided to bring Ann up as their own daughter, life had been idyllic. Their huge house had become a real home. Backing on to the beach, it had sea views from almost every room, and the land on either side sloped down to a rocky cove where Derrick and their sons had their boats moored. In the summer the beach was a paradise for adults as well as children, and it was also great to have the woods nearby. Everyone loved to see the wild animals and a great variety of flowers and birds.

Would this Belgian woman take Ann away from all of this?

Would she be allowed to?

Dee walked on, knowing she had no answers to her questions. When she finally reached the end of the beach, she had the choice of either turning back or climbing up the cliff, which would bring her out on to the main road. She decided on the latter. The climb was more difficult than she had anticipated and she slipped a few times, grazing her hands and knees. When finally her feet were safely on the road, she saw Michael Connelly and Danny Spencer coming towards her. With no hesitation, she ran towards them at full tilt, tears pouring down her face.

'Whatever made you come out on your own?' Michael asked, concern sounding in his voice as he pulled her into his arms. At the same time Danny was rubbing her back between her shoulder blades and murmuring words of comfort. They made a strange-looking trio, but Dee had never before been quite so aware of how lucky she was to have these two men in her life. Both were in their late forties, tall and well built, always immaculately dressed, and their manners were charming. They had a way of making a woman feel good, telling her that she was beautiful and talented even when they caught her on the hop, say with rollers in her hair. The two of them had been together for more than ten years, and every member of the Underwood family accepted them and loved them to bits.

'Let's get you home,' Michael said firmly. 'I think a cup of tea will do us all good.'

The telephone was ringing as they entered the house, and Dee quickly picked it up.

'Dee, we have to talk.' Jodie's voice was very brisk, very cool.

'What, what about? Has something happened?'

'Don't panic, Dee, it's something we have to get sorted. Laraine is going to fix dinner for all of us at her house this evening. Can you make your own way there, or do you want somebody to come and pick you up?'

'I'll drive myself. What time does Laraine want us?'

'She said we'll eat about seven, but to come earlier for drinks. Must go, I have to phone Michael now. Are you sure you're all right on your own?'

'I'm not on my own. Michael and Danny are here with me.'

There was a moment's silence, then Jodie's voice came back on the line. 'Put Michael on, please, Dee, I need to have a word with him.'

Dee held the receiver out to Michael and went to find Danny in the kitchen. By the time Michael joined them, the tea was made and the three of them drew up chairs and sat down at the table.

Dee opened up the conversation. 'Michael, did Jodie tell you what she was on about? Why Laraine is gathering us all at her house for a meal?'

'No, no, she didn't. She said she had some news that we should all hear, though why

86

she couldn't have told me what it was over the phone I just don't know. We'll find out soon enough. Are you sure you wouldn't like one of us to come and pick you up this evening?'

'No, really, I will be fine, but I am glad you both popped in this morning.'

'Well we'll be off soon, give you time to make yourself glamorous. You should run yourself a nice bath and try and relax.'

Having dutifully received their warm hugs and gentle kisses, Dee told herself she was going to do exactly as Michael had suggested. For the moment it was the best advice she was going to get.

# Chapter 7

When at home, Dee never locked her front door during the day. Friends and neighbours would pop in, always calling loudly, 'It's only me.'

Suddenly she was aware of footsteps in the tiled entrance hall. Someone had entered the house but had not called out. Alarm bells were ringing in her head as she got up from where she had been lying on the settee.

She recognised the woman from her TV appearances stating her side of the case. Although she had denied being in any way connected with the abduction, Chloe Warburg had lost no time in telling the world that she had every right to be acknowledged as Ann's birth mother.

Now, as she stood directly in front of Delia, Dee was thinking what a downright bloody intrusion it was. Chloe was in her late thirties, short and stocky with very broad hips. The clothes she was wearing were expensive and they suited her well: a silver-grey trouser suit worn with a black velvet top beneath the close-fitting jacket. Her hair was a dark chestnut colour and

Dee found herself being thankful that Ann had Underwood colouring. In no way whatsoever did she resemble her birth mother.

Dee had come to hate that expression. Birth mother! Just because she had carried the baby for nine months and had given birth to her, in no way did that make her Ann's mother. She had deserted that wee child before she'd even known what she looked like. At the time the family had agreed that this unknown woman had done the honourable thing by coming to England for the birth and making sure that the father knew of the baby's existence. So why was she here now, after all these years with no contact?

'You have no right to come into my house,' Dee told her with all the dignity she could muster. 'I have had more than enough of you pleading for sympathy, insisting you are Ann's rightful mother.'

'I thought if I could confront you face to face I might be able to make you see my side of the story.' The words had been blurted out and in no way had they softened Dee's attitude.

'I know full well what you are going to say. You've protested enough to anyone who will listen, including all the newspapers. Ann is almost six years old. You made your decision on the day she was born. She is truly loved, has a good life, a loving family. What the hell

have you ever done for her? She must be terrified being amongst total strangers. Derrick
and I are the only parents she has ever known
and that is the way it's going to stay.'

Having made her intentions clear, Dee
pointed to the door. 'I'd like you to leave. In
any case I am going to telephone the police.
Just by coming here you are admitting that
you know where our daughter is.' In spite of
her bravado, she was trembling. She wished
she wasn't in the house on her own.

At the mention of the police, Chloe Warburg's whole attitude changed, and she
became aggressive. 'She is my child. It was
me who gave birth to her. Why won't you
realise you won't have a leg to stand on if
you insist on dragging us into a court case?'

'Get out now!' Dee shrieked at her.

Chloe's face was like thunder and she was
breathing hard. 'Not until you listen to my
side of the story. Over the years nothing has
gone well for me. My fiancé was killed on the
docks. I was lonely. This year I came to England and rented a caravan for the summer.
Day in day out I've watched you and your
family. You have everything, including my
daughter. Both of you, you made of me one
big fool. All right, the baby was a mistake. A
genuine one. I went along with everything
you both wanted. Did either of you give a fig
for me? I had a lovely young man. He had a
good job; we were to marry, have children of

our own. Now what do I have? Nothing. Do you hear me? He's gone. I am not so young any more and am left without anybody.' Spittle was dribbling from the woman's lips and the look of pure hatred that she was directing towards Dee had her quaking.

Chloe wasn't finished yet. 'I know you have two grown sons, sons who will give you grandchildren. Why should you also have my child?'

The silence that followed was deafening.

Dee had to be honest and admit that at moments in Chloe's story she had felt sorry for her, but that in no way altered the facts. It was Chloe who had abandoned the baby and hadn't been near her in all these years. If Dee hadn't begged Derrick to let her take little Ann on, where would the child have been today? She would have been brought up in an institution somewhere in London, and on reaching school age a foster family might have been found who would have taken her into their home. At all stages of her life charity or state money would have paid for her care and well-being. Nothing like that had taken place. Derrick had proved to the magistrates that he was indeed her father and the judiciary had raised no objection to the baby being placed into his and his wife's care, having first ensured that the child would be going to a good clean home with an ample income to accommodate all her needs.

Dee was taken off guard as Chloe grabbed her arm. She was frightened when she saw that Chloe's other hand was balled into a fist. Dee tried to back away but was hampered by a side table and then a bookcase. She had no doubt that the woman intended to hit her; she wasn't as tall as Dee, but she was a much bigger build and her eyes now looked mad, almost popping out of her head, while her lips were curled back into a savage snarl.

Dee stared at her in utter confusion. Ann was everything to her. She had prided herself on what a fine job she and Derrick had made of bringing her up. How the whole family had closed around her, taken her into their hearts. The idea of sending her to a private school was not only to give her a good education but to protect her to some degree from learning too soon of how she had been born and deserted on the same day. It was supposed to have kept her out of harm's way. Now someone had made a telephone call, walked into the school premises and calmly taken her. Just one look at this angry woman and Dee felt sure her actions from now on would be unpredictable. She was vehemently denying it was she who had carried out the kidnapping, yet the fact that Dee and her husband were still being spoken of as the child's parents seemed to be acting as a red rag to a bull.

Angrily pushing furniture out of the way, her face contorted with rage, Chloe reached out and slapped Dee hard across the face. There was no room for her to turn away. She tried to cover her face with her hands, but now the blows rained down thick and fast. It wasn't just a fist; Chloe was brandishing a long, heavy object. The glass doors of the bookcase smashed, sending splinters in all directions. Suddenly a searing pain to the side of Dee's head sent her reeling, and no sooner did she feel the warm blood trickling down her forehead, clogging up her eyes, than everything became a blur and she slipped into unconsciousness.

'Mum, do we have to wait any longer for Auntie Dee?' Adele asked plaintively. 'It's almost half past seven and I'm starving.'

Laraine had already glanced at the clock many times, and she did so again now before saying, 'To tell you the truth, girls, I'm getting worried. This is not a bit like Dee.'

Annabel sniffed. 'Mum, your roast smells gorgeous. Won't it spoil if you don't dish it up soon?'

Michael and Danny came into the kitchen, and Michael lifted the lid of the electric slow cooker. 'Mmmm,' he murmured. 'Asparagus soup, gently simmering.' He replaced the lid and said quietly, 'I suppose something could have happened to Dee. It seems very odd that she hasn't phoned to say why she is delayed. What was it that you wanted to talk about tonight?'

'Just that I heard through the grapevine that Derrick's tanker has finally arrived in India; hence an impromptu dinner seemed a good idea. Thought we'd all raise a glass to his safe return.'

'But you never told Dee the reason for the get-together?'

'No, I wanted to share the news with all of you. With everyone worried sick over Ann, a dinner party seemed just the thing to brighten us all up, if only for a few hours.'

Michael looked very thoughtful before he quietly said, 'Laraine, you get on with the dinner, but I think it's best if I pop over to Dee's house, see if her car is still there.'

Laraine heaved a great sigh. She had so wanted the evening to go well, but at this moment she was feeling afraid. Dee would never deliberately not turn up. Something must have happened to her. Laraine didn't want to let her imagination run away with her, but there was a chance that Dee had been involved in a road accident. Oh please God, no! she hastily chastised herself.

'I'll come with you,' Danny said quickly to Michael as he made for the front door.

Jodie, who until now had remained silent, said, 'Ring us immediately ... whatever.'

'We will,' the two men said in unison.

They spotted Dee's car parked well up the drive and Michael pulled in next to it. Within seconds they were out of the car and running towards the front door, which they found to be unlocked. In the huge entrance hall they hesitated for a moment. The door that led into the main lounge was closed, but as Danny opened it and switched on the light, they both gasped, such was the shock they felt as they viewed the awful scene in front of them.

Dee was lying in a crumpled heap on the floor, and blood had been splattered everywhere. 'Mind all the broken glass,' Danny warned as Michael hurried to her side.

'Oh my dear God,' Michael exclaimed in horror as they knelt one each side of her. Danny felt her wrist, hoping to find a pulse.

'She's alive,' he whispered, 'but God alone knows for how long. Just look at her. This assault doesn't bear thinking about. Jesus, it must have been vicious.'

Michael bent low over her. 'This wound on the side of her head I'd say is especially bad. We'd better hurry and call for an ambulance.'

While Danny got to his feet and went into the hall to use the telephone, Michael remained kneeling by Dee's side. 'Poor darling,' he mumbled, his tears threatening to choke him. 'You've never done any harm to a single soul in your life, and now this.' He was feeling afraid. Dee was a complete and utter mess, her clothing soaked in blood. 'Dee, can you hear me, my darling? Squeeze my fingers if you can.' He was slowly stroking the back of her hand but getting no response. Once again he asked, 'Can you hear me, Dee?' even though he knew she was unconscious. The head wound really did look very serious. Who could have done this? It didn't look like a burglary; apart from an overturned table and the smashed bookcase, the room didn't appear, to have been ransacked.

'Oh you poor darling.' He was almost crooning to her as he spoke again. 'Dee, please stay with us, we're going to get you to hospital and the doctors will soon have you feeling a little better.'

Having made sure that an ambulance was on its way, Danny called Laraine and told her briefly what had happened. He then set about looking Martin's number up in the notebook that lay beside the phone. He had almost finished explaining the situation to Dee's elder son when the arrival of the ambulance could be clearly heard.

'You and Michael go with her, Danny,' Martin urged over the phone. 'I'll ring my brother and we'll meet you both at the hospital.'

The doctors were doing ward rounds with

several senior nurses in tow. The sister of the ward bent over Delia's bed. Poor Delia really did look a sorry sight. Her head was swathed in bandages, she was almost as white as the sheets on the bed, and she had a drip line in one arm. Beneath the crown of bandages her face was a mass of blue and black bruises and her eyes were swollen beyond belief.

'When the doctors have checked you over, your sons are waiting to come in for their daily visit.' The sister spoke gently, for her patient hadn't been fully conscious for very long. 'I've told them they may have just a few minutes with you. Do you feel up to it?'

'Oh yes please,' said Dee, doing her best to raise a smile.

She had woken up in hospital with a mouth so dry she couldn't have spat a six-pence. Her eyes had felt as if someone was poking red-hot needles into them. She was awake for some time before she realised she was wired up to a machine. She had a job to remember when and how she had got there. Had she had a nightmare? If she had, the person who had simply petrified her had been the woman from Belgium. 'Oh my dear God,' she groaned as her memory came flooding back to her.

It was now Tuesday morning. Delia had been rushed into hospital on Saturday even-ing and had been operated on that same night to remove small fragments of bone that had been embedded in her head wound. Jodie, Laraine and Adele and Annabel had joined Martin and Michael in the waiting room during the long hours of that first night. Come Sunday there had been a constant stream of visitors. Michael and Danny, together with Jodie's two sons Len and Reg, had kept up a supply of coffee and tea for everyone who had wanted to stay. They had only gone home late in the evening once the nursing staff had convinced them that Delia was out of any immediate danger.

Mid morning on the Wednesday.

'Jodie?' Dee queried softly. She was still very confused as to what exactly had happened to her, and her eyesight was not yet anywhere back to normal.

'Yes, Dee, it is me, I'm here,' Jodie hastened to assure her as she gently stroked the back of the hand that lay on top of the white counterpane. 'It has been a terrible few days,' she whispered, 'but you are going to be all right now. Hopefully the pain will get less from here on in. None of us could believe what that woman did to you. We all thanked God that Danny and Michael found you when they did.'

Dee was baffled, feeling all at sixes and sevens. She wondered if Jodie had been there when that woman had been battering her, and if so why she hadn't tried to stop her. She wanted some answers, mainly about Ann. Had she come home yet? But oh dear, she felt so tired, she wasn't up to discussing anything just yet. Her head was aching like mad. She lifted the hand that Jodie was stroking and tentatively touched the bandages around her head. She couldn't move the other hand because the drip line was attached to that arm.

'Have they cut all my hair off?' she asked, with a sob in her voice.

'No, my darling, honestly, only some of it from around where the wound is. Michael has taken the pieces away; he said he is going to plant them to see if they will take root.' Poor Jodie was doing her best to smile and to make her words sound mischievous. 'But right now you have got to rest. If you try and have a good long sleep you'll be fine, as good as new in no time.'

'Jodie, is Laraine here?'

'Yes, love.' Laraine answered for herself. 'I'm sitting at the end of your bed. Adele and Annabel have been in and out every day too. They will be so relieved that you are back with us again.'

Dee let out a long, soft sigh. 'Tell them I love them but I'm sorry I'm not really with it yet.'

'Not to worry, just close your eyes and try to sleep, that will be the best thing to do now.'

'Laraine, have you had any word about my Ann?'

Jodie and Laraine shot a sharp glance at each other. How the hell were they supposed to answer that one?

Confused and groggy as Delia was, their silence struck right through to her heart and her swollen eyes filled with tears as she said, 'If that woman has her way I am never going to set eyes on our little girl again, am I?'

With excellent timing the ward sister came back to stand at Dee's bedside. 'Well now,' she said. 'I think every member of the Underwood clan has had their turn at visiting today, and that is more than enough for my patient to be going on with. So I am going to ask you all to leave.'

Dee felt Jodie kiss her cheek, and then it was Laraine's turn.

Then someone was squeezing her hand and the loving, familiar voice of her mother was saying, 'Goodbye, my darling, God bless you. I'm going to move out of the way 'cos yer dad wants his turn.'

As her father picked up her hand, Dee felt a tear fall on to her skin and his gruff voice, thick with emotion, said, 'We're doing everything possible, Dee, and so are the police. Please believe that we will find Ann and bring her back to you.'

Her parents stayed a moment or two before they both leaned down and gently kissed her forehead, and then everyone left.

She did feel sleepy, but not so dozy that she didn't know they were no nearer to finding Ann than they had been before Chloe Warburg had paid her a visit.

Every member of the hospital staff had been made aware of the circumstances under which Delia Underwood had received her injuries. As members of the public they had read the history of the case in the daily papers, and had watched the interviews that had taken place on the TV. By and large most people seemed to be on the side of the woman who had taken on the wee baby abandoned at birth. Although the child was illegitimate, this woman had found it in her heart to forgive her husband and to take on the role of a true parent. Now look what she had got for her pains: a damn good battering at the hands of some foreign woman who had decided that after nearly six years she wanted her baby back.

The ward sister sighed heavily as she asked her nurses to get on with refilling the drugs trolley. She herself was going to administer the injection that was due to Delia Underwood. If nothing else, she was able to see that for the next few hours her patient would be sure of a long, peaceful sleep. God knew the poor woman deserved that much, she thought as she methodically prepared the syringe.

## Chapter 8

Two weeks had slipped by. Delia seemed to be getting better, although her eyes still held that haunted look. The hospital said they were going to keep her in a few more days for observation. She seemed to have only a little recollection of her ordeal, and everyone agreed that until she was ready to talk about it, it might be wisest to leave the matter alone, rather than try to force the memories.

This suited Dee down to the ground. 'Hindsight often gives us the wrong perspective,' she said very quietly to Jodie, who was sitting beside her bed. 'Sometimes I think I knew all along that the time would come when that woman would turn up again. It might sound strange to you, but it is true. The years Derrick and I have had Ann as our daughter, we have been so happy. After Derrick's horrendous injuries, it was a gift of a new life. A gorgeous little girl so full of fun, us watching her, loving her more and more as the months went by, as she developed and left her babyhood behind.'

Jodie nodded slowly. 'Makes us all realise that it was because of your determination that Ann became a unique gift. In the beginning a lot of us had our doubts as to whether you were doing the right thing in taking on a baby only a few days old. Even Derrick wasn't a hundred per cent sure. But not you, Dee, you never wavered. From the very outset you had the baby's best interests in mind.' Jodie's smile became wider. 'If it hadn't been for you, God alone knows where Ann might have ended up. You took something that was very wrong in the beginning and made it into something right for everyone concerned. Ann needed you and you have never failed her. You couldn't have loved her more, or done more for her.'

Dee felt choked up. Days and days it seemed that she had lain here, listening to folk telling her what a good mother she had been to Ann. It was all very well, and good to hear, but she felt ragged in herself, aches and pains all over her body, and she hadn't the strength to stand alone when the nurses got her out of bed. What good was she to Ann right now? And oh, how she wished somebody could tell her where Ann was. How could one little girl disappear off the face of the earth? Why the hell couldn't the police trace whoever it was that had taken her and find out where they were keeping her?

Dee let her shoulders slump and her head drop back to rest on the pile of pillows behind her. She felt as weak as a kitten, and lying here she was utterly useless. She should be up and out searching for her little girl. That last thought brought a sob into her throat, and try as she might she couldn't stop the flow of tears. She quickly covered her face with both her hands as she heard the door to this single bedroom open. She didn't want the nurses to see her upset.

'I think this might help,' said a deep male voice, familiar and yet strange.

Dee brushed at her eyes and peeped through her fingers. 'Derrick,' she whispered, afraid to believe what she was seeing. But sure enough he was standing there, her huge great suntanned husband, holding out a pure white handkerchief.

He stepped to the side of her bed, placed his right arm around her shoulders to raise her up a little and then used the handkerchief to gently wipe away her tears. 'Oh my darling,' he was murmuring as his wife gazed in disbelief at this husband she had thought was somewhere in India.

Jodie got to her feet saying tactfully, 'I'll leave you two to it,' and with the broadest smile she had managed in a long time she quietly left the room.

'Oh Derrick,' Dee murmured again. 'Is it really you?'

'You'd better believe it, my darling, and as soon as the doctors say the word, I am going to take you home. Our own doctor will visit you and if need be we'll engage a nurse.' Now he was gently pressing his lips to her forehead. 'Why did this have to happen when I was miles away? But if I have to move heaven and earth I will, I promise you; I'll get our Ann back.' Silently he looked at the bruises still visible on Dee's face. His wife had suffered badly and she did not deserve such treatment. Something would have to be done about Chloe Warburg. That woman might not have been personally responsible for the carrying-off of their daughter, but he would lay odds that she was involved in it right up to her neck.

But that was a thought he preferred to keep to himself, at least for the time being.

Right now he had to bring his handkerchief into use again, because the tears were once more trickling down his wife's cheeks.

Dee couldn't take her eyes off him as she softly said, 'Thank you so much, Derrick. You'll never know how much I needed to hear you say those words.'

It was three more days before the hospital doctors would agree to discharge Dee, and during that time Derrick scarcely left the hospital. He felt that the situation had been reversed. For months on end his wife had tirelessly nursed him through his horrific injuries; if only he were capable of doing the

105

same for her. The advice he had been given was that Delia was suffering mentally as much as anything, and as everyone was aware, only finding their daughter safe and sound was going to put an end to that.

When at last it was time for Dee to leave hospital, Derrick helped her from the bed into the wheelchair that would take her out to the car. He had so much to tell her about his travels, and she would gladly listen, but they both knew that they were skirting painfully around the biggest problem of all, that nobody seemed able to solve.

Who had their daughter, and where was she being kept?

So many friends, relations and people in authority were asking the same questions. The story hadn't died down; still the papers, the radio and the television carried the news. But there had been no answers to the many questions.

Everyone, it seemed, had decided to welcome Derrick home from his voyage and Dee back from hospital. As they all sat around in the lovely lounge at Marine House Derrick was answering as many questions as Martin and Michael could fire at him. It seemed as if by mutual consent the subject of Ann was to be left alone for the time being.

It was Michael Connelly who had started the ball rolling by asking, 'Was the tanker in good shape by the time you docked her in India?'

Derrick had been engrossed in telling Dee's parents how good the shipping line had been to him. 'Normally I would have had to take pot luck for the homeward journey, short trips from one port to the next; it could have taken me weeks to arrive back home. But as soon as the news hit the wires about Ann having been abducted, they came up with a first-class flight to Heathrow. So yes, I was more than grateful.'

Turning now to Michael, he let out a bellow of a laugh. 'Was the tanker in good shape? That was your question, yes?'

Michael looked a bit mystified as he said, 'Well, before you left these shores, your opinion was that she was a huge clapped-out iron giant. And you were worried as to whether the ship that was being used to tow the tanker would last the journey.'

'And at the time that was exactly what my feelings were. Surprisingly, though, we got through without too many mishaps. All went really well on the long trip out, and I was thrilled to have got her there in one piece.' Having said that, Derrick threw back his head and let out another great bellow.

His sons looked at each other and Martin asked, 'Are you going to let us in on the joke, Dad? Because there obviously is one.'

'There most certainly is, son,' Derrick said,

still smiling broadly. 'On arrival we had some top brass from the Indian government come aboard, and their congratulations on our voyage were freely given. I myself was thinking it was a job well done when one of them explained that the tanker was to be broken up. Yes! Don't look so astonished; he meant it, though at the time I thought it was incredible. Turns out that the ship's new owners intended to break it up to make pots, pans, gates, fencing and every other metal object you could imagine. The officials were quick to explain that every section and every panel, together with every nut, bolt and screw, would be melted down and put to good use.'

The room fell silent for a minute, then everyone burst out laughing.

'All that way to be broken up for scrap!' was the general cry.

'Damned expensive saucepans,' Martin joked.

His father grinned. 'I put in an order for a set to be sent home to each of my sons.'

Jodie was going around the room filling up glasses, and when she was satisfied that everyone had had a top-up, she said, 'Let's all drink to Derrick's safe homecoming and to having Ann back where she belongs, and then I think we had better make tracks for our own beds, because we have to remember this is Dee's first night back home.'

Kisses and hugs were given and received and soon it was just Derrick and Dee who remained. 'Let's leave everything for tonight. I'll carry you up to bed and we can talk properly in the morning,' Derrick said, sounding as tired as he felt.

It would only be a short reprieve, yet Dee felt comforted as Derrick picked her up in his arms and walked slowly up the stairs. She managed to get her dress off and her nightdress on and she watched as Derrick pulled the heavy curtains together. Then he took his clothes off and put on his pyjamas and got into bed to lie beside her.

'Been a long time,' he murmured as he pulled her in close to him and she nestled her head into his good shoulder. Simultaneously they softly sighed, each one feeling grateful that once more they had each other. Yet foremost in both their minds were still the same questions.

Where was their daughter and when were they going to see her again?

Derrick's hand continued to smooth her hair and several times he whispered, 'I love you so much, Dee.' That sentence was followed by the assurance, 'We will get our baby back, I promise you. We will have her back home where she belongs.'

There would be no lovemaking that night. It was enough that they could touch, feel and hold each other. Even words weren't necessary. Each knew exactly how the other one was feeling.

Even so, it was a long, long time before either of them slept.

# Chapter 9

Two weeks had slipped by since Delia had been discharged from hospital. Her bruises had faded and in herself she felt much better, but daily living was far from normal. Relations and friends still dropped in on any pretext, but the question of the whereabouts of little Ann was avoided. Everyone felt for Dee; that she was a good mother was never in doubt. As for Derrick, he was always respected and in the main he was well liked. Naturally there was plenty of talk concerning him and Ann. Coals would always be raked over in a case like this. A man who had two grown sons had suddenly found himself with a baby daughter. Most understood how he had come to love that daughter so very much.

But his wife, if all the stories were true, was a really remarkable woman. She had condemned no one and had taken on the role of mother to a newborn baby who had been abandoned. That hadn't been normal human nature. It had been an extraordinary kindness in what had been extreme circumstances. How could a stranger come to love another woman's child so very much?

111

Especially when she was well aware that it had been her own husband who had fathered the child.

And now it had become a drawn-out and heartbreaking situation to which as yet not a soul had come up with a solution. However, day-to-day living had to go on, even though there were times when tempers became fraught.

The police had worked hard when Ann had first gone missing, but as the days went by, obviously their commitment to the problem had lessened. That fact alone made things even tougher for Delia and Derrick, who were at their wits' end most of the time, feeling utterly useless.

It was eight o'clock on Monday morning, three weeks after Dee had been discharged from the hospital, when Derrick opened the front door to bring the milk in from the doorstep and found Peter Smith, their local constable, walking up the path.

Derrick was to say afterwards that at that moment his heart leapt with hope. He called out immediately, 'Have they found her?'

'Yes, they have. She was picked up in Dover in the early hours of this morning. May I come inside?'

It was as if Derrick was in a daze; he shook his head, trying to clear it, hoping he had heard right. 'Sorry, I don't know what came over me. Of course, come away in, my wife will be over the moon.'

Dee's face paled as the policeman stepped into the kitchen, but then she caught sight of Derrick's face, a grin spreading from ear to ear, and her heart almost missed a beat.

With two sets of eyes fixed firmly on him, the constable took a deep breath before saying, 'All I know, Mrs Underwood, is that your daughter is now in safe custody, at a children's home I think is what my sergeant said. A man was carrying her as he made an attempt to board a ferry bound for France. Being a weekend, the ferries were busy, but apparently a customs officer noted the child's long fair hair and insisted the man step aside for questioning.'

Dee was staring into space, dozens of questions rolling around in her head, but she made no attempt to speak for she was silently thanking the Lord Jesus Christ that at least she now knew that their daughter was still alive.

The constable broke the silence. 'I don't have any more details to give you, I'm afraid – the man in question wasn't brought to our local station – but I'm told that I can confirm that the child who is now in safe custody is without a doubt Ann Underwood.'

'Why couldn't the police have brought her straight home to us?' Dee was quick to ask, and the plea in her voice was enough to evoke sympathy in the hardest of hearts.

Constable Smith didn't answer for a moment, and when he did, he spoke gently. 'At least we've got the child back before she was whisked away from these shores, and that surely is something to feel grateful for.' He stepped closer to Delia and looked into her eyes. 'Your little lass has touched the hearts of so many people and the admiration for yourself shows no bounds. There's talk that folk are getting up a petition stating what a good mother you've always been from the day you took care of the child. Might help to get those in high places to make the right decision when it comes to court.'

Dee jerked herself backwards and said very firmly, 'I don't believe that after all these years I am going to have to appear before judges in a court of law to prove that my intentions when offering to take on an abandoned child were honourable. For Christ's sake, somebody should start remembering that at the time that little girl was born, nobody, not one single person, was prepared to give her so much as a second glance. It was me, only me, who took her and cared for her.'

Suddenly Dee was losing control. She flung her arms wide and her voice was loud and harsh as she said, 'These judges should be made to come here and see this home where our Ann has grown up. She's wanted for nothing, we've given her everything, but most of all we've loved her. Tell him, Derrick, please, we have to have our Ann back. They've found her and yet they haven't brought her home. We're still none the wiser as to where she is or has been all this time.'

Derrick came quickly to her side, and though in her distress she did her best to fight him off, he managed to wrap his good arm around her. 'Please, Dee, take some deep breaths and calm down. At least we know our Ann is alive and apparently well, and thanks to the beady eye of a customs officer she is still in this country. That was my one dread, that whoever had taken her had straight away whisked her off out of the country. At least now we know that is not the case.'

Peter Smith felt terrible. He knew none of this was anything to do with him, but who on earth wouldn't feel for this poor woman? No wonder she was half demented with all the worry she had suffered these past weeks. His voice held all the emotion he was feeling as he quietly said, 'Mr and Mrs Underwood, I'd better be off now. I've been on night duty. My sergeant said I should call in on you on my way home, bring you the news that your little girl has been found. He thought it would be a relief for you both. I'm only sorry I can't tell you more about what has happened.'

'Oh Constable, you know it is a great relief

and we really are grateful, both me and my wife. Sorry about Delia's outburst, though perhaps it has done her good to let off some steam.'

The policeman heaved a sigh of relief. 'OK then, I'll be on my way. I'm sure you will be getting more good news before the day is out.'

Both Delia and Derrick walked towards the front door with the policeman, but in the hall Dee stopped and looked about her. 'You know,' she began, still sounding very angry, 'the authorities can send any number of social workers and so-called do-gooders, but this has been a beautiful, comfortable, happy home over the years that Ann has been growing up, and I defy anyone to come here and try to prove differently.' She couldn't go on. Her heart was hammering against her ribs and her breath was coming in short, sharp gasps. She looked up at Derrick and her voice was barely audible as she murmured, 'It seems such a long time since we've listened to her chattering. Somebody has to bring her back to us. She has to come home, because this is where she belongs.'

Derrick practically pushed his wife down on to a chair, saying softly, 'Stay there, Dee, while I see the constable out, then I'll make you a nice cup of tea.'

Derrick himself had almost reached breaking

116

point when he heard Jodie and Laraine open the front door and call out loudly that they were coming in. 'Thank God,' he murmured. At this moment they were exactly what Delia needed. He had made tea for her and laced it with brandy, but she had hardly touched it. It seemed that she was feeling worse, if that were possible; all she kept repeating was, 'They've found her. Why can't she be brought home? Will somebody please tell me why?'

Derrick's thoughts were running along the same lines. Even though Ann had been found and they had been notified that she was safely tucked up in a children's home, they were still not allowed to know exactly where she was. 'God almighty! Who makes these bloody stupid rules?'

He had drunk his own cup of tea, then, unable to watch Dee still crying, he had reached for the telephone and dialled Directory Enquiries to obtain the telephone number for the police station in Dover. That had been no problem. With the number written down, he had swiftly dialled, but all he'd got had been a recorded message, an indifferent-sounding female voice telling him that the station was closed for business but that urgent matters might be dealt with on the following number. He had also dialled that number. The telephone had rung on and on but nobody had answered. It was as he'd put

117

the phone down and muttered, 'Damn, God give me strength,' that he'd heard the voices of Laraine and Jodie.

Walking towards them, he managed a smile of welcome as he said, 'You two are a sight for sore eyes. If ever Dee needed you both, she most certainly does today. Come on in and hear the latest news.'

The two friends sat down one each side of Delia. Laraine kissed the top of her head and then ruffled her hair affectionately. Jodie could see that Dee was at breaking point; she had seen it coming for a while now. She persuaded Dee to sit up straight and take some deep breaths, and finally Dee was able to speak calmly.

'Ann has been picked up in Dover,' she began, making a great effort to smile. 'She's safe, according to the police constable who came here and told us, but we're not allowed to see her yet. It's driving me and Derrick mad; Christ knows what it must be doing to Ann. She must be so frightened.'

Derrick came into the lounge bringing a tray of coffee and cups with him. His shoulders were hunched as he set the tray down on a side table. 'I presume Dee has told you that Ann has been found, but the buck seems to have stopped there. We're no nearer being able to see her. I've made two phone calls and got nowhere. Just look at what it's doing to Dee, and even I feel really buggered. How much more can either of us take?'

As usual, it was Jodie who took charge. She poured coffee for herself and Laraine, then, having taken a few sips from her cup, she got to her feet and stood in the centre of the room.

'It's Monday morning, the start of a new week, and I suggest that you get yourselves ready and go out and find some straightforward legal advice. No need to go tearing off to London, seeking the best that money can buy. Try one of the well-known solicitors in Brighton, lay the facts out and listen to whatever advice they have to offer. If it doesn't do any good, it can't do either of you much harm. Have a nice lunch out, talk to people who are paid to listen, who will look at this case skilfully and will be competent enough to give you the best advice. Come on now, the pair of you. Let's see you make a start.'

'Not leaving us much choice, is she?' Derrick smiled at his wife as he helped her to stand up.

It had been good advice that Jodie had offered. Both Delia and Derrick were feeling much better as Derrick drove into one of Brighton's many multistorey car parks.

Derrick seemed to know his way around Brighton very well. He had his good arm linked through Dee's, making sure that he held her close to his side as they walked through the famous Lanes. In less than ten minutes they found themselves in the business quarter, and with no hesitation at all Derrick, spotting a brass plate attached to the outside wall of a tall building, said, 'We'll try this one. They'll soon set us right if we're on the wrong track.'

In the outer office a very smart, clean-cut young man listened to Derrick's request for an appointment and asked him for a short outline of the business they wished to discuss.

'Please take a seat and I will see if anyone is free,' he said, smiling directly at Dee.

Only minutes later he was back, shaking his head. 'I am sorry,' he began. 'The first available appointment would be with Mr Richardson at ten o'clock tomorrow morning.'

'Tomorrow won't do! We have to get some advice today.' The words burst forth from Delia just as the door behind her opened and she was pushed forward.

The young woman who had opened the door had dropped a thick sheaf of papers, which scattered to the ground. However, she ignored the mess and immediately apologised to Dee that she hadn't taken more care when entering.

Having helped to get Delia steady on her

feet, the woman asked kindly, 'Can I help in any way?'

The young man leaned forward and explained that Mr and Mrs Underwood were just leaving because there was no lawyer free to see them.

'Well in that case, at least let me try and make amends for my clumsiness. Give me just a minute, please, John,' she said, smiling at her young colleague, 'and then bring Mr and Mrs Underwood through to my office.'

In a very short time, Dee and Derrick were seated side by side facing a desk in a corner of a large, businesslike office, one wall of which was mostly window.

'Jane Clarkson,' said the young woman, reaching her hand across the desk to Derrick and Dee in turn.

At that moment Dee thought she was staring at one of the most beautiful young ladies she had ever seen. Jane Clarkson was quite tall and slim, with well-shaped blonde hair and the most beautiful deep blue eyes. Her skin was lightly tanned and a few freckles were scattered across her perfectly shaped nose, which had Dee thinking that perhaps she had just returned from a foreign holiday. However, it was her smile that set Dee's mind at ease; it was so friendly, and it revealed absolutely perfect white teeth. All of which gave Dee the feeling that she was going to like this smartly dressed woman.

Derrick had answered Miss Clarkson's opening questions and had also stated his and Dee's full names and their address and given a very brief outline of why they were sitting here in this office.

Now Miss Clarkson held up her hand and said, 'I must stop you there, Mr Underwood, and declare that I have previous knowledge of the circumstances regarding the abduction of your daughter.'

The look she turned on Derrick wasn't one of mere curiosity, nor was it as if she were prying; it was definitely businesslike, and it left Derrick feeling that this young woman was totally in control.

'I have to tell you here and now that I have read up on what the media are saying, and I am truly sorry that you have suffered such an agonisingly long wait to find out where your daughter is. I also watched your appeal on TV, Mrs Underwood, and my heart went out to you.'

Fear clutched at Dee. Oh dear, was this going to be a rejection?

'So does previous knowledge of our case prevent you from acting on our behalf?' Derrick asked. His voice was low and he sounded totally defeated.

'I haven't previously discussed your case with anyone, and all the knowledge I have up until now has been available to any member of the public. Should you decide you wish to trust me with more details – in other words engage me to act for you in a case that might well be brought into a court of law – then I would be bound to act in your interest and to work only on information given to me by yourselves. In short, there would be a sworn oath of confidentiality between us.'

'Really!' Dee had uttered the word without thinking. She was astonished. They had walked into this office straight off the street, and already Miss Clarkson was more or less stating that she was on their side. She turned and looked at Derrick. He too was smiling as he leaned towards her and took hold of her hand.

At last someone was willing to listen to their side of the story, and maybe would even be able to offer a gleam of hope.

They were brought back to earth as Miss Clarkson asked, 'Is there anything I can get either of you?'

'No, thank you. Perhaps a coffee later,' Derrick replied. 'For now I would rather get down to the brass tacks of this business. What my wife and I really need to know is just where we stand legally. This whole rotten situation seems to be dragging on and we are both at our wits' end.'

'Well, as I have already admitted, I am aware of the bare bones of this case, but suppose you, Mrs Underwood, begin at the very beginning and tell me what made you decide to take on an abandoned baby who was only a few days old.'

Derrick smiled his encouragement to Dee. She cleared her throat and let her memory slide right back to the day two social workers had turned up on her doorstep armed with a slip of paper on which her husband's name and address had been written. They had been quick to give the information that the slip of paper had been left pinned to the lining of a cot in which a baby girl was lying in Hammersmith Hospital. The mother had apparently given birth to the girl the previous day and had then disappeared, abandoning her newborn baby.

Dee remained remarkably calm as she carefully related everything that had taken place since that day. When she paused for breath, Jane Clarkson cut in with a question.

'Mrs Underwood, were you on your own when you made your first visit to the hospital?'

'Yes, I was.'

'Mr Underwood, were you at sea during that period?'

'No, unfortunately I knew nothing of the birth of this child until much later. A matter of a good few weeks, as it happens. As soon as I was given the facts, I did immediately make all financial arrangements necessary for the baby's welfare.'

Miss Clarkson looked thoughtful for a moment before saying, 'I do have a little knowledge of your accident whilst you were at sea, but would you please give me details of what happened to you and exactly where you were when the mother gave birth to this baby girl in London?'

Derrick considered the question for a moment before he cautiously began to speak. 'I had a feeling that this batch of correspondence might prove to be useful,' he said, and it was only then that he withdrew a folder from inside his overcoat.

Derrick had shown great forethought; he had brought with him a portfolio that contained his complete medical history, from the day of the explosion until the completion of his treatment at the specialist burns unit in East Grinstead. His good hand was shaking as he leant forward and passed the folder to Miss Clarkson.

She gave the contents a quick appraisal before saying, 'It was certainly very astute of you to bring this with you today. It will be of immense help as I work my way towards getting a complete picture of the case. So, my turn to tell you a little about this firm, and then you will have to make a decision as to whether you wish us to act on your behalf.

'Saunders and Merchant are a large, reputable firm, well able to deal with cases that are brought before either a county court or a magistrates' courts. We also have one member of the firm who is an associate of the Law Society specialist family panel, whom I am sure will be of great help to you. Now, let's take a short break. I'll order us some coffee, give you time to get your thoughts together.'

Jane Clarkson had been studying Dee's face while her husband had been speaking, and she was shocked to see just how much she was suffering. The poor woman was a bundle of nerves!

While they all waited for the coffee to be fetched, both Delia and Derrick were busy with their own thoughts. It was Dee who broke the silence.

'If we can't persuade the authorities that Ann is better off with us in the only home she has ever known, will that automatically mean that the case will have to go to court?' she asked Miss Clarkson.

'Yes, I'm afraid it will.'

'And will you have to wear a white wig and a long flowing black gown?'

Jane Clarkson was having a job not to laugh. However, she pulled herself together and spoke softly to Dee. 'That get-up you have just described is for judges and barristers. I'm only a solicitor.'

'Oh, I thought if we did end up in court, we would need a bigwig of some sort to act for us.'

'And that is exactly what you will get if

126

need be. Please, Mrs Underwood, try not to worry. Today you and your husband have taken the first step towards getting help. Under your instructions I shall be with you all the way. I do the groundwork, you might say, prepare all the records we need for the barrister. Even in court I would be there with you for the whole duration of your case.'

At that moment a young lady dressed in a severe black suit and white shirt entered the office carrying a tray on which were three cups and saucers, a coffee pot and a small jug of cream, as well as a silver bowl containing sugar lumps. The young lady began to pour the coffee. Derrick had risen to his feet and was standing beside the small table ready to hand out the cups. Except for the rattle of china, the room had gone silent.

Once the young woman had left, Miss Clarkson asked, 'Mrs Underwood, are you aware of the identity of Ann's mother?'

'She was a Belgian prostitute,' said Dee. 'Her name is Chloe Warburg.'

'And from the very outset were you aware that your husband was the father?' asked the solicitor, very warily.

'No, of course I wasn't. As time went on and various events came to light, I began to realise that that might be the case.'

'Would you care to tell me how you eventually came to learn the truth?'

'Certainly. My husband's eldest brother, John Underwood, came to see me. None of us had heard a word from Derrick for almost a year. The shipping company still paid my allowances, but had never informed me that Derrick had been involved in an accident. I now know that Derrick himself had given the order; he didn't want any of us to see how badly he had been disabled.'

Dee sighed heavily, and Derrick came to her and refilled her cup. He also went to the desk and replenished Miss Clarkson's cup. When both woman had drunk from the fresh coffee, Jane nodded to Dee and said, 'You are doing exceptionally well. Can you please carry on for a little while yet?'

Another sigh escaped Dee's lips, but she sat up straighter in her chair, took a deep breath and began to speak again.

'Much later I found out that John had seen his brother on a few occasions; he was the only visitor that Derrick had allowed. John was well aware of all the facts. It wasn't until that woman came to England to give birth to the baby that he felt the truth should be brought out into the open. He paid me a visit. Believe you me, Miss Clarkson, he had the hardest job in the world trying to convince me that my husband had not had an affair on the side. In the end he did manage to convince me that he was telling the truth. It was only then that I learned just how ill

Derrick had been and how horrendous were his wounds. John also described in detail the mental anguish my husband had suffered. He longed to see me but was scared that I might reject him. That was something he vowed he would not be able to stand.

'To put it bluntly, just as John did when he paid me that visit, it was Derrick's orderly who had decided that sex might be the therapeutic treatment Derrick needed to improve his state of mind. He was in hospital in Belgium at that time, where prostitution is legal, and so this loyal man who had looked after Derrick twenty-four hours of every day since the explosion did what he thought was best and brought into the hospital a young woman, who he paid to have sex with Derrick. For the whole nine months not a word had come to light that the woman had become pregnant.'

Dee's head dropped forward and her shoulders sagged. It was a full minute before she was able to raise her eyes and look her husband full in the face. Then, in little more than a whisper, she said to him, 'I am so very sorry, Derrick, dragging all of it up again.'

He came across the room, dropped to his knees and took hold of both of her hands, looking straight into her eyes as he spoke tenderly. 'No need for apologies, Dee, we've come too far for that. Let's hope that we have revealed enough this morning for Miss Clarkson to start the ball rolling and so bring our little girl safely back home to us.'

Watching this couple, Jane Clarkson was almost moved to tears. 'Just one question and then I think we can leave it for today. I will speak with Russell Harwood, the barrister I mentioned, and on your way out you can make another appointment, say for two days' time. By then I should have all my notes printed out and have some idea as to the way we will proceed. How does that sound to you, Mr Underwood?'

'Fine, we'll do that, and meanwhile we would both like to thank you for the kindness and consideration you have shown us today.'

Derrick was shaking hands with Jane Clarkson when Dee spoke up. 'You said you had one more question?'

'Yes, yes I have. You say you had Ann in your care for the whole of her young life. Did you ever have her christened? And did you on any occasion leave her in the care of other people for a period of time? Oh, sorry, that's two questions!'

Dee smiled and shook her head; it didn't matter. 'Yes, we had her christened Ann Kathryn Underwood, in the old church in Rye in June 1985. As to leaving her for a period of time, never. If we went on holiday then she came with us. For a day at a time, yes. We have a large extended family, and each and every member loves our child dearly.'

'Thank you, Mrs Underwood. We'll meet again in a couple of days. Meanwhile, try not to worry too much.'

It was in silence, with arms linked, that Derrick and Dee walked slowly through the Lanes until they went down on to the seafront. Derrick suggested that they have lunch at the Old Ship Hotel.

Having eaten a really good meal, they returned to the car. Derrick was driving the short distance home when he asked, 'Dee, do you feel any better for meeting up with Miss Clarkson?'

'Yes, I think I do, though I do wish we had thought to ask her if she could get the authorities to grant us permission to visit our daughter, wherever she is being held.'

'Please don't start worrying again. I will telephone Miss Clarkson as soon as we get home. She did give me her card and said to ring if anything more occurred to us. She will soon find out if it is possible.'

When Derrick had turned the car into their driveway, he switched off the engine, got out and went to the passenger side to help Dee out. 'You go on in, love, I'll put the car away and I won't be far behind you.'

# Chapter 10

It was February and the weather had not got any better. Back in October it had rained continually; not just showers, but a continuous deluge, causing severe flooding in many parts of the country. Today it was bitterly cold and during the night there had been a really heavy fall of snow. Jodie was having to walk through snowdrifts on the way to the local shops. The winter was flying by, except that this unexpected snowfall was going to delay the start of spring.

She had been thrilled this morning to hear that at last Derrick and Dee had been granted a permit to visit their daughter in the children's care home in Dover where Ann was being kept. Safe custody was the description the authorities had chosen to use. But try telling that to Ann's parents! How could anyone argue that a child who had known a happy home with good caring parents from almost the day she had been born would be better off in council custody?

However, Jodie wasn't at all sure that this first visit since Ann had been so cruelly abducted would turn out to be a good thing. How heartbreaking was it going to be? Seeing the little girl for a couple of hours at most, and then having to leave her again. It was enough to tear any parent apart. And naturally it would be a great wrench for Ann too who would want to cling on to her parents when the time came for them to leave her.

Poor Dee and Derrick were having the most awful time one way and another. That bloody Belgian woman who had seriously beaten Dee should have been arrested. As the police were fond of saying, though, they had to find her first. She had put herself in the limelight enough when trying to whip up sympathy for herself, and the newspapers had loved her. But now she'd gone to ground, knowing full well that she had done serious damage to poor Dee. It was a good thing that Derrick and Dee were so close, so happily married; if they hadn't been, this chapter of their lives would have truly driven them mad.

These thoughts drew Jodie to think of her own personal life. Things were still going well with Philip, who was always attentive, charming, generous to a fault. He managed to get hold of tickets for the latest London shows. He wined and dined her at the very best restaurants and hotels, and the gifts he insisted on buying her were tasteful and expensive. Yet always there was that lingering doubt. Philip was reluctant to make a commitment.

When their names had first started to be linked together, he'd cooled off, hadn't been quite as enthusiastic. Jodie had put it down to the fact that she had two teenage boys. As time went on, Philip seemed to accept Reg and Lenny, was comfortable with them at a party or when in a group of family members, but he still mostly shied away from one-to-one situations. The trouble had always been that her sons were well aware of his feelings.

It was probably too late now to wish for anything different. Too much water had flowed under the bridge.

Both her sons seemed to have settled down happily. Neither of them had chosen to get married yet, though they both had a mortgage, had each bought a nice property and were living with their partners. They earned a good living, with their boat and their fishing as a lucrative sideline.

Things were viewed so very differently in this day and age. Neighbours didn't huddle together on their doorsteps and talk in whispers if a young unmarried couple moved into their street. It was the same when babies were born. Not a soul turned a hair if the parents weren't wed.

Although Jodie got on very well with both the young ladies her sons were now living with, she still hoped they would very soon lawfully become her daughters-in-law. And if her sons were to become fathers, she would much rather that the new members of the family were automatically entitled to take the name of Underwood. Otherwise there was always the chance that when the children were of an age to go to school, some clever-dick might tell them they were bastards. That would be one step too far for Jodie! But if ever the situation did arise, she knew she would let fly, she wouldn't be able to help herself. For the moment, better that she kept her thoughts to herself. This was a new, modern era and she was beginning to show her age, was what her Len and Reggie would be quick to tell her in no uncertain terms if she was daft enough to voice her thoughts out loud.

It was John, their father, and thoughts of him that were really keeping her awake at night. Since he had spent that short spell in prison, it appeared that he had altered. Turned over a new leaf, as her mother-in-law would like everyone to believe.

Jodie also wanted to believe that this new John was genuine, because it would be a whole new side to him, one she had never seen before in all the years she had been married to him. Could he have changed so much, so late in life? She'd dearly like to believe he had.

Maybe it wasn't too late; at fifty-two perhaps he really had had a change of heart and had begun to mend his ways and think about others rather than himself. If that was so, it would be the first sign of John acting as a responsible adult, and Jodie felt it was the least she could do to listen to what he was saying and help him with what he was aiming to do.

Trouble was, for all her reasoning, she still had her doubts about trusting her husband. One question repeatedly came into her mind: where had he been all the early years of her boys' lives? In the Royal Navy most of the time; that had been the one and only period of her life that she had been sure of regular money being paid to her. Though that wasn't anything to do with John; it had come to her through the government. But when he had been home on leave, had Reg or Lenny ever seen him? Not very often. Too busy chasing other women, gambling money away, even stealing from her and never showing any sign of regret. When her thoughts ran along these lines, which they did far too often lately, Jodie would find herself getting angry, even though she knew full well that raking over the past was never going to be of any use.

Much to her utter frustration, she still felt undecided, and indecision was so pointless. Either she was going to listen to John, and think long and hard before making any commitment, or she should keep her distance. The trouble was, although she tended to remember all the bad things about him, in the early stages of their marriage they had actually been very happy. At that thought Jodie caught herself laughing. John had been like a big kid; he'd loved taking her dancing and ice-skating. He really had been a nice bloke. Just irresponsible, especially when it came to money matters. Everyone, except her own parents, had really liked him. He had been fun to be with, and always amusing.

Legally John was still her husband, and they were always going to meet up and be thrown together whenever there was a family get-together. The fact would always remain that he was the father of her sons, and these days the two boys had a lot of time for him. Was she being cynical when she let herself think that John's money had a lot to do with the relationship that had recently formed between him and his sons? If it was money that had eased things, where had it come from? Since his release from his short stay in prison, John had never seemed to be short of a few pounds. Never once to her knowledge had he tapped any family member for a loan, and he certainly had not approached her for money. But Reg had a brand-new car which his father had paid for, and Lenny had been quick to let her know that John had put a large amount of cash into the building business that he and Reg had set up together. Was it dodgy money? She truly hoped not.

When Jodie got back home from doing her shopping, she was freezing cold and her clothing was very damp. She turned the central heating up but she also put a match to the fire that was laid in the lounge. She loved an open fire, and as she was likely to be on her own this evening due to the weather, she might as well make herself comfortable and cosy.

She put the dry goods she had bought into the kitchen cupboards and most of the rest into the fridge or deep freeze, leaving out on the worktop the ingredients she would need to make herself a lasagne, which she would eat this evening with a green salad. Most of the afternoon slipped by as she sorted out the clothes that needed to be washed, which included the white jackets and coats she wore when working at Shepperton Studios or in her own salons. Two loads had soon gone through the washing machine and she spent a couple of hours ironing it all. By then darkness had closed in, and she went into the lounge, threw a few more logs on to the fire and drew the heavy floor-length curtains, shutting out what on a clear day would have been her view of the Epsom Downs and the famous racecourse.

She then decided she would indulge herself. She checked that the cheesy topping of her lasagne was browning nicely and began to lay up a large tray. For once she was going to carry her evening meal into the lounge and eat from a tray laid across her knees.

At seven o'clock, having finished her solitary meal, she decided it was time for a check-up on her mother-in-law.

Marian sounded tired, distracted even, as she complained that she couldn't hear what Jodie was saying.

'I'm calling to make sure that John is taking good care of you, Mum,' Jodie said, raising her voice to a higher level.

'I haven't seen John for four days and he hasn't rung me either. I can't get out; I'm stuck indoors, the weather is so terrible.'

'Have you had much snow at Camber Sands?' Jodie asked.

'Probably nowhere near as much as you have, but more than we usually get. This close to the sea the snow hardly ever settles. It's the wind that's so terrific; it would knock me off my feet if I ventured outside the door. The sea is really rough and we're having very high tides.'

'Well, as long as you're warm and cosy indoors. Have you no idea where John might be?'

'No, I really don't know, but it will be such a shame if he has gone off the rails again. He's been so good for ages now. Don't you agree?'

'Yes, I do. He has been very different lately, but I think it is far too early for us to start worrying ourselves. He'll turn up when he's good and ready. It's you I'm concerned about. Have you had a hot meal today? And have you got enough food in the house to keep you going?'

'Yes, I'm all right, love. John stocked me up with tinned food a couple of weeks ago. Thinking about it now, it seems to me as if he knew he was going away somewhere, and yet he never said a word.'

'How about Mary and Jack next door, are they all right?'

'Yeah, good as gold, as always. Jack came round yesterday with a roast dinner for me, and this morning Mary came in to have a cuppa and brought me a hot bread pudding. I couldn't ask for better neighbours. They're still worried sick over little Ann, though, like the rest of the family. I just wish for every-one's sake that the authorities would let her come home where she belongs, then per-haps we'd get the whole damn mess sorted once and for all.'

Jodie sighed heavily and took her time before answering.

'Yes, Mum, I know. It's been a hellish time for all of us, but at least now they have found Ann the matter will soon be resolved.'

Talking about who should have custody of Ann was the last thing Jodie wanted to get tied up with over the phone. She hadn't yet got an inkling as to how Derrick and Dee's

140

visit to the children's home had gone, and she was terrified of saying the wrong thing. She took a deep breath and did her best to end the conversation safely.

'I will try and get my car out tomorrow. If it doesn't snow any more tonight I should be able to get over to you. If you think of any shopping that you need, make a list and keep it by the telephone, and I'll ring you in the morning. I'd better go now, but if John should ring you, Mum, please ask him to give me a call.'

'I will, Jodie, thanks for ringing. Good night, love.'

Jodie had scarcely replaced the receiver when the phone rang.

'Hi, Jodie, it's only me.'

'Where are you, John? What do you think you're doing? Your mother is worrying herself sick over you,' she said loudly.

'I'm in Lewes, there's been a terrible disaster here. What with all the rain we've had recently and now this heavy snow, the river has burst its banks again. You have to see the damage to believe it. It is all so unfair. It's less than two years since Lewes was last flooded and the authorities promised to move heaven and earth to make sure it didn't happen again. Some folk haven't even got back into their homes yet, and those that have are heartbroken. They've only just got their properties dried out, repaired and replaced their

141

furniture and belongings, and now they're finding themselves going through it all over again. It's the stench that is so diabolical, and the muck and slush that is all up the walls from the broken sewer pipes. None of us know how to begin to help; everywhere you look it is just appalling. You can't imagine what it is like.'

'Yes I can,' Jodie said sadly. 'I was watching the news on TV earlier on. What are you doing there?'

'One of my mates owns a boat, quite a large one, and we've been out and about picking up folk who were stranded, taking those who were injured to the Red Cross places which have been set up and generally assisting the men in the lifeboats. I phoned to ask you if you would give my mum a call.'

'Oh, I've only just put the phone down, have been speaking to her for some time. Apart from worrying as to whether you've gone off the rails again, she is fine, perfectly OK. I know it will be difficult for you to phone, but keep in touch as much as you can, and let me know if there is anything I can do.'

'Let's see what tomorrow brings. If the weather improves, there is a lot you could do. The WVS are pleading for helpers.' John sounded more serious than he had in years. 'I have to go now, Jodie. There's too much going on here to hang about talking and phone.'

Before she had the chance to say another word, he was gone.

Jodie settled herself down in her armchair, all the while thinking about the unfortunate people who had bought homes in Lewes. It was such a beautiful town, with so much history attached to it. The very steep narrow streets and the unusual shops had always fascinated Jodie and her sisters-in-law. This latest tragedy was so hard to accept. When these disasters happened almost on one's doorstep, it did bring it home very vividly.

In spite of all that John had said, it still seemed strange to Jodie that he was there, in the midst of other folk's utter misery, apparently doing everything he possibly could to help. It didn't sound like the John she knew, and although she was pleased, she couldn't help thinking that it would be almost a miracle if it were true.

Even later that night as she climbed the stairs to go to bed, she was still wondering if John was finally growing up and late in life was aiming to become a decent man.

Be nice if he were.

After all, it was long overdue.

The main roads had been well gritted and plenty of salt had been laid down by folk who lived in the side streets. Jodie hadn't had too much trouble getting her car out of the garage and on to the road. Before leaving, she had phoned her mother-in-law and spent a few happy minutes telling her the good news about John and the way he was helping people who had found themselves homeless for the second time in less than two years.

'I'm on my way to Shepperton Studios, though I'm not looking forward to the journey,' she had told Marian. Then, having ascertained that her mother-in-law didn't need any shopping and promised to phone again later, she had cut short the call.

Having seen more than one car that had skidded on an icy patch and was now lying useless on the side of the main road, Jodie was driving carefully and was more than pleased with herself when she and her car arrived at the studios all in one piece.

Philip was waiting for her in the reception area that was reserved for important guests. He looked entirely at home in the opulent surroundings, wearing a light grey suit, white shirt and dark blue striped tie.

'Despite the weather, you still manage to look a million dollars,' he told her as she handed him her sheepskin coat.

'So do you, Philip. I only brought that coat in case we have to go out in the open from one lot to another. It was nice and warm in the car. My footwear might not come up to scratch, though,' she said, laughing as she gazed down at the leather boots she was wearing. 'Good job I keep a decent pair of shoes in my office.'

He bent his head and kissed her cheek. 'First things first: coffee?' he asked, already leading her into the bar.

Jodie couldn't take her eyes off him. This was the first time they had met up this year, though they had frequently spoken on the phone. Philip had been home for Christmas, and today he looked every inch an Italian, with his glowing tanned skin.

The waiter brought them a pot of coffee and two brandies, and Jodie listened to all that had gone on in Philip's family life over the holiday period. When a news flash came on to the TV screen showing the disaster caused by the flooding in Lewes, she immediately began to explain that John was there in person.

'He really does seem to have knuckled down and is trying to help,' she concluded. As Philip made no comment, she went on to tell him how pleased Marian Underwood was with the way her son had been acting of late.

Very abruptly Philip cut her short.

'Don't tell me that you believe a transformation of John Underwood into a saint is in process,' he said sarcastically.

'No, it isn't that at all,' Jodie quickly protested. 'We all know it will take time for

ın to adjust. But it could happen. He is
ɔt all bad, you know.' She was sounding
really upset.

Philip looked furious. 'I think the time has
passed when I have to listen to you singing
your husband's praises. Whatever he does
now will not alter the fact that John Underwood wouldn't know how to behave hon-
ourably even if he read a book on the
subject. Once a rogue, always a rogue.'

The atmosphere had become unpleasant.
There was no way Jodie could form an answer to Philip's accusations. With as much
pride as she could muster, she got to her
feet, gathered up her belongings and said
quietly, 'I shall be in my office if you need
me, Philip.'

Where did she go from here? Jodie asked
herself. As yet she had no idea.

# Chapter 11

Derrick had driven the car to Dover. It had been barely seven o'clock when he and Dee had left the house. The main roads had been cleared of snow, and traffic-wise it had been a good journey, but the atmosphere in the car had been strained and for the most part silent.

It was only when Derrick pulled the car over to the side of the road and switched off the engine that Dee realised they had arrived.

'I'm just going to take a look at the drawing that Jane Clarkson sent us. It shows the road that runs behind the children's home.' Derrick was looking very thoughtful as he added, 'She seemed to think there might be some reporters about and it would be best if we tried to avoid them.'

'She's been so very kind, hasn't she?' Dee murmured, not expecting an answer.

Having quite easily found the building they were looking for, both Dee and Derrick were pleasantly surprised. The grounds at the back of the building were obviously tended with great care. Tall trees, ample shrubs, some even flowering despite a covering of snow, with lots of greenery showing in the midst of harsh winter, while off to one side was a ...dren's playground, with several swings, ...e-saws and even a roundabout.

Holding hands tightly, they walked slowly up the short flight of stone steps that led to a very large wooden door. As they reached the top step, the door opened and a very motherly-looking woman wearing a wrap-around pinafore urged them to come in out of the cold.

The friendly welcome and the offer of a hot drink went some way to putting both Dee and Derrick more at ease.

'I am the housekeeper, Mrs Collins,' the woman informed them. 'Visiting hours are from ten to twelve, but for you they have been extended until two o'clock. I take it that you would like to go along to see Ann without any delay.' She sounded as if she had a very warm heart, and both Dee and Derrick quickly said, 'Yes please.'

'Very well, I shall get Sister Marie to take you to her, and after you have reassured yourselves that Ann is doing well, I shall have some refreshments sent along to you.'

Derrick hesitated a moment before speaking, and when he did, he sounded reluctant. 'Mrs Collins, you spoke of a Sister Marie. Is this a Catholic institution?'

'Not at all, Mr Underwood, we rely on all sorts of outside help to keep the place up and running, and although we are a regis-

tered religious organisation, we do not sho
any preference.'

Derrick was saved from having to answer
by the arrival of Sister Marie. She was aged
about thirty, wearing a uniform that was not
unlike that of a nurse, except for the head-
dress, which was white, wide and flowing,
making a frame for her quite lovely, peace-
ful-looking face.

'If you'd like to follow me,' she smiled, as
soon as introductions were out of the way.
Dee scrambled out of her chair, aware that
at last she was going to get to see her little
girl but also conscious that her limbs were
shaking. Sister Marie led them down a hall-
way past a row of open doors. Although
small, the rooms looked colourful, neat and
tidy, and it pleased Dee to see that on each
bed there lay a couple of soft toys.

At the end of the corridor double doors
were flung open to disclose a very large
lounge, one wall of which consisted of three
huge picture windows from which there was
a good view of the grounds.

Turning their eyes to the fireplace brought
a sudden smile to the faces of both Dee and
Derrick. There was a big squashy-looking
armchair, and sitting in it was their beloved
little girl.

'Oh!' The word came from both of her
parents and it was more of a cry than an ex-
clamation. Dee found she couldn't walk

roperly, but she lurched across the carpet until she was standing looking down on the child who at times she had dreaded she might never set eyes on again. Rooted to the spot, she gazed at the solemn little girl, waiting for her to hold out her arms and smile. Instead, Ann's eyes were downcast and her appearance was one of total dejection. The sight was enough to break any mother's heart, and the lump that had formed in Dee's throat was threatening to choke her.

Derrick had sunk down on to his knees and with arms outstretched he tried to enfold Ann to his chest. She shrank from him, wriggling back as far as she could get into the padding of the chair.

The look of despair on Derrick's face was as much as Dee could stand. She herself felt defeated. It was awful! They were Ann's parents. Whatever had they done that their little girl should cringe away from them? Or perhaps more to the point, what had been done to her to make her react like this?

With tears running down her face, Dee murmured her daughter's name over and over again. She longed to take the little girl into her arms, yearning just to smell the scent of her soft skin, to lay her hand on her silky hair, to hear her say her name, but Ann's eyes were closed now and she hadn't uttered a word.

Should she try to hug her? Delia asked

herself. What if Ann were to flinch at her touch? Already she had recoiled from her father. Oh dear God! To be able to see their child and yet not to be able to touch her was a situation that neither of them knew how to cope with. It was unbearable. Intuition told Dee that if she were to persevere and do the things she had set her heart upon, the result might well turn out to be devastating.

Sister Marie had returned and both parents heaved a sigh of relief.

Sensing the vibes, the sister calmly suggested that they take Ann outside to the play area for a short while.

They walked separately, all three of them well wrapped up in woolly scarves and hats, all solemn and thoughtful, and just when even the adults were beginning to feel the cold, Ann slipped one tiny hand into her mother's and the other into the willing grasp of her father. Over the top of their daughter's head Dee and Derrick exchanged glances, with eyes that were brimming with scalding tears.

When they reached the roundabout Ann indicated with a nod of her head and the teeniest smile that she would like to have a ride. With his heart in his mouth, Derrick enfolded his daughter in his arms, holding her very gently as if at any moment she might break. Then he sat himself on one of the wooden seats and placed Ann on his knees, her back resting against his broad chest, still keeping his arms close around her little body. It fell to Dee to push the roundabout, which she did with much huffing and puffing but also with great joy.

Back inside in the warm, hot drinks and refreshments were provided, but parents and child each only managed to nibble at a biscuit.

Both Dee and Derrick became anxious as visiting hours came to an end and still Ann had not uttered a single word. Together they had done their best to act as normal parents, singing songs she had learnt at school, telling her how much her big brothers missed her, and her cousins, Adele and Annabel, Lenny and Reg. How her aunt Jodie was making a new frock for her to wear at the big party they were going to have when the time came for them to bring her home. And Auntie Laraine was looking in the shops to find some pretty silver sandals for Ann to wear with the new dress.

God above! It seemed hopeless. Not only did it appear that their baby had been struck dumb, she had also lost the power to show facial expressions. Only once had she smiled, a small, barely noticeable smile when her father had lifted her on to the roundabout. Had she been locked up for hours on her own? Had she been frightened or even threatened? Had she been hurt? Neither parent could let their thoughts flow along that train of thought!

Dee could tell by the look on Derrick's face that the same kind of thoughts were running through his head and the very prospect was making him blazing mad. His one good hand was clenched tightly into a fist and she could see that resentment of how inadequate he felt was burning him up. She felt quite sure that if they could only get Ann home, amongst everyone who loved her so dearly, they would soon be able to break down these barriers, make her forget what had happened to her since she had been abducted. Every member of the family would work wholeheartedly to help their little girl get back to a healthy, happy childhood.

Dee felt incompetent, useless, stupid and weak. She wanted to pick up her little girl and run like the wind. But what good would it do if she were to try? Where would she take her? All these years of being a good mother, and now it seemed that she just had to wait until some judge in a court of law decided whether Ann could return to the only home she had ever known, or whether the woman who had given birth to her and abandoned her on the same day had the right to turn up almost six years later and demand that she be allowed to take the child out of the country to live with her in Belgium.

Now it was Delia who was blazing mad,

ready to spit blood, asking herself why she had been so bloody weak when that damned women had attacked her. Why oh why hadn't she retaliated? Given as good as she had got? It might not have done any good at the time, but it would have made her feel a damn sight better if she could have said she had fought for her own child.

And now to have to walk away and leave little Ann alone amongst a whole lot of strangers. It really was too much for any mother and father to have to bear.

Derrick at least had the comfort of knowing that he had held his daughter close, whereas all Dee had been given was the joy of holding her tiny hand.

Mrs Collins joined them for the last ten minutes of the visit, asking, 'Would you like to come along to the dining room and have a hot meal before you set off back home?'

'Thank you for the offer, it's most kind of you, but we'll get on our way, maybe have a halfway stop depending on the weather,' Derrick told her, doing his best to smile.

'Very well. I suggest you leave while Ann is still here in the lounge. Sister Marie and I will stay with her.'

Dee couldn't hold her tears back any longer. 'Oh God, I just can't leave her here and walk away.'

Derrick, whose thoughts were running along the same lines, swore beneath his breath. He got down on his knees again in front of Ann. 'Darling, will you try and understand? Mummy and Daddy will be back soon, and after that we hope to be able to bring you home. We miss you so much. All your aunties and uncles miss you, and next time we come, your big brothers want to come as well. You'd like to see Martin and Michael, wouldn't you?'

To the great joy of everyone watching, at the mention of her brothers' names she lifted her head and nodded. Yet still no words came from her lips.

Derrick and Dee stood in the doorway, unable to believe that their little girl was going to let them walk away without any show of emotion whatsoever. Surely she would burst into tears when she realised that they were leaving without her? Had she been punished for making a scene, or for crying? Or was it because she blamed them for whatever it was that had happened to her?

They both stepped nearer, longing for a cuddle before they left, but Ann leant backwards, and as she did so, her mother became distraught. Her child wasn't speaking to her, didn't want her to touch her; it was all too much. Dee was beyond the point of despair; she didn't know how to cope.

'Please, Mrs Underwood, it is time for you to leave now. We have to hope your next visit will be more satisfactory.' Mrs Collins spoke softly.

'But what if it turns out to be just as bad?' As Delia asked that question, she brushed the tears from her eyes and looked over to where her daughter had been sitting. Ann had gone.

Derrick put his arm tenderly around his wife's shoulders and led her from the room. 'Come on, darling, we have to leave now.'

It was the hardest thing they had ever had to do.

Derrick was sitting with his long legs tucked underneath a small table in a busy coffee shop in the heart of Dover. Without thinking he took a great gulp from his mug of hot coffee. 'Damn and blast,' he muttered, holding a paper serviette to his mouth.

Dee had more sense; she was still blowing on her coffee before taking a sip.

'Derrick, what are we going to do?' she asked softly.

Derrick shrugged. 'What choice do we have? Leave it to the solicitors now, that's all we can do. And any day now I expect the police will want to speak with us again.'

'Are you saying we've tried our best and got nowhere so let's leave it and walk away?'

Derrick thumped his fist down on to the table and Dee's coffee spilled over the top of her mug. She felt her face muscles tighten;

one look at Derrick's face and she was truly frightened. With good cause, too!

'How dare you, Dee?' he bellowed, so loudly half the customers in the shop turned to look at him. 'I'm as much at the end of my tether as you are! This case will never be classed as black and white, and you as well as everyone else have got to come to terms with it.'

Dee raised her eyebrows but did not answer him.

'Well?' He was still shouting. 'What do you expect me to say?'

'Calm down first,' Dee replied simply. 'There wasn't any need for you to go off the deep end like that.'

Derrick rolled his eyes. 'What the hell am I supposed to do? Neither of us can begin to imagine what our little girl has gone through. For her to be with us for more than three hours and never say a word; it was as if there was no connection between us.'

Dee pushed away her mug, although she had barely touched her coffee, then grabbed her handbag and her coat. 'The last thing we should be doing is having a go at each other,' she said. 'Let's go back to the car. The sooner we get home, the better. In the morning I will ring Jane Clarkson, let her know how we got on today and see if she or Mr Harwood has made any progress with the court hearing.'

Once outside the coffee shop, Derrick shrugged himself into his overcoat and did the buttons up quickly. Looking very sheepish, he said, 'Sorry, darling, anger got the better of me.'

Dee stood on her toes, reached up and tenderly kissed his cheek before saying, 'You're entitled. It's been a wonder to me that you have kept your temper in check for as long as you have.'

He put his big, brawny arm around her and pulled her close to him. 'Not much of a day, was it? Let's get to the car and make for home.'

'Yeah, new day tomorrow, new start, let's see what that brings,' she said.

As they reached the car park and Derrick was unlocking the car, they heard someone calling to them. They both looked up as a flash bulb on a camera went off.

There were two reporters, and it was almost as if they were offering an olive branch. 'Thanks,' they both called as they lowered their cameras. 'Hope the visit went well.'

Derrick slid a smile into place and took a firm hold on his wife before he answered.

'Early days yet, but it was great to see our daughter.' And even as he was speaking, he placed his arm firmly across Delia's back and guided her into the passenger seat.

Within seconds he was sitting beside her in the car and had turned the key in the ignition. As the engine started, he leaned over, squeezed his wife's hand and said, 'Things will get better, Dee. We have to believe that we will soon be bringing Ann home with us, and then we'll look back on this period in our lives as just a brief nightmare.'

Dee couldn't bring herself to form an answer, but she did in turn squeeze his arm and managed a smile.

Albeit a very watery one.

# Chapter 12

Delia Underwood was giving herself a damned good talking-to, getting more embittered by the minute.

Just because there's been a catastrophe in my life doesn't mean that everyday living has to come to a halt. If only Martin and Michael were still small boys, I would have so much more to occupy my time. As it is, the thought of Ann being in a care home when she should be here with me and Derrick is just about driving me mad. There are still the boring, menial tasks that have to be done – preparing the vegetables for one – but now it's only the two of us for dinner each night, and neither one of us has what could be called a hearty appetite. Twice a week is enough to load up the washing machine and there are no pretty little dresses to iron, and it's far too cold to go out and do a bit of gardening. I'm not able to go to any of the salons and work because we are waiting all the time for telephone calls, though Michael and Jodie are always pleading with me to do a few shifts, and as for Laraine, she practically begged me last night to go with her to Shepperton Studios; she said there were no end of slots where she could get me fixed for a day's work.

It was kind and thoughtful of Laraine and I did appreciate her offer, but it wouldn't seem right. I always have such a great time whenever I do a stint at the studios. But now, whatever I do, nothing blocks out the fact that I have no idea what has happened to our daughter. Of course I enjoy having a drink with the girls, but I do feel guilty, and somehow I don't feel things are going to get any better, not until the matter of getting Ann safely home is satisfactorily resolved.

I would have given my right arm once to have time to myself. Now look at me. Afraid to sit and be idle because of all the horrible things my mind keeps conjuring up. Will we ever get our daughter back? And if we do, will she be normal, because at the moment she's a long way off from being that! What on earth happened to her? Three times now Derrick and I have visited her, taken her presents from everyone, and yet she shows hardly any emotion. And to touch her is nigh on impossible. It wouldn't be an exaggeration to say that she recoils from us if we attempt to take her in our arms.

I don't think anyone can begin to imagine, let alone understand, what that does to Derrick and me. If either one of us comes out of this chronic situation with all our sensibility intact, it will be a miracle.

God above! I never knew there were so

many hours in a day, or just how lonely one can feel.

I know I've been driving my poor mum mad, and she's right to remind me of what she used to say to me: be careful what you wish for!

Nobody seemed to be in the least bit of a hurry to get this case to court. I listened to Jane Clarkson speaking to Russell Harwood on the telephone, and they seem to be of one mind that Chloe Warburg is the chief suspect regarding Ann's abduction. Personally, I don't believe that woman would have compromised herself by actually taking part in the kidnapping. Does the opinion of Miss Clarkson and Mr Russell count? Does mine?

I'm listening and watching with the objectivity of someone who thinks they know what will happen next. But is praying almost every hour doing any good? No evidence so far.

Meanwhile Derrick, my loving husband, tells me daily that I shouldn't attempt to prejudge this case. What would he have me do? Sit back and watch while Ann is taken away from us? Jodie and Laraine keep saying the worst is almost over. With the best will in the world, how can they think that?

In two days' time we make our first appearance in court. The nightmare is only just beginning.

As if her thoughts had conjured him up,

Derrick walked through the door and to stand beside Delia's chair. Having kr her cheek and put his arm around shoulders, he looked straight into her ey as he said, 'Are you quite sure that you're willing to go to court to fight for custody of Ann?'

Dee got up slowly, and when she spoke, her voice showed how sad she was feeling. 'Do you really have to ask that question of me? I couldn't love that child more if it had been me that had given birth to her. I can't bear the thought of her never coming home to us ever again. I think that would break me. In fact I know it would just shatter me. The quicker we get a court decision, the better.'

'That's a relief,' Derrick said, kissing her tenderly.

'Why is it a relief?' she asked, puzzled. 'Surely you didn't think for one moment that I would agree to hand our daughter over just like that to a complete stranger?'

'No, of course I didn't. Dee, let's go upstairs and have a lie-down together. Neither of us slept very well last night, did we?' He held out his hand. For a moment she almost rejected his suggestion, but then he smiled at her and that was all it took to melt her heart.

Holding hands, they went up to the bedroom. For a while they sat side by side e edge of the bed, staring out at the The snow had mostly cleared but heavy n was now sweeping in, pounding the each, running in torrents down the cliffs, then being swept out again with the high tide until it seemed that the whole area sparkled, leaving the beach fresh and clean.

Dee felt safe and secure, more content at that moment than she had been for a long time. She knew she hadn't been at all well. Every moment of those first weeks after Ann had gone missing had been a time of sheer terror for her. Her imagination had run riot. Then gradually terror had eased to anxiety. She was tired of pleading and praying, and seemingly getting nowhere; she wanted Ann home where she belonged.

Derrick was slowly undoing the buttons on her blouse and she smiled as she watched him. Maybe their lovemaking was not as frantic and energetic as it used to be; but for Dee it was always good, sometimes comforting and cosy, other times joyous, even passionate. She adored the slow, tender way Derrick loved to explore her body, the endearments he murmured, his moans of pleasure, and when he entered her, all she ever cared about was that she wanted him as badly as he wanted her.

Later, as they lay close to each other, Dee said, 'I could murder a cup of tea.'

'If that is all it takes to please you, then I

shall go downstairs and make you
Derrick was laughing as he put his dre
gown on and slid his feet into his slippe

Alone, Dee lay listening to the waves s
pounding away on the beach below an
took to thinking how lucky they were to own
this lovely house. It wasn't long before
Derrick was back carrying a fully loaded tea
tray. He poured a cup for each of them, then
brought Dee's cup round to her side of the
bed and set it down on her bedside table.

They drank their tea in companionable
silence. When their cups had been drained,
Derrick spoke. 'Maybe now that we have a
barrister acting for us, he might be able to
get together with the legal team acting for
Chloe Warburg and work out a deal.'

'A deal!' Dee repeated, and she sounded
really irritated. 'Our daughter's future is to
be decided by a group of men making a
deal? Ann is an Underwood. That has been
proved beyond doubt. Can you even begin
to imagine what our little girl will have to go
through if she is told that the court has
decided she should go to live with the
woman who gave birth to her? That we shall
no longer be her parents? She would end up
living in a foreign country, knowing no one.
Unable to converse with anyone because the
language would be strange to her. Jesus,
they'd probably give her an entirely new
name! No, I'm sorry, Derrick. It is not going

open,' she vowed defiantly. 'I don't , and nor do I care, what I have to do: find some way to keep our daughter safe thin the only family she has ever known nce she was a tiny baby.'

Derrick was well aware that she meant every word she had uttered.

There were times when he wished he could show his feelings as much as his wife did. Never an hour passed when he didn't think about the little girl who had brought so much happiness into their lives. He even let himself imagine her being grown up. At times like that his mind would leap over the years and allow him to wonder what it would feel like to have Ann's arm linked through his own as he proudly walked her down the aisle of the church on her wedding day.

However, there was a heap of trouble that needed to be set straight before he could look to the future, he reminded himself. Someone had to sort out this unholy mess. Bad enough that several adults were suffering because of mistakes of their own making, but what about the little girl whose very life had been snatched away from her? He wouldn't openly admit it, but it was tearing his heart out to have to visit Ann. The poor little mite was bewildered and confused and all he could do was sit there and try to coax her to speak or even smile.

The fact that he had no control over
was happening to his daughter was wr
ching at his guts. As to what might have ha
pened to her while she was missing, that wa
something he had to try and bury deep
within his mind. Thinking about it only
served to swamp him in utter misery. Disgust
came first, quickly followed by murderous
thoughts.

He was Ann's father. He should be taking
care of her, protecting her, loving her, and
yet although she had been found, he wasn't
being allowed to bring her home where she
belonged.

Who could blame the child if she never
again felt she could put her trust in any
adult?

Over the years, Dee had often grumbled
that Derrick took far too many photographs.
He had never agreed. Right now, the family
album was his most precious possession. If
the worst came to the worst and the court
did decide that Ann should be passed over to
the woman who had given birth to her,
then– He pulled his thoughts up very
sharply. No way would he contemplate going
down that road. A catastrophe such as that
didn't bear thinking about. It would affect so
many people, not the least Delia and himself.

In all probability it would destroy their
marriage.

# Chapter 13

'The final day has arrived,' said Delia softly, as she and Derrick made ready to leave the house at nine o'clock on Tuesday morning.

'In actual fact this will be just the beginning, probably the first of several hearings,' Derrick told her. He knew he sounded cruel, but it would be daft to let her think that everything would be finalised, done and dusted today.

The short journey to Lewes Crown Court was uneventful The car park seemed to be a long way from the main building. Halfway across, there were several flashes, which at first made Dee jump as they almost blinded her.

'Keep your head down,' Derrick advised. 'The newspaper photographers are here in force.'

As soon as they walked through the main doors, there were uniformed men ready to usher them into a side room. Once seated, they were informed by court officials that there was going to be a delay. 'How come, for what reason?' Derrick asked, but his question went unanswered.

More than an hour later, Jane Clarkson

popped her head around the door. 'I'm going to take you both downstairs for a coffee. It seems there has been an unavoidable delay.'

Derrick expressed his heartfelt thanks. His throat was dry, and just sitting here with a stony silence between him and Delia was driving him mad.

'I don't want to go. I'll stay here,' Dee said, her eyes cast down. It could well have been fright that was making her sound so contrary.

'Delia, you can't stay here. If our case is called at all today, it will have to be in another courtroom. The time allocated to us for courtroom number three has run out.'

Reluctantly Delia rose to her feet and in total silence the three of them walked along several corridors. Finally they came to a door that opened on to a very large, bright cafeteria. Derrick remarked that all the tables situated along the back wall were occupied by throngs of reporters.

'Of course they are,' Jane Clarkson said before going on to explain. 'This case is the sort that sells newspapers. That is a fact of life. A small child has been abducted and there is an ongoing dispute as to who are her rightful parents. And as if that is not enough, there is a great deal of animosity between the parties. That is how the reporters see this case, and to them it is just another job.'

Delia was not feeling at all well. She really

had convinced herself that today would see this whole matter resolved. The most pressing issue for her at this moment was Ann. It hadn't occurred to her that their daughter wouldn't be allowed to be at the hearing, and her eyes were darting everywhere, hoping for a glimpse of her.

The door opened and a policeman put his head round it. 'Miss Clarkson,' he said formally. 'Mr Harwood requests that you join him in the judge's chambers.'

As Jane left with the policeman, a well-dressed man entered the cafeteria. The expensive-looking dark suit he was wearing marked him out as a man of authority. He extended his hand to Derrick. 'Thomas Paterson, from the Law office. I have come to offer you an apology and to give you an explanation,' he said, smiling at Delia.

Apparently wires had got crossed. Chloe Warburg had been ordered to appear in court by ten o'clock, but had arrived an hour and fifteen minutes late, a fact that didn't sit too well with the judge. She had been charged with illegally entering premises and remorselessly and excessively wounding Mrs Delia Underwood with intent to kill.

Delia gasped. Paterson nodded. 'Miss Warburg admitted the charge of wounding but pleaded extenuating circumstances and even protested that she had severe provocation. However, there wasn't enough time

170

left in the judge's schedule for the case to be heard this morning, and it's now been adjourned until two o'clock this afternoon. The court wishes to be clear as to whether you, Mrs Underwood, are well enough to participate in the hearing.'

Delia exchanged a glance with Derrick but left it to him to answer the question.

A muscle tightened around Derrick's jaw, and quite forcefully he said, 'I presume you haven't seen the hospital report. That woman almost killed my wife.'

'Would it be possible for you to provide a copy of the report, and also the follow-up notes from her GP? There would be time for you to go home and fetch the necessary papers if you have them; they would go a long way to helping in this case.'

Derrick reached down and slid his briefcase out from beneath his chair. With a smile he faced the official, tapped his fingers on the case and said, 'Everything you have asked for I have here with me. I brought the papers along as a precaution.'

'Well done. I don't think there will be any need for your wife to testify; if you're able to provide evidence as to how badly Mrs Underwood was hurt, that should be sufficient. I'm sorry I am not able to say that it will be as cut and dried when it comes to the custody case the lady has involved you both in. If you could sort out the relevant papers

171

and hand them to Miss Clarkson, she will see that they get into the right hands for appraisal before the commencement of this afternoon's hearing.'

'No problem, I'll sort that out straight away.' Derrick sounded not only firm but very strong-willed.

'Thank you so much,' Dee said to Thomas Paterson. She felt as if a weight had been lifted from her shoulders. This man had shown that not all officials were hard-hearted.

Paterson was a gentleman, with children of his own. He knew about the Underwood child having been abducted; who didn't? Of course he had to appear to be totally im-partial, but that had never before stopped him from adopting a humane approach. He nodded his head and said before leaving, 'Mrs Underwood, please try not to worry. I can understand a little of what you and your husband must have suffered and I am truly sorry that your case didn't go forward this morning. In the meantime, I'll let you into a little secret. Because Miss Warburg turned up very late today and was not at all helpful or pleasant when she was ordered to apolo-gise to the court, she hasn't done herself any favours with the judge.'

Delia was pleased with the kindness shown to them both by this very considerate man, but right now she felt she never wanted to put a foot inside a courthouse ever again. However, she also knew that if doing so meant the fight for their daughter wasn't over, there was nothing on this earth that would keep her away.

Quite suddenly the whole building seemed to have gone quiet. The corridors were empty and silent.

'It appears that everything stops for lunch,' Derrick said, smiling. 'We might as well go and find something to eat, too.'

Derrick chose the White Hart, which was right opposite the courthouse. Once inside, he guided Dee over towards the bar.

'What would you like to drink? I'll ask for a menu while we're here, and I can see there is a nice dining room at the back there.'

'I think I would like a whisky and dry ginger,' Dee answered with a weak smile, flopping down on to the big squashy cushions of one of the huge sofas that were set against the wall.

Having taken a good sip of her drink, Dee sighed as she set the glass down on the table. 'That tastes good and I think it's just what I needed,' she said, looking up at her husband and laughing for the first time that day.

'Well make it last, because you can't have another. We're going in to eat just as soon as you look at that menu and decide what you'd like for your lunch. Then we'll be in court and it wouldn't do for you to be smelling of booze. By the way, my darling,' a very serious look had suddenly come across Derrick's face, and his voice had hardened, 'you do realise that you are going to come face to face with Chloe Warburg this afternoon, don't you?'

'Yes, but Mr Paterson said I will not have to give evidence, and anyhow you'll be there with me, won't you?'

'I most certainly will. I'll even hold your hand, if that would help. There is one other thing I should make clear to you. The case before the court this afternoon is in no way connected with Ann's abduction. I doubt very much that will even get a mention. This is Chloe Warburg being put on trial for assaulting you.'

'I know,' Delia said, shuddering, her voice little more than a whisper.

'All right. Now we've got that settled, will you please decide what you are going to eat, because one thing we daren't do is be late for the hearing this afternoon.'

The meal of fresh salmon and salad that they had both decided on was excellent, but neither Dee nor Derrick did justice to it. Derrick was waiting for his wife outside the ladies' powder room and commented on how lovely she looked. Delia felt more relaxed, having been able to freshen herself and repair her make-up.

'Time to settle a few scores,' Derrick remarked as they entered the courtroom.

Dee wasn't thinking along those lines. What had been done couldn't be undone, and as much as she detested the fact that Chloe Warburg had beaten her half to death, there had been times of late when she had felt a small pang of regret that things had turned out the way they had for that woman. But the other side of the coin was that the decision to abandon her baby had been Chloe's own choice. Nobody had influenced her, one way or another. When she had walked away and left a day-old baby to fend for itself, had she given a single thought to what might happen to it?

Delia was brought up sharply from her thoughts as an official put his hand on her shoulder and escorted her towards a row of chairs, passing a long table where several legal-looking people were sitting in a line.

'Still a great number of reporters here this afternoon,' Derrick murmured.

Delia turned her head to look up at the gallery. Every seat had been taken, but she recognised no one. Suddenly she faltered, feeling as though she couldn't take another step. The usher took her arm firmly and guided her forward to a seat. Derrick sat beside her and put his hand over hers.

Silence fell, then the usher commanded loudly, 'All rise,' as the judge made his appearance.

As soon as everybody was seated again, the judge rapped his gavel and asked, 'Is the prosecution ready to proceed?'

The solicitor acting for Chloe Warburg, Patrick McGregor, nodded and replied, 'Yes, your honour.'

'Will the defendant please come forward.'

Chloe Warburg didn't move. An usher hurried over and practically hauled her out of her seat. By the look on her face, he had badly wrenched her arm.

Dee felt cold shivers run down her back. This was the Belgian woman's chance to lie about her, she realised, and she dreaded what was to come.

Chloe climbed the steps, entered the box and turned to face the court. The sight of her brought Delia's head up sharply. She hardly bore any resemblance to the person who had come into her home and attacked her so fiercely. She was wearing a white linen suit that made her look taller, slimmer and much more sophisticated. Her hair was styled very differently, twisted into a French pleat at the back but leaving a springy fringe scattered along her forehead. All in all it gave her a much younger and softer look. Dee formed the opinion that Chloe was more than pleased to have this chance of dressing herself up in expensive new finery in the hope of gaining sympathy from the court. Though if that were so, she should have made more of an effort and been on time this morning.

Patrick McGregor rose slowly to his feet. 'Please state your full name?

Chloe hesitated, then said quite loudly, 'Chloe Ursula Warburg.'

'Will the clerk please read the charges?' asked the judge.

'This court of law hereby charges that on or about the thirtieth day of July 1987 the defendant Chloe Ursula Warburg did acrimoniously assault and severely injure Delia Underwood in her own home at Newhaven, East Sussex.'

'How do you plead?' asked the judge.

'I was greatly provoked,' Chloe answered, sounding offhand and giving the judge a look that showed she was uninterested in these proceedings.

The judge drew himself up to his full height against his tall chair-back before saying sternly, 'That is not what you were asked. I say again, how do you plead?'

'Guilty, I suppose, but she deserved it!'

'Miss Warburg, will you please just answer the questions put to you and refrain from adding any further remarks.' His voice was harsh, but it softened as he asked, 'Who is appearing on behalf of Mrs Underwood?'

Jane Clarkson rose to her feet and faced the judge, stating her name.

'Thank you, Miss Clarkson. As the defendant has pleaded guilty, are you looking for a custodial sentence?'

'Your honour, after this hearing there is to be a further case in the Crown Court which has much bearing on the matter before you now. Due to the severity of the beating that Mrs Underwood received at the hands of the defendant, she was hospitalised for two weeks. However, we would agree to bail for the defendant, subject to your discretion, rather than delay the second hearing, which involves the welfare of a small child.'

'Thank you, Miss Clarkson. I see that Russell Harwood is seated at your table. Is he to appear as barrister for Mrs Underwood in the Crown Court?'

'Yes, your honour, he has agreed to do so.'

'Very well then.'

Jane Clarkson sat down and the judge turned to face the defendant, who had remained standing in the witness box. He made a point of shuffling a sheaf of papers before looking up, and when he did speak, his voice was loud and clear. 'I will suspend a prison sentence on the accused for two years, and in the meantime, Miss Warburg, as you have admitted the offences, you are ordered to pay Mrs Underwood five hundred pounds in compensation and sixty-five pounds court

fees. You must pay the full amount to t
court within fourteen days. As to the sen
tence, it will be two years, suspended for two
years, which means that should you commit
any unlawful act during that time, the
sentence will immediately become viable. Do
you understand?'

'Yes,' Chloe said, now sounding not quite
so defiant.

Russell Harwood turned to Jane Clarkson
and half smiled. Both Derrick and Delia felt
like smiling too. If Chloe Warburg had been
sent to prison, it might well have set back
the hearing for the custody case, and that
would almost certainly have meant a much
longer stay in the care home for their little
girl.

That was something that had to be
avoided at all costs.

The judge now leant forward and spoke
quietly. 'Mr McGregor, Mr Harwood and
Miss Clarkson, will you please approach the
bench.'

All three stepped forward and two ushers
stood behind them. The judge put his hand
over the microphone, making sure that the
press couldn't hear what he had to say.

'Obviously,' he began, 'there is not a person in this court today who is not aware of
the Underwoods' pending custody case. I
have acted in good faith by not sending
Miss Warburg to prison. I do not think she

all disappear and I don't think she will risk harming Mrs Underwood again. There have to be two sides to this further court case, and I have taken the view that the sooner it is brought to completion the better it will be for all concerned.'

Russell Harwood gave the judge a gracious nod. 'Your honour, I feel sure I speak for us all when I say that we appreciate your sensitivity. This forthcoming case is a difficult one for everyone involved.'

The judge acknowledged the words with a slight inclination of his head as he stood up.

'The court will rise,' the usher called.

Derrick turned to Delia and hugged her as if he would never let her go. Delia started to cry, but they were gentle tears and were accompanied by a watery smile.

Russell Harwood approached Derrick, his hand outstretched, and the two men shook. Then the barrister smiled at Delia and said quietly, 'That wasn't so bad, was it? You have taken the first step to sealing the future of your daughter.'

# Chapter 14

The next few days at Shepperton Studios were crazy ones for Jodie. She had been allocated an early breakfast slot and a two p.m. magazine show. For each programme she was styling the hair of the stars of the show as well as the presenters. As luck would have it, Laraine was advertising the products that were being used and also demonstrating false hairpieces and wigs, endeavouring to convince ladies who were watching the broadcast just how easy it would be not only to change one's hairstyle, but to obtain a completely different look entirely. Her advice was also of great help to ladies who were acutely ill and had suffered great hair loss.

Jodie and Laraine had lunch together, and agreed that as they were both facing a busy week, it made sense to stay up near Shepperton rather than face a tedious journey twice a day. The studio had rooms in a local hotel always provisionally available for staff to use at reasonable cost. Over a drink that evening, they agreed that both sessions had gone well, and then Laraine asked Jodie about Philip.

'I didn't need to be a clairvoyant to see

you two were at loggerheads. Bit emrrassing really. Philip brought my coffee ver to me but didn't even glance your way. How long has this been going on?'

'Ever since he came home from Italy.' Jodie said, doing her best to make light of it. 'First off he didn't even pick up the phone to tell me he was back. Then when we did meet up, he was absolutely charming until I mentioned that John was doing a great deal of good helping out with the flood victims in Lewes. The very mention of John's name never did sit well with Philip, and because for once I said I was proud of John, he really let rip at me. Since then he's adopted a dog-in-the-manger attitude.'

Laraine had known Philip for a long time, and she was aware that he and John were as different as night and day. She picked up the bottle of wine that she and Jodie were sharing and replenished their glasses before saying, 'Jodie, no one could accuse you of settling for the steady type. You could have got yourself free from John years ago – he certainly gave you enough justification – but you've clung on. As for you taking up with Philip, he's not the marrying type, I'd say, but if he did propose, would you finally divorce John and marry him?'

After careful consideration of that question, Jodie at last said, 'Probably.' There was another pause, both girls deep in thought,

until Jodie murmured, 'John and l
good together when we were young. We
some great times and two wonderful boy
knew my responsibilities after they we.
born. John didn't. He felt he was too young
to settle down. The Royal Navy and the
chance to see foreign shores gave him the
opportunity to play away from home. That
was when everything between us went down
the drain.'

Laraine was fearful that she had upset
Jodie, and she quickly responded, 'No it
didn't. As you say, you got two marvellous
sons out of the marriage, and you can feel
proud of the way they've turned out. From
what I hear, they are getting along fine with
their father these days, too.'

'Thanks, Laraine, I agree with what you're
saying, but at the same time I'm a bit wary.
Lately John seems to be quite flush. I'm not
knocking what he's doing for Reg and
Lenny – it's only what they deserve and it's
long overdue – but where is all the money
coming from? I just can't help asking myself
that question.'

Laraine coughed and gave Jodie a very
cheeky-looking grin. 'I may be able to shed
some light on that. Do you remember Isaac
Rittman? He owned several draper's shops,
years ago. From what I've heard, he started
off with stalls in Chapel Street market in
Islington, and his first real shop premises

n Brixton.'

s, of course I know the family. I went to ool with Rachel, his daughter, but she ed soon after we were old enough to start vork. It was all so sad. Her mother was distraught and followed her to the grave, she was that heartbroken.'

'Well,' Laraine sighed softly, 'seems Isaac was left with just Wally, his only son, and he was well on the way to going off the rails. Hard to believe, but word has it that your John took Wally in hand in more ways than one, kept him on the straight and narrow. Apparently Isaac was always grateful to him for that. Father and son got back together and were doing fine by all accounts.'

'Laraine!' Jodie felt she had to stop her. 'You've got my head in a whirl,' she complained as she picked up the wine bottle from the table to top up their glasses. 'We were talking about John being flush with money and you've started on about the Rittman family, I can't see the connection between the two.'

'Oh, you will,' Laraine told her with a broad grin. 'If you just listen to me for a minute, I promise you will.'

Jodie laughed, picked up her glass, took a good swig and said, 'Go on then, I'm listening.'

'Well, a few months after your John got out of prison, old Isaac Rittman didn't wake up one morning. Died peacefully in his sl... turned out that the will he had made short and simple. Apart from the local sy... gogue being a beneficiary, two thirds of r... remaining assets he left to his son Wally an... the remaining third to John Underwood, and make no mistake about it, there appears to have been plenty for each of them.'

'Laraine, you *are* joking?' Jodie sounded as shocked as she felt. 'How come you know all this?'

'It's common knowledge in some quarters. I've often wanted to ask you and Delia if you'd heard about it. Adele first told me; she got it from a boyfriend. It was about the time that Ann was kidnapped, and it didn't ever seem appropriate to bring that kind of subject into the conversation.'

'Thanks for that, Laraine, you did right. I'm finding this hard to believe, but if what you're saying is true, John has behaved remarkably well, knowing full well that he couldn't ask everyone to celebrate his good fortune because of the anguish and misery that poor Dee and Derrick were suffering. I am more pleased than I am able to put into words. At long last he has done some good in this tricky world. No wonder there has been such a change in him.' She smiled broadly as she added, 'Let's hope it lasts.'

'It's a long time since I have seen you look so happy.'

, well, thanks for telling me. We'll con-
e to keep it from Dee and Derrick for
time being, and from our dear mother-
-law, bless her. She has been on and on at
ne saying what a difference there is in her
son. I think she's afraid it won't last.'

'Do you feel that way too?' Laraine asked
cautiously.

Jodie gave a knowing smile before reply-
ing. 'I would like to say no, but let's just say
I think John deserves the benefit of the
doubt this time.'

By half past seven the next morning, Jodie
and Laraine had all their equipment set out
and were ready to go when Jeffrey Hutch-
ison, the newly appointed manager of advertising at Shepperton, appeared and looked
directly at Jodie. 'Do you know where Philip
Conti is?'

'Sorry, no, I don't. Is he due in as early as
this?'

Steve, who had been the stage manager for
years and was known for his tolerance and
easy-going ways, piped up. 'Did you two
have a disagreement over something yesterday?'

'I haven't seen or spoken to Philip since
early yesterday morning, when I first arrived
at the studio,' Jodie pointed out calmly.

'Well he was hard put to be civil all day,
and whatever had upset him, he was taking

it out on everyone in sight. He was
rude to me twice. He hasn't been the
man since he returned from his holiday
Italy; he's been irritable and acting like
owns the place.'

'He is not a bit like that usually,' Jodie said
quietly, before turning away. She was thinking to herself that when grown men got
upset at each other, they were worse than
little children.

She had slept well last night, delighted at
the news that Laraine had given her. Now
she was hoping against hope that this new
John would continue with his good works
and turn himself into a man you could trust
and rely on. It would be wonderful for so
many people, especially his mother.

All that was needed now was for the decision over Ann's future to be the right one.
Then the whole family would be able to
rejoice and set about thinking of a homecoming party that would be long remembered by everyone.

# Chapter 15

It was Sunday morning, and the phone was ringing in Jodie's house. Everyone was still sleeping. Finally Michael Connelly heard it and got out of bed to answer it.

'Hello?' Michael said, barefooted and in his pyjamas, as he yawned loudly. He was having difficulty in remembering what had happened last night. They had all been up late and had been drinking, and Jodie had insisted that everybody stay.

'Hello, Uncle Michael.' It was Adele. She sounded wide awake. 'Would you mind asking my auntie Jodie if she knows where my mum is?'

Michael shook his head, hoping to clear it. 'Adele, your mum is here, no one went home.'

'Can you go get her, please, I need to ask her something.'

'All right, pet, but I'm not sure that she will be awake.' Michael put the phone down and padded off to see which room Laraine had slept in. There were bodies in all three of the bedrooms, but no sign of Laraine. 'Last try,' he murmured as he opened the door to the dining room and looked in. Laraine and Alan

Morris were lying on the floor sound asleep, with all their clothes on. He didn't want to wake them, so he went back to the phone and picked up the receiver.

'Adele, my darling, they're still sleeping,' he told her firmly.

'They, who the hell is they?'

'It's all right, babe, your mum is with Alan, Alan Morris. They are on the floor and they do have all their clothes on.'

'Uncle Michael, I am not worried as to whether or not my mother is dressed, but Alan Morris! Annabel and I thought he was a thing of the past. When did they get back together again?'

Somebody was banging a drum inside Michael's head and he needed a coffee before he could think clearly. 'Why don't I tell her you called when she wakes up, and then she can phone you back.'

'Sounds like Auntie Jodie's running a great sleepover. Bye.' The phone clicked in Michael's ear before he had the chance to hang up. He glanced up the stairs. It didn't seem worth going back to bed now, but since nobody else was awake, he'd go into the kitchen and put the kettle on.

Danny was already there, wearing a silk dressing gown over his pyjamas. 'Sit you down, Michael, a cup of strong black filtered coffee will be in front of you within the next few moments.'

Michael did as he was told, placing his elbows on the table and clutching his face with both hands. It was the aroma from the hot steam off the coffee that made him sit up straight, and as he looked up at Danny he said, 'We've lived together for many years now, yet you still have the ability to amaze me.'

Danny smiled. 'I heard you get up to answer the phone, and I knew coffee would be in order for both of us. When I've showered and dressed, I'll make some more for everyone and take it around the rooms.'

It was midday before everyone was assembled in Jodie's lounge. Jodie was wearing a sarong that Dee had brought her back from abroad. Around her shoulders she had wrapped a huge colourful shawl, another gift from foreign shores. On her feet were soft flatties. High-heeled shoes were definitely out of order today. Laraine had settled for jeans and a polo-necked jumper, both borrowed from Jodie.

There were four men present: Danny and Michael, who in the main had been responsible for clearing up the aftermath of last night's impromptu party, John Underwood and Alan Morris. Derrick and Delia should have been there too, but were feeling the strain of waiting for the custody case to begin.

The six of them had started the evening by having dinner at the Grand Hotel in Brighton. The four men were all good-looking and the two women had done them credit. Alan had said that Laraine looked like an angel, and indeed she had, with her long blonde hair and pale gold dress. Jodie always stood out in a crowd; last night she had worn a slinky black dress set off by silver accessories. There had been a good band playing and everyone had enjoyed themselves.

Before they had gone in to dinner, John had taken the trouble to explain what had been going on in Lewes since the floods had once again hit the town.

'Jodie said you had been working with a boat, John, is that right?' Michael had asked.

John had explained that because the streets had been turned into rivers by the torrent of floodwater, the boat had come in very useful when rescuing stranded folk. Throughout the whole of the evening he had behaved well, precise about what he had been doing but in no way boastful.

They had taken a taxi back to Jodie's house in Epsom, and then the really serious drinking had begun. Jodie smiled to herself. Everyone looked under the weather. The blame for the state they were all in could be laid at John's door, for it was he who had brought back three bottles of champagne. Still, it had been good champagne, and today being Sunday, they had all day to let the effects work themselves off.

'I think it is about time one of us gave Derrick and Dee a ring,' Laraine suggested. 'Or would it be better if we piled into a couple of cars and went over there?'

'I don't think it would be a good idea for us all to land on them today,' Michael ventured. 'Better to ask them to come here, get them out for a while, away from their own home. Danny and I could rustle up a light lunch and we could all laze around, maybe go down the pub later.'

'I'll go and phone them,' Jodie said, getting to her feet. 'See how they're feeling. I'm sure they will agree to come here.'

Laraine followed Jodie out into the hall and with a sheepish grin said, 'I suppose I've got some explaining to do to my girls. Comes to something when your own children pass comment on what their parents get up to.'

Jodie smiled. 'Michael told us he had let the cat out of the bag, telling Adele that you were asleep with Alan. What difference does it make? I always thought Annabel and Adele liked Alan; surely they realise it hasn't been a great life for you left on your own at such an early age?'

'When Alan and I first got together they did think he was great. He took them around the House of Commons, gave them lunch, opened doors to all sorts of places they'd never have got into without his say-so; he is quite well known in the West End, mixes with all the right big names.'

'So what went wrong?'

'Remember the time when he proposed to me out of the blue?'

'Don't I just!' Jodie laughed. 'You were afraid he was looking for a submissive house-keeper, not a wife.'

'Well I learnt afterwards that he had suggested to the girls that they find their own accommodation after we were married. Oh, he wrapped it up nice enough, said they'd have a much better life, more freedom away from their mother, anywhere except in his house.'

'Bloody cheek!' Jodie let fly.

Laraine laughed loudly, then held her head and sighed before saying, 'What you've just uttered doesn't come anywhere near to what my girls apparently said to him.'

'So how come you've got back with him?'

'I wouldn't say I have, but I do hate to be the odd one out everywhere I go. There are times when I really feel that I am intruding. Michael and Danny are such dear friends and they are the most excellent dance partners anyone could wish for. Last night at the Grand I knew all the ladies were envying us when we were dancing with them, but unfortunately we can't spend our entire lives on the dance floor. Anyhow, Alan has been really persistent and he's promised so much. We'll see how we go. Meanwhile, you phone Dee and then I'll ring Adele and listen to what she has to say to me.'

'Talk about reversed roles,' Jodie laughed as she dialled Dee's number.

'Thank God for that,' Delia said out loud as she replaced the telephone receiver. The quietness of their house today was driving her mad. Were folk deliberately ignoring her and Derrick? Or were they just afraid that if they came to visit, they might say the wrong thing? This terrible business with Ann being away from home was making life a sheer misery. The sooner they got a date for the hearing at the Crown Court, the better it would be for all of them. Or would it? she wondered sadly. If the outcome should go against them, what then? The alternative just didn't bear thinking about.

She had been up early this morning and had done some baking. Once she had cooked because she enjoyed it and because it was something all mothers and wives did. These days she cooked to give herself something to occupy her mind rather than dwelling on her terrible fears and longing for her little daughter. Today she had whipped sugar, butter and eggs in a bowl, added vanilla pods and finally the flour. While the sponge was in the oven,

she had prepared the filling: thick clot
cream she had sent to her from north Dev
once every month, and strawberry jam sh
had made herself. She sampled a little of
each, rolling the taste, especially the cream,
on the tip of her tongue. She would take this
cake with her today to Jodie's house.

Now all she had to do was persuade
Derrick to get himself ready and drive them
over to Epsom. An outing in the fresh air
would do them both good, and it would be a
pleasure to have company for the rest of the
day.

Derrick was being obstinate, which came
as no surprise to his wife, but she had long
ago learnt how to handle him.

'You'll enjoy yourself once you get there,'
she said, as she pleaded with her husband.

'Will I?' Derrick asked, sounding much as
he had done during the whole of this horrid
period of their lives: tired, worried and sad.

'The fresh air will do you good. You know
everybody who is at Jodie's, and it will make
a change for you to see your brother.'

He looked at her, his face blank.

Dee laughed. 'You might as well give in
graciously, because I am going, whether or
not you decide to come with me. You'll be
the loser, left all on your own on a Sunday
afternoon. It won't be much fun. Still, you
will have the papers to read.'

She turned away, then quickly turned

ĸ. 'Caught you.' She waved a finger at
.n. 'You smiled.'

'I did not.'

'Oh yes you did, and it shows you still have a few human feelings left.'

'Not many,' he grunted.

Dee chuckled. 'I am going to take this cake out and put it on the back seat of the car, and then I am coming back in to fetch my coat and handbag, and if you are not ready by then, I really will drive off on my own.'

She stood for a moment staring at the man she had loved ever since she had been sixteen years old, and her heart ached for him. He was a big man not only in stature but also in the way he led his life. He had always looked to the future and made provision, and most of all he took care of his own. Now, however, he felt utterly useless. His daughter needed him, and he would give his own life if it would make hers happier, but whichever way he turned, he got nowhere. Day by day he had to keep functioning and hope to God that one day soon he would be able to pick his little girl up in his arms again and bring her home.

Back inside, Dee didn't need much imagination to know what was going on in Derrick's mind. She couldn't speak – she couldn't find any words that would bring comfort to him – but the sad look on his face was so hard to bear. She knew that if

she opened her arms and clasped him
they would both end up crying their h
out. They had done that so often since ⁄
had been taken from them. And what go.
had it done?

Instead she shook her head, doing her best
to clear out the thoughts that were torturing
her just as much as they were him.

'Well, I see you've put a decent suit on,
and that tie does go very well with that shirt,
so are you going to drive or shall I?'

'Depends on which car you've put the
cake in,' Derrick said mischievously.

Dee gave him an impish smile before
saying, 'I thought you weren't coming, so I
got mine out.'

Derrick gave her a playful swipe as he
walked down the garden path. 'Good, I can
sit back and enjoy the ride.' Before he
lowered his head to get into the passenger
seat, he turned and pulled Dee close enough
to be able to place a gentle kiss on her lips.

'What was that for?' she asked.

Looking straight into her lovely eyes he
said quietly, 'To say I am sorry that I have
been acting like a bear with a sore head.'

There was even a smile on his face now,
and this almost broke Dee's heart.

Derrick was enjoying himself far more than
he had expected.

By two o'clock Jodie was bringing a gor-

Sunday roast dinner to the table. ...t people now were sitting around her ...ng table, hangovers forgotten thanks to ...e hair of the dog.

Of course, Derrick told himself, he was pleased to see his brother. It was John who had been his solitary visitor when he had been going through hell. Michael and Danny? He loved those two guys. They never put a foot wrong or said a word out of place, but were always there whenever they were needed, and on a day like today they were damn good company, which was something that both Dee and himself were badly in need of.

Alan Morris was an unknown quantity, but as he didn't know him at all well, Derrick decided to give him the benefit of the doubt. As for Jodie, Laraine and his own wife Delia, it really was an outstanding friendship that existed between these sisters-in-law. You'd travel many a long mile before you came across three women who were as talented, as beautiful and with such big loving hearts as they were blessed with.

Later, Jodie made afternoon tea. She signalled to John that she could do with some help in the kitchen.

'Close the door,' she said. 'I have a confession to make to you, John, I know all about your inheritance from Isaac Rittman. Laraine mentioned it to me. And if you don't ⟨...⟩ my saying so, I thought it was great news ⟨...⟩

'Whether I mind or not, you've alw⟨...⟩ struck me as a woman who says what sh⟨...⟩ feels and to hell with those whose views happen to differ.' John spoke in an offhand way because he wasn't sure whether she was truly pleased or not.

'You're right about that. And you've struck me as a man who goes his own way and more often than not puts his needs before those of others. But since talking with you about helping out down in Lewes, and then Laraine telling me how you've held back from celebrating your windfall in consideration for Derrick and Dee, I feel I am in danger of beginning to alter my opinion of you.'

John laughed, but it wasn't a cynical laugh, and he straightened his face before he said, 'Thanks for the vote of approval. Perhaps from now on we will be more at ease with each other. One more thing before we rejoin the party. Why don't you let me take you out for dinner one night next week?'

'What? Just you and me?'

'Would that be such a bad thing?'

'I suppose not; bit strange though, you kind of asking me on a date.'

'Even old married couples like us can sometimes feel they'd like to rekindle their first love. Besides... No, I've said enough for now.'

ease, John, I *would* like to have that
ner with you, but I would also like you to
ish what you were about to say.'

'Well, as you have agreed to our date – and
I am holding you to that – I will tell you
right now, Jodie. I am going to enjoy watching my wife trying to figure out my rehabili-
tation.'

'Not before time, is it?' she quietly reminded him.

'I agree,' John answered, a little too quickly.
'We've been at loggerheads for a long while.
A truce is overdue.'

Suddenly he held his arms out and Jodie
reached for him. For a moment they stood
close together, just holding each other. John
was a true Underwood, broad-shouldered
and well over six feet tall. She had forgotten
how well her head fitted into the hollow of his
shoulder, and the feel of his brawny arms
around her body was a joy she was happy to
recall. It was when his lips met hers in a soft,
gentle kiss that she began to wonder if she
was dreaming all of this. John had never been
a gentle lover. Not in her memory.

Reluctantly they broke apart and went
back into the lounge to join their friends
and relations.

At seven o'clock they linked off into pairs
and walked the few yards to the nearest pub.
Tomorrow would be a normal working day
and tonight some of them had to drive

home, so the men decided on a game of darts over half a pint, while the girls were happy enough to settle for orange juice and a good old natter.

Back at the house by nine, everyone refused Jodie's offer of coffee. Fond farewells were said, and Jodie found herself standing alone on her doorstep.

She watched as four cars drove away from her house. John had kissed her cheek, much as the others had, but he was the only occupant of the car he was driving, and she couldn't help wondering whether he felt as lonely as she did at this moment.

Later, as she lay in bed, she let her mind fly back to the short time she had spent in the kitchen alone with John. Had it been for real? Surely one couldn't go back and pick up the pieces of a life that had been lived so very many years ago?

She laughed heartily and told herself they had been young lovers then. A repeat of those years was totally impossible. No one could suddenly pick up the threads of the kind of life they had led in their youth. For one thing they had two grown-up sons now, both living their own lives with their partners.

It wasn't out of the question that before too long she and John would become grandparents!

That was a thought that brought her up

ply, but one she wasn't going to worry
out tonight. Instead she leant over,
itched off her bedside light and pulled the
edclothes up around her shoulders.

She wasn't ready to sleep yet, so she lay
there letting her mind roam. Did she really
believe there was even a slight possibility
that she and John could have a stab at being
a couple once again?

John had been so different tonight: so loving, almost caring. He had certainly woken
feelings in her that had lain dormant for too
long.

Who could tell? Second time around might
turn out to be all right.

Wine was known to improve with age.

Why not people?

# Chapter 16

Derrick was trying to figure out how to handle himself in this awkward situation of his own making. He had driven to Camber Sands to collect his mother and bring her home to stay with Delia and himself for a few days. Trouble was, Dee's parents lived in the house next door to his mother and they had come out to greet him almost before the wheels of his car had stopped turning.

He hadn't had any option. Over tea and home-made cake he had extended the invitation to Mary and Jack Hartfield. After all was said and done they were his wife's parents, and Dee would be pleased to see them. He hadn't given it a thought, and apparently neither had Delia.

He was now on the way back to Newhaven with his mother sitting in the front passenger seat of the car and Jack and Mary seated in the back.

Marian Underwood was smiling as she looked across at her son, with her head tilted the way he'd seen her do when she was thinking about something. Or someone.

'You know, son, it is true what Mary tried to tell you about that Belgian woman.

parently she has been in Camber Sands quite a while now, staying at one of the ed and breakfasts along the seafront.'

'Mother, I never said that I disbelieved Mary, I just asked you all to hold back on what happened until we get home. For one thing I need to concentrate on my driving, and for another surely you want Delia to hear all that has been going on.'

What Derrick kept to himself was that he couldn't bear to hear all the details, and then have to sit and listen to the story being told all over again to Delia.

He had telephoned Dee from his mother's house to say that he was bringing her parents to stay for a while, so there was no problem. Delia had sounded more than pleased.

Jack Hartfield was a good man, not given to talking much, but his many kind deeds spoke a lot more than words. When his wife had started to talk about Chloe Warburg, he had squeezed her hand and signalled for her to remain silent. Marian Underwood, though, was a different kettle of fish. A good-hearted lady, but one who would rush in where angels feared to tread. 'There's another woman with her,' she said, sitting herself up straight and puffing her large chest out.

'Mother, please, we are not yet halfway back to Newhaven and the traffic is getting really bad. Just lay your head back and close your eyes and try and have a little sleep will be able to tell both Dee and me ev thing that has been going on once we home.'

Marian did as her son had asked, but she had to have the last word.

'Poor Delia! She's been through a terrible ordeal. I don't think anyone can begin to imagine how she must feel.'

At last they were home. Derrick tooted the horn but Delia was there already, opening the front door wide.

Mary Hartfield undid her seat belt and glanced across at her daughter standing on the step. Good gracious, hadn't she lost a whole lot of weight! Mary got out of the car and put her arms around Dee, hugging her for a brief moment before Jack took his turn.

Derrick was helping his mother out of the car.

'Hello, Marian, you look extremely smart today, but then you always do when you come to visit,' Dee said, smiling her welcome. 'I've just put a leg of lamb in the oven for dinner tonight, but I've got a few tasty things ready now for our lunch, including some sausage rolls straight from the oven.' She had her arm linked through that of her mother-in-law as she led her up the path and into the house.

ıch was over and several cups of tea had
en drunk – none of these house guests
ere coffee drinkers. Bedrooms had been
sorted out. Marian had her usual ground-
floor room, which normally served as a sew-
ing room for Dee but was always made very
attractive and comfortable whenever her
mother-in-law came to stay. Close by was a
bathroom, a godsend at the best of times, but
more so when it saved older guests from having to climb the staircase, which was steep,
wide and winding. On the windowsill of this
ground-floor bathroom Dee had set out
Yardley's Old English Lavender soap, bath
salts, talcum powder and hand cream.
Everything that Marian liked.

Her own parents knew full well which room
they would be using: one of the first-floor
sea-view bedrooms. They had often stayed
here when Derrick had been in hospital and
Delia had been away visiting him. Jack
especially loved it here, more so when Martin
and Michael, his two grandsons, had been a
bit younger. They had had great times together, often taking the boat out and coming
home with a good catch of fish.

Derrick had warned Delia that there was
news regarding Chloe Warburg. She'd done
everything and anything she could think of
to keep her mind off the forthcoming
gossip.

It wasn't working.

It was Mary Hartfield who started the rolling.

'Dee, love, you remember Jean Witney she's a bit younger than you but she has worked for Mr Barrett as a legal clerk for a good many years – well, she came to see me and your father to let us know that a Miss Warburg had been into the office seeking advice. There is no way she would have told us about it if Mr Barrett had taken the woman on as a client. But as he turned her down flat, Jean felt she was at liberty to contact us. The reason he gave for refusing to act on her behalf was because he was familiar with the people who were involved. Jean said if she hadn't been in full possession of the facts of the case, she might actually have felt sorry for the woman.'

'More fool her.' Marian had found her voice.

'Were any of you aware that this Chloe was living locally?' It was Derrick who had asked the question.

His mother jumped at the chance to enlighten him. 'She stands out like a sore thumb, what with her foreign accent when she speaks. It's not difficult to work out who she is, and although the press have let the story die down recently, there were enough photos of her in every daily paper not so long ago. The fact that she's now living in llage – well, the news spread like wild-

'Mum, what made Jean say she almost felt orry for her?' Dee sounded really puzzled.

Mary pondered the question for a minute and sighed heavily before she spoke. 'She said that the minute Chloe became aware that Mr Barrett was going to turn her down, she changed her tune and started to plead with him. Told him that no matter what his charges were, she would pay them if only he could promise to win this case for her. She told him she could get hold of the money, any amount, as long as she got custody of her daughter.'

Delia stared straight ahead. She could understand Chloe's feelings to a certain degree, but nowhere near enough for her even to consider giving up her daughter to this stranger. Dear God, she thought, how much longer do we have to go on living with this terrible ordeal hanging over us?

'I don't think we've skipped anything in the telling,' Mary said quietly to her daughter.

'Yes we have.' Her mother-in-law butted in again. 'You said that Jean heard this Chloe say she was getting married to a man who was very rich, and that money would be no object.'

'Nothing wrong with your memory, is there, Marian?'

'Did Jean tell you that, Mum?'

It was her father who answered. 'That a ‎ a darn sight more, but none of it has an bearing on your case.'

Jack Hartfield looked across at his son-in-law. His heart ached for him just as much as it did for his daughter. They were a good pair, Delia and Derrick, and they didn't deserve this terrible thing that was happening to them.

'Dad, why do you think Chloe Warburg has taken lodgings in Camber Sands?' Dee had sat and watched the various emotions flicker across her father's face, and now she wanted to know what he thought about it all. Her dad had always been a quiet man, never had a lot to say, but when he did speak, nine times out of ten he was right.

'Well,' Jack Hartfield sighed softly, 'with hindsight we all know that during the summer months that woman rented a caravan in the area, and who knows who she got friendly with, or what tales she told other people. Maybe she was just spying on all of us, working out a plan of action. We don't know what's going on in her mind.'

Marian and Mary decided to clear away the used cups and plates, and when Dee heard the water running in the kitchen, she assumed they were washing up.

Derrick announced that he was going to walk to the village to fetch an evening paper.

ee moved on to the settee to be next to
r father. Her lips were trembling as she
poke. 'Dad, I'm scared, really scared, and I
don't like it.'

'It's OK, Delia.' He put an arm around her
and pressed his lips to the top of her head.

'It's not OK, Dad. If they take Ann away
from us, I just don't know what I will do.'

Suddenly her breath seemed to get caught
in her throat. She tried to push herself up,
but the muscles in her arms felt like
meringue. She struggled, and finally col-
lapsed to her knees on the floor, rolling over
on to her back.

'Dee, what happened?' Her father dropped
to the floor beside her. Dragging a cushion
from the settee, he lifted her shoulders and
placed it beneath her head.

'I can't breathe,' she murmured. 'Can't
breathe.'

'Yes you can.' Her pupils were dilated, and
her face was dead white and very clammy.
Jack put a hand on the back of her head and
slowly brought it up until her torso was bent
forward and her head was almost touching
her knees. 'Come on now, Dee, deep breaths,
slow and easy, that's it, and again, slowly,
deep, deep breaths.'

'No more, I can't.'

'Yes you can. Come on, breathe in, and out.
Keep going.' He continued to gently hold her
head down.

'I'm feeling better. I thought I was go
to choke. I'll be all right now.'

'Like hell you will, you are far from bein
steady. I am wondering if I shouldn't call an
ambulance.'

'Dad, don't you dare, and don't even think
about telling Derrick. I just got something
caught in my throat.'

He helped her to her feet and gently pushed
her back down on to the sofa, arranging
several cushions behind her shoulders and
head.

'Stop babying me,' she pleaded.

'Both you and Derrick are heading for a
whole pack of trouble unless you start to
ease up and give yourselves a break. You've
had nothing but stress, shocks and hard
knocks for months now. It can't go on, you'll
both end up really ill.'

'I know, Dad, but it has been hard.' She
took one long deep breath, and was relieved
when it didn't catch in her lungs or her
throat. 'I am going to ask Derrick whether he
thinks it would be a good idea to hire a private detective to delve into Chloe Warburg's
background. After all, we don't know all that
much about her, and yet it looks as though
she has been spying on us for months. What
do you think, Dad?'

'Clutching at straws probably, but what
harm can it do? And there is always a chance
that something might come to light about her

kground that will prove useful if brought
.o the court case.' Jack breathed a thankful
.gh, and smiling broadly he continued, 'I'd
say you've probably hit on a winner. At least
you'll be able to tell yourselves that two can
play at her game, and it will give you
something different to think about. Yes, my
girl, I'd say I'm all for it.'

'Oh Dad, I do love you,' Dee said as she
flung her arms around her father and kissed
him.

'Do you, pet? Because if you do, then show
it by slowing down. No more panic attacks;
you frightened me half to death.'

# Chapter 17

Wednesday morning, and the first thought that came into Jodie's head as she got out of bed was that this evening she had a date with her husband. The notion had her laughing. How many years had it been since she'd had anything to do with John on a one-to-one basis? More than she cared to remember.

She reached up and took down her dressing gown from where it was hanging on a hook behind her bedroom door. Having wrapped it tightly around herself, she slid her feet into her slippers.

The marriage had worked well enough all the time that John had been in the Royal Navy. Once he had been demobbed, he'd made it perfectly clear that he had no intention of settling down to lead a decent family life. Even his two growing lads had not received much attention from him. The queer part about their break-up was that neither one of them had thought about seeking a legal separation, let alone applying for a divorce, and on the numerous occasions over the years when they had met up at family get-togethers, there had never been the slightest show of animosity on either side.

Jodie sighed, feeling really sad for a moment as she leant over and threw back the bedclothes to allow them to air before she remade the bed. She made her way downstairs, thinking as she went that this house really was far too big for just her to live in now that Reg and Lenny had left home.

The problem between her and John was that they challenged each other personally. Yet for the first few years of their marriage they had complemented each other. The bad times had started when she had first found out about John going with other women. That had been tough enough, without the thought that he had been spending money they could ill afford on cheap tarts when she was working seven days a week to keep a roof over their heads and shoes and clothes on their two boys.

That had been the period when they had fought like a pair of mad dogs.

When they hadn't been at each other's throats they had been falling into bed, and at times like that John had been so lovable! It had been ridiculous for them to get married. They both knew that now. She had been a crazy teenager with her head in the clouds. But what had seemed romantic, exciting and sexy had soon turned into stark reality. It hadn't helped that she had been pregnant even before they got married. It was understandable that she had given birth twice before she was eighteen years old, because for the first few months of their married life they hadn't been able to keep their hands off each other. Jodie caught her breath as she remembered what a wonderful lover John had been.

But then it had become painfully obvious that he had a roving eye and he hadn't been particularly selective about who he slept with. Oh yes, Jodie warned herself, stop kidding yourself and admit it. During that period he had been a right bastard, and what had made it all ten times worse was the fact that when she collected proof and confronted him with it, he hadn't had the guts to confirm or deny her accusations. Had said she only had herself to blame.

What was it he had called her? Oh yes. She shuddered as she remembered.

An unresponsive frigid bitch.

She had never been sure which part of that accusation had hurt the most.

The rest of that day had been a complete blur. All she clearly remembered was telling him to get out. Had he showed any remorse? Hell, no. Had he promised it wouldn't happen again? No chance.

From that day on he had gone his own sweet way. But then so had she. She had been successful, bought two businesses and more than one nice property. She could also look her sons in the eye, knowing that she had always made sure that they were well fed and clothed.

Now that she'd made herself all hot and bothered from recalling these old memories, she hastily filled the kettle and switched it on and went to have a quick shower while it boiled. As she covered her body with shower gel, her hand touched the ring she wore on a gold chain around her neck. It had been her grandmother's wedding ring. It had also been the ring that John had placed on her finger in the registrar's office on the day they had got married. He hadn't had enough money to spare to buy her a new one.

She had yanked the ring off her finger when she had yelled at John to get out and leave her alone. But she hadn't felt able to part with it. Over the years she had thought of it as a symbol of her worst failure.

Having dried and dressed herself, she suddenly questioned whether she was doing the right thing by going out to dinner to-night with John. Was there any reason why she shouldn't? Of course there wasn't. They had both moved on. A lot of water had run under the bridge since they had made an attempt at being a married couple.

Jodie could not have had an inkling, but the truth was, the same kind of thoughts were worrying John. He had met up with Laraine yesterday and over a cup of coffee he had done his best to sound her out. After all, these three sisters-in-law lived and breathed as one person. Hurt one and you upset them all!

He had kept his voice low as he'd asked, 'Has Jodie finished with Philip Conti?'

'Who can tell? Why don't you ask her yourself? I have heard that Philip is thinking of going back to live permanently in Italy,' had been Laraine's cautious reply.

'Give me a break, Laraine. Is she seeing anyone else?'

'If you're so damned concerned, so very much interested, why the hell don't you ask her, instead of playing the fool all the time?'

John had shrugged his shoulders. 'Good question, Laraine. A flipping good question. Let me tell you something. I loved being married to Jodie, but I admit I also loved women, and God knows I was young and selfish in those days. That's the long and short of it, and if a man is able to combine the two, well, life can be as perfect as it is ever going to get. But it is no recipe for a happy marriage. We were both far too young. I didn't think I had to answer to anyone but myself in those days. I was such a fool. For months after Jodie told me to get out and stay out, I kept telling myself she'd come crawling after me. Stupid, wasn't I?'

'Yes, if that was what you were thinking,

you certainly were stupid.' Laraine had laughed heartily before she'd added, 'Jodie would never crawl. Not to anyone. Any more than myself or Delia would. That is one thing we three have always had in common.'

The more John listened to his sister-in-law, the more he realised he hadn't handled everything quite as skilfully as he could have. Should have, he corrected himself. It didn't really make him feel any better to know this, but it did warn him to consider making a different approach when he met up with his wife on their date.

There was definitely a current still running between him and Jodie. He had been aware of it for some time, mainly since it had fallen to him to be the arbitrator between Dee and Derrick. It didn't really shift the blame away from him, but it did open up the door to considering another approach.

As he took his best suit out of the wardrobe and searched for his cufflinks, he vowed to himself that he would do his best to make tonight so special that they would both want to repeat the occasion.

Jodie was staring out of her front window and she drew a deep breath when she saw John drive up and park a brand-new Range Rover alongside her front wall. He had phoned twice since the weekend to confirm that they were still on for this evening.

'Well here goes,' she told herself, with a wide grin on her face as she picked up her gloves and her handbag and went through the hall to open the front door.

John was already standing on the doorstep, and the long look of appreciation he gave her said more than a host of words. It told her that the time and effort spent in getting herself ready for this evening out had been well worth it.

John cupped her face in his hands, and his touch was so gentle it threw her off balance. His lips touched hers, but it was a light kiss that seemed to be more one of affection than anything else. A fact for which she was grateful. At least he had set the pattern for the evening; he wasn't going to rush in all guns blazing. He was still acting the gentleman as he took hold of her arm and led her to the car.

John had chosen well, a smart hotel far out in the country, renowned for the quality of its food. The waiter showed them to a table close to the huge fireplace in which a coal fire was burning. However, John drew him to one side and in an undertone asked if it were possible for them to eat at a table with a little more privacy. The location was changed to the satisfaction of all concerned.

The first course was excellent, and when they had finished, John pushed his empty plate aside, reached over and took Jodie's hand in his. His fingers tightened when she tried to jerk free.

'Don't be so damn prickly, Jodie. I will admit that I have been a philanderer in my time, but you must know that I would never physically hurt you.'

'I know that, John, but you were squashing my fingers.' She let out a breath and then laughed before she added, 'Would you like to know what I've worked out?'

'About what?'

'About the two of us. It suddenly occurred to me that over the years we have been a lot of things to each other, yet we never got around to being friendly. Since you have decided to change your ways somewhat, I'd like to alter that. From now on, let's try being good friends.'

If she had told him that at her age she had become pregnant, he couldn't have been more surprised.

'You want us to be friends?'

'To start off with, yes.'

'And then?'

'Take it as it comes.'

'Stop playing games, Jodie. I thought that we *had* remained friends, whatever else had gone wrong between us. I know I made your life miserable when we were together; you were unhappy, and that's something I've thought about quite a lot since we split up.'

Jodie sighed softly. 'I suppose we should admit that we made each other unhappy.'

'Maybe we did. But I know one thing for sure: I was a darn sight happier with you than I have been without you.'

For a moment she couldn't gather together the words he had just said. He was cool, calm and collected, which was so unlike the John she had lived with. 'I find that hard to believe,' was all she managed to say.

He laughed. 'Thought I would just warn you that since I have become a man of means, I have come to realise that there really are some things that money can't buy. And being as smart as you are, and knowing what I've just told you, you'll be able to work out that I prefer being happy to being unhappy. That's enough of my confessions for one evening. Just let me remind you that this is my new beginning. From now on I'm working on, even banking on, the possibility that you might find it in your heart to forgive me.'

When she made no comment, he smiled sheepishly, and timidly asked, 'How am I doing?'

'Actually not too bad,' Jodie replied on impulse. To herself she added a warning. Don't be a downright idiot! Before you know it he'll have you believing that you were also happier with him than you've been since you split up.

As big a man as John Underwood was, to

Jodie at that moment he resembled a sad, lost little boy, and just looking at him was pulling at her heart strings. Was he too old to change his ways? At least he deserved a chance. Perhaps the fact that he had gone a long way towards helping Wally Rittman back to a sensible way of life had brought him up sharply. It was soon after that episode in his life that he had been locked away for six months inside a prison cell. He must have had plenty of time whilst in there to reflect on his own past life and to contemplate his future. Now, if he needed help, or even encouragement, perhaps she should be feeling good that he had turned to her.

Jodie was saved from saying any more; their main course had arrived. They ate with relish. John was attentive but not pushy, and suddenly Jodie realised that she was enjoying his company as well as the beautiful food.

They both refused the offer of a sweet and settled for cheese and biscuits and a pot of coffee. It was while Jodie was pouring coffee into their cups and John was buttering his water biscuits that he looked up at her and asked, 'How did you think Delia and my brother were holding up when they were with us last Sunday?'

Oh dear! Jodie had hoped they could lay off that subject, just for one evening. Then she rebuked herself sharply: don't be so mean.

She hadn't intended to think such sharp thoughts, but it seemed such a useless topic to keep going over time and time again. There was nothing in this world that she and the rest of the family wouldn't do if they could end this nightmare and bring little Ann home to her rightful parents again. Trouble was, the case was dragging on and everyone was beginning to feel so helpless.

Doing her best to smile, she said, 'Your brother looked like he hadn't slept in a month of Sundays, and as for Delia, well, I just wish I could find the right words to say to her. Although when I saw her yesterday, she told me she has come up with a brain-wave.'

'Really? That sounds great. Or is it just that she is clutching at straws?'

'Maybe she is, who knows? On the other hand, both of them are sick and tired of not being able to do anything. Dee's idea is to hire a private detective to delve into this Belgian woman's background. I laughed when she started to tell me; I know I shouldn't have, but it sounded a bit melodramatic. Then Dee's mum explained that Chloe Warburg was here all last summer, living in a caravan, spying on the family. It now seems she is back again in Camber Sands, staying at a guest house. Lord only knows what she is up to. I don't know what Dee is hoping to find out if she does go ahead with this idea.

What do you think?'

'My first reaction is that it's a damn good idea. My brother should have thought of it at the very start of this mess. Even with the little we already know about this woman, it stands to reason her past hasn't been as white as the driven snow! She's certainly caused our Dee a great deal of aggravation, not to mention the savage way she attacked her. Yes, I'd say it is about time that Dee retaliated.'

Somewhere in the hotel a band had struck up.

Jodie leaned back against her chair and closed her eyes. The music was great, soft and familiar, and she told herself it had been a very nice evening.

Sitting opposite her, John was deep in thought. He had loved being with Jodie tonight. She looked beautiful and smelt gorgeous, that lingering fragrance of her perfume that he used to know so well. So many times he had told himself that he was better off without his wife; she was a stickler for tidiness, for daily grind and all sorts of other things that had got on his nerves. In truth he now realised that he missed her, had always missed her. What could he possibly do about it now?

He told himself to calm down. If he acted at all, it had to be slowly and calmly. They were no longer spring chickens, and no

224

matter how much he wanted her to say that maybe they could resume their life together sometime in the future, he wasn't going to allow sex to muddle the affair, not this time. He knew full well he had to give Jodie time. He mustn't rush her, even though patience had never been his strong point.

He couldn't take his eyes off her as she sat humming along to the popular tunes. He wanted his wife back; he wanted to start over. And this time he would make sure they both knew that it would last for the rest of their lives.

Feeling better, he poured them each a second cup of coffee. He would have liked to call for two brandies, but he had the car to drive home and he knew that Jodie wouldn't drink alone.

As he passed her cup back to her, she widened her eyes and smiled at him. 'I don't know when I have enjoyed an evening more. Thank you, John.'

It was enough.

For now.

## Chapter 18

Delia leaned back against the seat in Derrick's car and shut her eyes. She was glad he'd insisted on driving. She just didn't have the energy. She was upset, her mind in a whirl. Derrick wasn't keen on this idea of consulting a private detective. He said it was an invasion of Chloe Warburg's privacy. But what about my privacy? thought Dee. That woman walked into our house uninvited and ended up nearly killing me.

Derrick shoved the car into reverse. 'You're hoping that if we dig deep enough, we'll come up with a load of shit in her past, is that it?'

Now she knew his temper was getting the better of him; he didn't usually resort to swearing, at least not in front of her.

'Let's just seek out this private detective, tell him as much as he needs to know and take it from there.'

'Fine.' He shot backwards out of the driveway.

They shouldn't be acting like this, Dee realised. She no more wanted to quarrel with Derrick than fly in the air, but she was entitled to her own opinion once in a while.

The trouble was, she was so tired and she felt she could only be pulled in one direction at a time. 'All right, we won't go any further if you feel so strongly about it,' she said, doing her best to remain calm.

He stopped the car and pulled over to the side of the road until he had fought down his anger. This business of the Crown Court case looming up was driving them both over the edge.

He reached out, rubbed his fingers over Dee's cheek and said, 'Sorry.'

'What are you apologising for?' she asked crossly, but she did turn her face towards him.

'For being a selfish pig. Will that do?'

'Fine. Now you decide. Are we going to keep that appointment that you went to such lengths to make, or shall we just go back indoors?'

'All I did was look up a number in the Yellow Pages,' he muttered.

'Yes, but we were both taken by the name of the firm, "Discretion Foremost", and as we seem to have calmed down, we might as well take ourselves off to Brighton.' Dee was getting good at the art of persuasion.

He managed a smile as he turned the key in the ignition.

'No, wait.' Derrick switched off the engine. Dee stared straight ahead without saying a word until she was certain she could speak without breaking down.

'I am sorry for that woman – there are times when I'm desperately sorry for her – but I am also very angry with her. Nobody forced her to walk away and leave that baby. Nearly six years, never an enquiry about the child, not one gift or a birthday card. The anger wipes the pity out when I think how she attacked me. What wrong did I ever do her? Except take on a dear little baby that no one else could be bothered with and made her our daughter. Was that so wrong?'

She fell towards him, pressing her face into his chest, and he gathered her to him, because by now she was crying. God above! His Dee never used to cry, but since all this business had started up, she had shed so many, many tears and they were all because of him and what he'd done in the past.

She turned her hot, damp cheek on to his shoulder. 'Why couldn't that woman have left well alone? I couldn't bear to have Ann taken away from us for good, not after all this time. I just don't know what's going to happen, and it scares me.'

Derrick felt utterly useless as he murmured, 'It's the same for both of us.'

There had always been a tenderness between him and Delia. He had never experienced anything like it in his own family. Underwoods, he thought, weren't able to express their feelings. His father had been a man of few words who worked hard and rarely complained. Derrick had never doubted that his parents loved each other or their children, but he wasn't sure he'd ever heard his father actually say so. He'd shown his love by making sure there was food on the table, a warm fire in the grate and clothes on his children's backs.

Maybe that was why Derrick made sure that he often told Delia that she was beautiful and that he loved her. In these last few years he had tried to show his appreciation for all she had done for him. Not many women would have been able to stand the sight of him when he'd first been allowed home from the hospital.

'You know what, Dee?' he suddenly exclaimed.

Dee took the handkerchief that he was holding out to her and rubbed at her eyes. 'No, I've no idea, but I am sure you are about to tell me,' she answered weakly.

'Seeing as we're in the car and ready to go, why don't we call in to that address I got over the phone, say our piece and listen to the reaction we get. Then, good or bad, I suggest that we have lunch at the Old Ship Hotel on the seafront again. All right with you?'

'Yes.' She managed a smile as he tucked the car rug around her knees before switching on the engine again.

They found the premises they were looking for in Hove, the moneyed part of Brighton. The office they were entering had the feeling of being very exclusive. The reception area was vast, with dark wood panelling and comfortable chairs, and the table positioned in the centre of the room had been polished so much it gave off a glossy sheen. The lady sitting behind the enormous desk looked graceful, expensively dressed and as well cared for as the furnishings. Her smile was pleasant and her tone of voice was certainly upper-crust.

Derrick approached her and said, 'Mr and Mrs Underwood. We've got an appointment at eleven thirty with Mr Anthony Wilbourne.'

'May I ask the nature of your business?'

Derrick glanced down at the brass name plate on the desk and forced himself to smile as he looked up again. 'Ms Baldwin, I gave the necessary details to Mr Wilbourne. It's personal business,' he added, which earned him a mild glare of reproof from the elegant Ms Baldwin.

'Please, take a seat,' she said, this time smiling directly at Delia. 'I'll let Mr Wilbourne know you are here.'

Hardly had they seated themselves than Ms Baldwin came from behind her desk saying, 'If you'll follow me, I'll take you to

Mr Wilbourne.'

'Thank you.' Derrick took Delia's arm as they started down a carpeted corridor.

The office was even more expensive-looking than the reception area. Derrick had already pegged Mr Wilbourne as being rich, classy and very successful, though he told himself that this outward show of wealth didn't necessarily make the man good at his job.

Anthony Wilbourne was lean, with not a spare ounce of fat on his body. He looked to be nearing fifty, because there were a few streaks of grey showing in his thick dark hair. His suit was a dark navy pinstripe and looked expensive; a white shirt with cuff-links and a light blue tie completed his attire. His accent was sharp, or as Dee was later to say, 'rather posh'.

'Is this a personal or professional enquiry?' was Mr Wilbourne's first shot once they were all seated.

'Depends on which way you look at it,' Derrick replied, 'but first off I have to ask: if my wife and I agree to tell you the reason we're here, will whatever we discuss be totally confidential?'

'Without a doubt, Mr Underwood.'

'Whether we decide to hire you or not?' Derrick persisted.

'I can certainly promise that whatever either of you chooses to tell me will be

231

treated as strictly off the record until such time as you decide otherwise.' He opened a drawer and took out a writing pad. 'Now then,' he said, pencil at the ready. 'Why don't you start, Mr Underwood, and tell me what problem has brought you to me?'

Derrick opened his briefcase, leafed through it and took out several sheets of paper. Leaning forward, he placed the pages on the desk directly in front of Mr Wilbourne.

There was a lengthy silence while the investigator read through the typed notes. When he looked up, there was a very serious expression on his face as he began to speak. 'I gather the lady in question was brought to you whilst you were in a Belgian hospital. The facts are clearly laid out in these notes. She was paid to have sex with you. Are you hoping to find details of her earlier life?'

'Yes.'

'In that case, I can initiate a search with no problems and get you some answers without any more information than what you have given me here.' He tapped the pages. 'But I can work more quickly, and more effectively, if you decide to trust me and give me more information.'

Derrick frowned. 'I did not know Miss Warburg; it was just the one meeting, purely for sex. I would like you to delve into her former life and see what you come up with.

Her full name is Chloe Ursula Warburg.'

Delia was squirming in her seat. Why oh why did she constantly have to sit through meetings such as this? It was so embarrassing, at least for her, though Derrick seemed to take it all in his stride.

Suddenly Anthony Wilbourne smacked his hand against his forehead and burst out loudly, 'I am so sorry! Why has it only just this minute dawned on me!'

Derrick and Delia glanced at each other. They needed no telling that the investigator had suddenly realised who they were.

It was Mr Wilbourne's turn to feel disconcerted, and he struggled to get his thoughts in order before he spoke.

'With all the reporting in the media and the coverage from the TV stations, how could I not have grasped who you were as soon as my secretary said your surname? Once again I do apologise, and I have to ask if you wish to continue this meeting or not. I won't be offended if you would prefer to bring the session to an end.'

'Mr Wilbourne.' Derrick paused and gave a cynical laugh. 'My wife and I would be hard pushed to find anyone who doesn't know our history. We are willing to carry on if you are.'

Delia added her weight by nodding her head.

Derrick continued. 'I would like to enighten you as to what has brought us here to you. We have been made to suffer in so many ways. Despite the fact that our daughter has been found, the authorities have decided that she should remain in a children's home until such time as a court of law decides who her rightful parents are. We have been continuously spied upon. Miss Warburg illegally entered our home and assaulted my wife so badly that she had to be hospitalised for two weeks. We are now facing the possibility that a court of law may decide that our daughter will never be returned to us. Both my wife and I feel it is time that we retaliate.'

Complete silence followed that statement.

Anthony Wilbourne was overcome. He had heard the tremor in Derrick's voice and he at once became a sympathiser. Yet it was to Delia that he turned. 'Mrs Underwood, I would like you to chat to me for a few minutes, if that is all right by you?'

Dee nodded her head. She had been half expecting him to question her from the moment she had sat down.

Mr Wilbourne gave her an encouraging smile before saying, 'I can appreciate that in all probability you have been asked many times to tell the story of how you came to take on the role of being mother to a newborn baby, but would you mind repeating it once more?'

Delia cleared her throat, but no wo
came.

'Take your time,' Mr Wilbourne encou...
aged her.

Derrick stood up and, speaking very quietly, said, 'Sorry, Dee, yet again it is all falling back on to you. I'll wait outside; that way it won't be so distressing for you. Just remember, my darling, no shame can be attached to you. I'm the one who should be feeling mortified.'

With Derrick gone from the room, Delia swallowed hard and asked, 'In the papers my husband has given you, did you find notes on the strange way that I learnt about the baby in the beginning?'

'Yes, I saw that social workers came to your home address clutching a slip of paper with your husband's name and part of his address on it that had been discovered pinned to the inside of the baby's cot. Is that an accurate account of what happened?'

'Yes. The social workers took it for granted that my husband was the father of the abandoned child.'

'And did you go along with that assumption?'

'No, I did not, but I was concerned for the baby and I paid a visit to Hammersmith Hospital. From my first sight of her, that wee baby tugged at my heart strings and I did everything possible to make sure she s well taken care of.'

'Even though you strongly believed she was not in any way your responsibility?' Mr Wilbourne felt he had to verify this fact.

'At the time it seemed to me that not a soul in the world cared about that child. I couldn't have just walked away from her; she needed to know that at least one person loved her.'

'Personal question now, Mrs Underwood: how and when did you become convinced that your husband had fathered that baby?'

Delia laughed, though it was a hopeless sound. 'How can I possibly make you understand?'

'You could try starting at the beginning and going right through to the end.'

'That would take all day.'

'I have all day.'

'Oh, Mr Wilbourne, most of it would bore you to death.'

'I'll be the judge of that.'

'You are being extremely kind to me. So if you insist...'

Once more Dee repeated the story of the explosion at sea, Derrick's terrible injuries and Bob Patterson's belief that sex with a prostitute would boost his morale. She explained how John had finally managed to convince her that the story was true.

'Derrick and I already had two grown-up sons,' she continued, 'but somehow that baby wormed her way into my heart. Derrick was allowed home for a couple of days every now and again, and I began to make sure that the baby was at our house under my care at the time of his visits. We named her Ann, and from day one she captivated our hearts. She became our daughter, accepted and dearly loved by every member of our family. For almost six years she has been the light of our lives. The fact that her mother was a prostitute no longer bothered me. Over the years I have often thanked God that Chloe Warburg abandoned her child. Ann has turned out to be a blessing for us both. We couldn't love her more if it had been me who had given birth to her.'

Delia slipped forward in her chair, lowering her head to rest on her cupped hands. After a few minutes of silence she looked up and said very softly, 'Now after six years, that woman wants her back. How can she do that? She doesn't even know our child. If the courts grant her custody, I just don't know what Derrick and I will do.'

Anthony Wilbourne had taken out a white handkerchief from his pocket and wiped his eyes before he could bring himself to speak.

Then, picking up the telephone, he spoke into it. 'Miss Baldwin, would you ask Mr Underwood to come back into the room, and then will you bring tea for three, please.' As he replaced the receiver, he smiled at

237

Dee and asked, 'Is tea all right for you?'

'Oh yes, please,' she murmured, and she even managed a weak smile.

The tray was enormous, the cups, saucers and plates of the finest bone china. There was a silver tea strainer laid across a slop bowl; another bowl held sugar lumps and a pair of silver tongs for handling them. A three-tiered cake stand held the smallest, daintiest fancy cakes that Dee had ever seen.

'Thank you, Miss Baldwin,' Mr Wilbourne said as she put the tray down on his desk. 'I'm sure Mrs Underwood won't mind waiting on us men.' As Miss Baldwin walked towards the door, he gave a sly wink in Dee's direction and suddenly her hopes rose.

Delia poured the tea, offered the bowl of sugar lumps, gave each man a side plate, a serviette and a silver cake fork, all before passing round the selection of fancy cakes.

Derrick chose a chocolate square and Mr Wilbourne laughed. 'Good God, man! That's not even a nibble. Take three or four, please do.'

It was a happy half-hour before he rang again for Miss Baldwin to remove the tray. Then, settling back behind his desk, he turned to Derrick and said, 'I take it I may hold on to these papers? I shall get on to this case straight away. The very fact that the lady in question was earning her living as a prostitute, whether legal or not, must throw some light on to her way of life. I honestly do not think we have a lot to fear, but if we have some cannonballs in readiness, it won't hurt our case to threaten to fire them. I will be in touch within three days at most.'

They all shook hands, and once outside, both Derrick and Dee let out a deep, deep breath. It was a sigh of relief. At last somebody had listened to them. There was someone with them now, batting on their side.

'Come on, my love, we're going to have a slap-up meal,' Derrick said, still grinning.

'So it wasn't such a bad idea of mine to come and see an investigator? But how can you talk about food when you've just scoffed a load of fancy cakes?'

'A load! Put the whole lot together and you wouldn't make one good one, but they were delicious, weren't they?'

'Of course they were, and he was a very nice man, wasn't he?'

'If you say so. Bit of a toff, I thought, but I'll reserve judgement until we see what he comes up with.'

Linking arms, they set off to the car park, and their footsteps were lighter than they had been for many a long day.

# Chapter 19

Another month had gone by, the cold snap had passed and spring was on its way, yet the Underwoods were all feeling down in the dumps. No matter what efforts they made, they always turned out to be ineffective. A date for the court hearing had still to be set, and hopes that Ann would be returned to live with Delia and Derrick were deteriorating.

A cloud of sadness was hanging over the three sisters-in-law as they walked arm in arm along the glorious seafront at Bexhill-on-Sea. Yesterday they had gone together to visit Ann in the care home at Dover. Each woman had been holding several presents, sent by aunts, uncles and grandmas. They hadn't been given enough passes to enable them to take anyone else with them. Laraine and Jodie had been looking forward to getting down on their knees with arms flung wide open and calling to Ann to run to them. Nothing of the sort had happened. There had been a tiny reaction when her mother and two aunts had entered, but then Ann had immediately gazed up at the nurse who had come into the room with her, and almost at once her dear little face had become blank, almost lifeless.

It had been heartbreaking to sit across a huge table from Ann, telling her how much everyone loved her and missed her, and yet not one flicker of emotion did the child show and not a single word did she utter. To be honest, Jodie and Laraine had been thankful when they were able to take hold of Delia and leave. If they had remained any longer in that huge silent room there would have been no telling what action Dee might have resorted to. It had been agonising for all of them.

This morning Jodie had come to Bexhill to view some premises that were up for sale. It had been her suggestion that Laraine and Dee accompany her.

'What's the matter?' Laraine flinched as Dee squeezed her arm tightly.

'Christ almighty! It's her,' Dee gasped.

A few minutes later they had drawn level with Chloe Warburg. The three sisters-in-law stood gaping at each other. They were so stunned they were utterly speechless.

It was Dee who finally broke the uncomfortable silence. She took a deep breath, then said, 'I'm glad they didn't send you to prison.'

Chloe gave the women a deadly look and in a voice so loud it could have raised the dead she shouted, 'How dare you all gang up on me?' Not bothering to hide her hostility and loathing, she leaned forward and hissed straight into Delia's face, 'You are a wicked bitch. You stole my baby.'

The angry words, shouted out so violently, the undisguised hatred on Chloe's face and her threatening manner had frightened Dee. She quickly took a step backwards, shock and dismay showing on her face, which by now was as white as a sheet.

Chloe wasn't finished, not by a long chalk. 'I'll get the better of you yet, no matter what it takes. You stole my only child.' By now her face was a brilliant red, her voice shrill and far too loud.

'And it took you six years to decide you'd done wrong by abandoning her?' Laraine reminded her.

In a flash, Chloe turned and faced her next opponent. 'You can mind your own business. You're another Underwood, like the rest of the bloody family determined to take my child. You are all horrible people; you have cheated me out of what is rightfully mine. You're thieves, the whole lot of you. Now get out of my way.'

Jodie pulled Laraine away, fearful that she was about to strike the woman. Chloe must have realised she was outnumbered. Clenching her fists tightly, she pushed between Jodie and Laraine, almost knocking them over as she went, and swept on along the seafront without a backward glance.

Delia was badly shaken, and there was a sick feeling in the pit of her stomach. She was momentarily paralysed, powerless to move. Laraine put her arms around her and shook her gently.

Jodie let out a deep breath before muttering, 'Phew! That was awful. She can't be right in the head.'

'No, she can't be,' Laraine agreed. 'Doesn't she realise that if she had assaulted any of us, we could have called the police and she would have been arrested? She needs to remember she is out on remand.'

Delia pulled herself away from Laraine and ran almost blindly across the main road, up the steps and through the front door of the nearest hotel. She wanted to put some distance between herself and those passers-by who had witnessed that awful scene. She had never before felt so humiliated and she was still shaking inside.

Her two sisters-in-law ran after her and found her standing just inside the door, striving to calm herself. They each slipped an arm through Delia's and drew her across the reception area.

It was Jodie who spoke. 'At least we didn't know any of those people who were listening and gawping at us, Dee, so let's forget it. Come on, we'll have a nice cup of tea, it will do us all good.'

Once they had been shown to a table in the lounge area of the hotel and had settled down, Jodie ordered a pot of tea. As the waiter walked away, Dee sat back and gave a great sigh of relief before saying, 'What a nasty shock that was.'

'Yes, could have turned real ugly,' Jodie said. 'And that would have been even more embarrassing. You'd have thought that once she had spotted us she would have done her best to avoid us. I could hardly believe it when she raised her voice and started to shout at us.'

Laraine was quick to say, 'It wasn't as if any of us goaded her. In fact, I thought Dee bent over backwards to be nice, telling her she was glad the judge hadn't sent her to prison. I wouldn't have been so nice. I probably would have told her she should be behind bars!'

Jodie nodded and gave Dee a careful look. 'Why on earth did you speak to her in the first place?'

'I didn't know what else to do. We were so near, her face was almost touching mine. It was terribly awkward,' Dee replied, and then she paused and shook her head slowly. 'I suppose I've always felt a little bit sorry for her, deep down. I've never really thought she was wicked, just that maybe she was confused all those years ago and somewhat stupid now by attempting to turn the clock back six years. Come what may, it isn't going to happen. Or at least I pray to God it isn't.' As Dee said that, she felt the hackles rise on the back of her neck and shivered involuntarily.

'I agree with you, Dee, about the stupidity, but I don't feel sorry for her and neither should you,' Laraine exclaimed, sounding exasperated.

Fortunately, the waiter arrived with a tray and they were all glad of the distraction as he started to place cups and saucers in front of them. He departed, but almost instantly returned with a large pot of tea and a jug of hot water. He went away again and came back, this time pushing a trolley in front of him.

None of them could resist the temptation. The trolley was three tiers high, each tier loaded with scones, delicious-looking pastries and gorgeous gateaux.

'Mmmm,' they each murmured before making their selection.

Once they had finished their tea, the three women re-emerged from the hotel, and with shoulders back and heads held high, they marched off towards the car park. To passers-by they looked what they were, a very formidable trio.

## Chapter 20

For the fourth time in three weeks, Jodie was having dinner with John. Tonight they were seated facing each other in the dining room of the Fox and Hounds hotel, which lay at the foot of the famous Downs at Epsom.

They had finished their meal and were now having coffee and brandy. They had also enjoyed an excellent bottle of wine with their dinner, because tonight John had arrived to pick Jodie up in a taxi so that they didn't have to worry about who was driving.

As was usual of late, John was doing everything possible to convince Jodie that he had indeed become a reformed character. His voice was low but firm as he spoke.

'Lots of events happened so quickly, all of which made me view my life in a totally different way. First off it was a shock when I looked back and realised just how badly I had treated you, our two boys, and yes, even my own mother.'

John sounded so very sincere every time he broached the subject of why and how they had split up all those years ago. But to Jodie it was important that she remembered

246

the hell they had lived through prior to the break-up. She wasn't going to allow him just gloss over the past. On the other hand this man sitting with her now didn't bear any resemblance to the husband she had lived with when she had been in her teens.

Since they had taken to going out as a couple, they had both been more relaxed and had come to appreciate their evenings and some weekends together. Yet Jodie, if asked, would have been the first to admit that she was still not totally convinced of the change in John. The very thought made her feel guilty. Poor John, he had been trying so hard, and she hadn't shown much faith in him. That was the sad truth. If there truly was a change, what had brought it about?

True, thanks to Isaac Rittman, John no longer had any money problems. But just what was it that he had done to earn such a legacy?

Word was that Isaac's son Wally had been out of his mind on drugs. If that was so, had John lived through a terrible time with Wally? Just holding his hand would never have been enough. Not a soul had set eyes on either of the two men for weeks on end. Perhaps that was how long it had taken to get Wally clean. I am being irrational about this, Jodie decided, and there and then she made a resolute effort to dismiss her doubts about John and accept that he really was a ormed character.

His voice broke into her thoughts. 'Jodie, I'm asking you to at least think about it. Please give me a chance.'

Jodie sighed. He was being such a dear. Taking a deep breath, she said, 'I have so enjoyed being with you these last few weeks, but I still don't know if I have the courage to trust you enough to start all over again.'

John was looking into her eyes, and the smile on his lips was so sad that she almost gave in, but he continued before she had a chance to speak. 'I look at the home you've made; it is truly beautiful. You have your own thriving businesses. And then there are our two sons. You alone bore the burden of their upbringing. They have turned out to be self-sufficient and successful young men. The credit for that is entirely down to you. So, looking back, how could I, or anyone else for that matter, doubt your courage? It is a big decision, though, isn't it?'

'Yes, John, it is, but I am thinking seriously about all the reasons you've given me,' she said, trying to make her laugh sound a happy one.

'That will do me for now,' he said, rising to his feet. 'We'll talk more later in the week.' He made an elaborate show of holding her coat, and as she put her arms through the sleeves, he pulled her back so that her whole frame was tight up against his chest.

'Mr Underwood, your taxi has arrive the waiter quietly told him, and was rewarded for his attention during the evening by a folded note that John discreetly slipped into his hand.

Back at the house, John asked the taxi driver to wait. He took the keys from Jodie, unlocked her front door and stepped inside to switch on the hall light. Jodie moved to stand directly in front of him and as his arms went around her, she gave a deep, soft sigh. His lips on hers were not demanding, they were sweet, and Jodie was hungry for someone to really love her.

'Good night, my darling.' John's voice sounded hoarse as he broke away from her. 'Just say you will think about what we've said, and I'll ring you in the morning.'

'Send the taxi away; stay here tonight.' Jodie's voice was little more than a whisper. She stepped nearer to him and wrapped her arms around him.

'Are you sure this is what you want?'

'Yes. Yes, I'm sure.'

He led her towards the lounge, switched on the lights and said, 'I'll be back in a minute.'

It wasn't long before they were sitting opposite each other at the kitchen table with hot toddies in front of them.

There was a grin on John's face that would have done credit to a Cheshire cat.

Oh my darling Jodie! I messed up so badly the first time around. But I realise now that I never stopped loving you. At times it's driven me mad thinking of you going out and about with Philip. The very thought of you and him drives me crazy.'

Jodie leaned forward and ran a hand over his hair, and now she really was laughing. 'I think you'd find that Philip feels the same way about you. You two should become friends.'

'I heard that he is going back to live in Italy; perhaps when we get back together, we should go there to have a holiday and look him up.'

'Shouldn't you be saying *if* and not *when?*' she said quietly.

'Stop teasing, Jodie. Whoever said that love is supposed to be sane or even sensible? I have admitted that I messed up badly. As things are now, do you think I deserve a second chance?'

'Ask me again in the morning.'

John got to his feet, came around the table and took her in his arms. Then very gently he kissed her, and suddenly it was such sweet pleasure. Long, lingering kisses, his lips moving softy and slowly. They stood swaying, melting into each other.

He did stay the night.

Next morning, like an old married couple,

they sat opposite each other at the kitc
table eating bowls of crunchy cornflakes.

John broke the silence. 'Jodie, I am goir
to do my best to prove that I really do lov
you, and I've got some things I want to say
to you.'

'OK.'

'I want us to get back together again.
Properly, as man and wife.'

Jodie didn't make any reply.

'Really, I want to make things up to you.
Make everything all right between us. I will
even ask Reg and Lenny what their feelings
are if that would help. And I promise not to
screw up this time. I really want us to try and
get back to the way things were when we
were first married. Honestly, Jodie, I must
have been mad not to realise just how much
you meant to me. I was the one in the wrong.
All along the line I messed up, and when you
told me to get out, I only went because I was
damn sure you'd come running after me. But
you never did! You were so self-reliant, such a
good businesswoman. You never needed me.
You never needed anyone. And I was a right
big-headed fool, wasn't I?'

'Yes, you were, we both were. But this
morning you're doing fine.' She had to stop
and blink away her tears before she was able
to say more. 'If we do manage to revive our
marriage, I promise to involve you in every
aspect of my life. In future we will talk

...e, and we must never again assume that each know what the other is thinking. I promise to tell you whatever I am involved in no matter what it entails, and whatever is on my mind, providing you promise to do the same.'

John stood up, came around to her side of the table and lowered his head to gently kiss her, but she pushed him away.

'What now?' he asked, wondering at how Jodie's moods could change so quickly.

'I think you should propose to me all over again.'

'If that's what it takes,' he said, sounding dead serious. He moved a chair out of the way and knelt down.

'Will you marry me please, Jodie?'

'No, you know I can't, I am a married woman.'

'God above!' He huffed and puffed as he stood up. 'You really are getting your own back good and proper today.'

'Well it's true, and another thing, you haven't told me whether you love me.'

'Good God, Jodie, you are enough to drive a man to drink. But do you want to know something? I love you even more when you become cantankerous; in fact I love everything about you, and this time around, if you will only say yes, I will buy you two rings – one right now, today, an engagement ring, and then later a wedding ring. I can afford one this time.'

'Are you trying to show off?'

'No way. It will be no more than you deserve.'

'I still have my wedding ring.' She put her hand inside her jumper and lifted the chain over her head. Then, taking hold of his hand, she dropped the chain and the gold band it held into his palm.

He stared at it, absolutely overcome with emotion. It took a while before he was able to ask, 'Is this what I think it is?'

'Yes, the very same. You put that ring on my finger the day you married me.'

'You yanked it off and flung it away the day you told me to get out of your life.'

'That was what I led you to believe.'

'You've been wearing this all these years?'

'Mostly, though I took it off sometimes if I was wearing a low-cut dress. Had to wear other jewellery occasionally. Suppose you're going to tell me I'm daft, too sentimental.'

'Not at all. If possible, I love you even more. Do you want to keep wearing it or would you like a new one?'

'I wouldn't change it for the world. It will be a good reminder of time lost. Though I would like to take you up on the offer of an engagement ring or even an eternity ring, something to prove that this time it is going to be a lasting marriage.'

'I'll buy you both. Today. You can come

me to choose what stones you'd like.'

'Oh John, you're a real darling, and please may we have a celebration? A proper wedding this time. And we're buying a house.'

'What for? We have this one.'

'Oh no, definitely not! *I* bought this one. Our new house will be one that we have chosen together, one that we'll make into a real home where family on both sides will always be welcome. Somewhere we can grow old together.'

'I don't care where it is, Jodie, just so long as it is *our* house. If we're lucky, it might yet be overrun with our grandchildren.'

Jodie gasped. 'You're jumping the gun a bit, John, but by all that is holy I do like what I'm hearing.'

'I do love you,' he said. 'Are you quite sure that you love me?'

'It was me who asked you to stay the night. I am taking all of this very seriously. First and foremost, yes, despite everything, John Underwood, I do love you dearly and I want to have you as my husband. But full time, mind you!' She said the last five words with a smile, but he had gathered the full meaning of them.

He undid the clasp of the chain and slid the gold ring off. 'Suppose from right now, this very minute, you start to wear this ring again. If you agree, you will make me the happiest man alive.'

Jodie held out her hand and sprea[d] fingers, and as John slid the ring on t[o] appropriate finger he murmured, 'Till de[ath] us do part.'

'Yes,' Jodie murmured, adding softly, 'Please God.'

Within seconds, John had swept her off her feet and up into his arms as a groom might carry his new bride. Then he lowered his lips to her upturned face and kissed her. It was a long, lasting kiss. One that she knew she would remember and cherish for the rest of her life.

As he set her down on her feet, he grinned. 'Come on, Mrs Underwood, we have a couple of rings to buy, and we're going to start off the right way by choosing them together.'

They hadn't wasted any time. John had driven his car as far as Clapham Common, then parked and hailed a taxi that would take them into the West End of London. 'Hatton Garden, please,' he said to the driver.

Jodie was surprised as she stepped out of the cab. Hatton Garden lay between Holborn Circus and Clerkenwell Road. This was a moneyed area, in a class all of its own, full of beautiful old buildings, many with bow-fronted windows with small circular panes of thick glass. Having read all the shop signs, it didn't take long for her to realise that this was the centre of the diamond merchant ... e, with gold and silver as a sideline.

... ohn seemed to know exactly where he ... as heading, but when he stopped, Jodie was almost afraid to walk up the steps and into the shop. She was well used to London, but not familiar with premises such as these. It was as if she were dreaming. Within minutes, John had held a quiet conversation with a well-dressed elderly gentleman who introduced himself as George Lieberman. Now John was holding her forearm, urging her to take a closer look at several sparkling rings that had been placed on a bed of black velvet.

'Darling, there's no hurry. Just take your time, try on as many as you like. What do you fancy? Just diamonds, or an emerald or a ruby in the setting?'

Jodie wanted to stop him. This was going too far. God knows what any of these rings would cost! She had never discussed with John the amount of money Isaac Rittman had left him, but from the way he was carrying on, it would have to be a bottomless pit.

Meanwhile Mr Lieberman was holding out a ring card. 'May I try this card on your finger, please, madam? It is essential we get the right size.'

Jodie finally settled on three diamonds on a gold band, the centre stone in a square

setting with a smaller stone on each sid
actual ring was far too big for her finger
Mr Lieberman explained that that was a
the good. It would be made smaller and t
gold band would become wider.

'How soon will we be able to pick it up?'
John, as usual, wanted everything done and
settled at once.

'I will have it sent straight to our work-
shop, and it will be ready for you tomorrow,
at any time to suit you, sir.'

'Hang on a minute.' John had put out a
hand to prevent Mr Lieberman from clearing away the rings that were still out on
display.

Jodie gasped; the way John had spoken
was a bit sharp. It was obvious that Mr
Lieberman was also taken aback, but before
he had time to comment, John smiled and
said, 'Our business is not quite finished. We
need two eternity rings, one for my wife and
one for myself.'

Relief all round was obvious. 'I'll have my
assistant bring a couple of trays in. Do you
have a preference for gold, and would sir
prefer the rings to be self-designed or set in
with diamonds?'

Jodie almost choked! However, she swallowed and managed to say clearly, 'Plain
gold will be fine.'

Mr Lieberman remained silent until a
younger man had laid out two trays of rings

e glass counter and departed. 'Madam
notice that none of these rings are per-
tly plain; that would be a wedding ring
ach as the good one madam is wearing.'

Jodie felt she was getting out of her depth
and it made her uncomfortable; she was
used to being the one in charge.

'Come on, my darling, try some on. Shall
we have the same or would you prefer something really fancy?'

Jodie was lost for choice. Each and every
ring was beautiful, some narrow, some wide,
and each one had been engraved with a pattern. The third one that she tried on had her
smiling. When she slipped it on it was a
perfect fit, sitting snugly next to her own
wedding ring and yet leaving enough room
for her new engagement ring. The gold band
had a decorative scroll design all the way
round it. She loved it.

John laid his hand on her shoulder, making her jump.

'Is that the one you would like, Jodie?'

'Yes, if that is all right by you. Have you
chosen one?'

'Yes, but not from those trays.' He held
out his left hand and on his third finger he
was wearing a thick plain gold wedding
band. 'I am saying to the whole world, I am
a married man.'

Jodie would have dearly liked to have
thrown her arms around him but the pre-

sence of Mr Lieberman and the grande
her surroundings prevented such a sho
emotion.

John knew what Jodie was thinking but r
told himself there would be plenty of time
for that later on. Turning to face Mr Lieberman, he said, 'These two rings fit so I think
we'll keep them on.'

Mr Lieberman smiled, then very discreetly
lowered his voice and said, 'Sir, would you
care to come through to my office to complete the transaction?' Turning to smile at
Jodie he then asked, 'Would madam care to
sit down? I shall have a glass of champagne
brought to you.'

In her head Jodie was laughing. Talk about
money speaking all languages. It was an
entirely different world inside these premises.

By the time John had re-joined her and
they had both had a glass of champagne, she
was ready to believe that whatever John was
promising her might just come true.

Outside on the pavement, Jodie stood still
and took a deep breath, while John laughed.
'Would you like to go and do some more
shopping?' he asked her, still grinning.

'I don't think so,' Jodie answered em-
phatically, still troubled about the amount
of money he must have just spent.

They had a late lunch at a new restaurant
that John wanted to try. It was in Stockwell,
not too far from where he had parked the

he menu was excellent, not at all ex-
sive and the atmosphere was friendly.
ie was still on cloud nine. She kept rub-
ng her wedding ring that was back on her
inger and the eternity ring that had now
joined it. In her mind she was reliving every
moment she had spent choosing a diamond
ring to go with them. Was it all real?

She looked at John and she knew that he
was fully aware of what she had been thinking and suddenly they both burst out laughing. 'Here's to our great future,' he said,
raising his glass of juice with his right hand
and wiggling the third finger of his left
hand, showing off his wedding ring.

Their main course arrived and they ate in
silence, both busy with their own thoughts.
To Jodie it still seemed strange to be out
shopping with John. She'd been taken aback
when he had introduced her to the jeweller
as his wife, telling him that when they had
got married he hadn't been able to afford an
engagement ring.

By the time they arrived back in Epsom,
Jodie was exhausted. She was so happy, but
also a little dubious. It had been a great day
and the night preceding it still had her
tingling as she recalled their lovemaking.
Were they going at too fast a pace? For years
they'd had hardly anything to do with each
other and now, suddenly, they were re-
married. Was it all too good to be true?

John saw her safely to the house, but he couldn't stay and Jodie said she had to at Shepperton Studios by seven thirty the next morning so they agreed to part.

'I'll phone you tomorrow,' he promised as they stood in the doorway. Then as a parting shot he added, 'Don't forget we have to search for a house to buy.'

Jodie wasn't able to answer that because his lips had covered hers with a final lingering kiss. As they drew apart Jodie smiled and spoke in a whisper. 'Good night, John. Thank you for everything.'

'Good night, my darling. It won't be long before we set up our own home.'

As he walked to his car, John vowed he was never going to lose Jodie again. He truly loved his wife, more than ever before.

The morning was misty but a sliver of light was shining through a gap in the curtains. Jodie yawned and sat up in bed. Running her fingers through her thick dark hair she glanced at the clock. 'Oh my God!' It was ten minutes to seven. She had set the alarm for a quarter to six.

She was supposed to be at the studios for seven thirty.

After one lengthy phone call, two cups of tea and a very quick shower, Jodie drove off in her car at a quarter to eight. It was as she approached Wimbledon that she sensed she

in trouble. The engine of the car didn't
⎡nd right. She checked the fuel gauge,
hich was fine. As she drove along Merton
High Street, the car just shuddered and
died.

Other drivers were honking their horns
behind her and she was tempted to get out
and give them a piece of her mind. Instead
she held her temper and slowly but surely
turned the steering wheel with her left hand
and walked pushing the car to the edge of the
road. She had no option but to abandon it.
Thank God for her mobile phone. She made
a quick call to the AA, gave them all her
necessary details and the location of where
she was leaving the car. She told them she
would finish her journey via the underground
and would phone them later to get details of
where they had moved her car to.

Gathering her briefcase and only the
things that were essential for her day's work,
Jodie locked the car and walked to Colliers
Wood underground station. This local line
would take her to Clapham, where she
would have to change trains. If the car had
to break down why the hell couldn't it have
been in town? Then she would have been
able to flag down a cab. Out here, no taxi
driver would want to enter the centre of
London at this hour of the day. They could
end up stuck in traffic for hours and if the
passenger decided to abandon the cab, the

driver would still be stuck but without
and therefore well out of pocket.

Inside the station, Jodie bought a tic
and boarded the first train to Clapha
Common. As she sat in the carriage, wedge
between two portly gentlemen, she told
herself she was lucky to have got a seat.

Jodie hadn't been on the underground for
a long time. She studied the route that was
mapped out on the wall, found she needed
to follow the red dots to get herself on to the
Northern line. Everyone seemed to be
travelling by tube today, and all were in a
hurry. The noise, the heat, the steam: how
glad she was that she didn't have to do this
journey day in, day out.

When she changed lines she managed to
find a seat again, this time she was seated
next to a young lady who had a dear little boy
sitting on her lap. He reminded her of her
own two sons, now grown-ups. She wondered how Reg and Lenny would feel about
her and their father getting back together.
She really hoped they would be pleased. She
was very much lost in thought about yesterday's events as the doors of the carriage
kept opening and shutting. She wasn't going
to let herself get all het up; she was hours late
already and worrying wouldn't alter that fact.

Jodie was thinking about who would be
standing in for her this morning at the
studios when there was what sounded like a

explosion ahead of them and immedi- the lights went out. The little boy that s sitting on his mother's lap started to cry; die could hear him but she couldn't see him. Folk were terrified and it was quickly getting worse. Sheer panic. Women and men were shouting and screaming. Jodie tried to stand up but bodies were so tightly packed it was as if the blast from the explosion had squashed everyone into a tight mass. Her case of equipment and heavy handbag were wedged tightly against her shins so she couldn't even move her feet.

Suddenly the long dark tunnel reverber-ated with a series of explosions and a great accumulation of fire could be seen through the windows as it swept along the walls of the subway. Inside the carriage the heat was unbearable, and the noise was deafening. It was a total nightmare. Pandemonium en-sued as some of the men tried their best to open the doors of their carriage. Jodie's eyes were fixed on the moving wall of flames on the other side of the carriage. Better the doors were left closed, she said to herself but as she thought the words, the sliding doors smashed, sending fragments of glass everywhere.

The heat really was suffocating Nudge, push, shove. Everybody wanted to get out, yet outside some people had turned into fire-balls. Jodie had no option as she was shoved

out through the shreds and huge piec⸺
glass. All she could see was a mass of bei⸺
and flames surrounded her.

She was living a nightmare. The carriag⸺
she had just been on burst into flames. There
was black smoke everywhere. She couldn't
breathe, her chest hurt, her feet were killing
her, she only had one shoe on. As she bent
down to remove that one, her legs buckled
and a man pitched into her, sending them
both down.

Moaning and groaning could be heard
from all around, people were trying to run,
somebody trod on Jodie's chest. The smoke
had become incredibly dense. No matter
which direction Jodie looked in, there
seemed to be nothing but flames. What
frightened her most was the number of
bodies that were lying near her. She had no
way of knowing if these people were alive or
dead and she couldn't tell whether she had
fallen on to the platform or the railway lines,
because she was so firmly squashed up
against the man with whom she had collided.

What had happened? She was burning hot
and she was having trouble breathing. Would
she and all these other poor souls ever get
out? Of course they would. Ambulances
would soon come and they would all be rescued. Suddenly, above all the commotion,
she could hear somebody screaming. The
sound was blood-curdling and Jodie badly

ed to cover her ears with her hands but arms were wedged. Wearily she lay still, opped trying to move, closed her eyes and t herself drift into oblivion.

# Chapter 21

It was time to face facts. Derrick and Delia were having a lazy late breakfast, during which they had already had two phone calls. The first, which Derrick had taken, had been from Jane Clarkson, their solicitor. He had come back into the kitchen deep in thought, but the very look on his face had told Dee that it hadn't been bad news. Before he had even sat down, the phone had rung again and Derrick went back out, to the hall to take the second call.

This time when he came back to the table, he was smiling. 'Darling, would you please put the kettle on and make a fresh pot of tea. Jane Clarkson has given me quite a bit of good news, but I need to make a few notes while the facts are still straight in my head. Oh, and the second call was from Anthony Wilbourne. He wants to see both of us; I said we'd go in this afternoon.'

Still talking, Derrick was rifling through one of the kitchen drawers. He didn't seem over-pleased. 'Why the hell is it I can never find a writing pad or a pen when I need them? The ones usually kept by the telephone were missing,' he complained.

they weren't,' Dee laughed. 'I moved
down on to the shelf underneath when
dusted the table this morning.'

'Now you tell me,' he roared at her.

You could have looked, was what Dee was
thinking, but she had the sense to keep that
remark to herself.

When the kettle came to the boil, she
emptied the teapot, rinsed it out with boiling water and then made a fresh pot of tea.
Leaving it to stand for a couple of minutes,
she walked into the larder and took down
from the shelf a bag of croissants. She laid
two on a plate, which she popped into the
microwave for thirty seconds. Bringing two
fresh cups of tea to the table, she set out a
warm croissant for each of them and placed
a jar of her home-made Victoria plum jam
on the table.

Her timing was perfect. Derrick was walking across the kitchen, but he didn't immediately sit down. Instead he came to his
wife, put his good arm around her and
pulled her close. Lowering his head so that
he could look into her lovely eyes, he
smiled, a smile the likes of which she hadn't
seen for so long, and then kissed her, gently
at first, but as she clung to him, his arm
tightened, and when he finally did take his
lips from hers, Delia was left gasping.

Derrick looked as happy as a sandboy as
he said, 'Let's drink our tea before it gets

cold, and I'm going to butter my cr[...]
and sample that new jar of jam, and t[...]
shall tell you all that Jane Clarkson ha[...]
say.'

Dee smiled but hesitated for a moment.
can guess that she has given you good news
and I know you'll tell me all about it when
you're good and ready. For now, well, I am
just so relieved that you're sounding happier.'

When Derrick had finished eating, he
drank the remains of his tea and wiped his
lips.

'Dee, it's funny, but I could hear the excitement in Jane's voice the minute she started
to speak this morning. Her first words were
that she had some really great news, and she
went on to tell me that the venue for our
court case has been changed and that it will
turn out to be to our benefit.' He paused and
glanced at the notes he had made.

'Got to get these facts right,' he mumbled.
'Oh yes, here's the next bit. Since Miss Warburg was first up in court, charged with
assaulting you, Judge Rickworth, who heard
the case, has been concerned. Jane said that
without going into too many details or giving
away what happened behind closed doors,
she was now able to tell us that he wasn't the
only one who had felt concern; there were
others, and they used their influence. The
result is that the custody hearing will no

be heard in a criminal court. Our soli-
ʒ have been given notification that the
ʒ has now been referred to the Law
ʒciety specialist family panel, which means
ʒ will be heard before a panel of magistrates,
all of whom will be barristers or solicitors of
at least seven years' standing.'

Dee's feelings were mixed as she watched
Derrick again refer to his hastily written
notes.

'Oh yes, Jane reminded me that at our very
first meeting she mentioned that Russell
Harwood is a long-standing member of this
family panel.'

As Derrick came to the end of relating
what Jane had told him over the phone, Dee
sighed heavily.

'What on earth is the matter, Dee? I
thought you would feel the same way as I do,
that at last there is a glimmer of light at the
end of the tunnel. This kind of court hearing
will be very much more informal. We will be
allowed to call our own witnesses, or any that
our solicitors think will be of benefit to our
case, and the magistrates will listen to what
everybody has to say.'

'That's all very well, but it will also work
for the other side, won't it?' Dee protested
gloomily.

Derrick was dumbfounded. It was true
they had suffered many setbacks, but surely
this had to be good news. In the short time

he had been acquainted with Jane Cla
he had come to feel that he could trus
and that they were working together v
He thought it was good of her to have te
phoned this morning; she could just a
easily have sent them a letter. There was no
getting away from it: Jane cared about the
predicament they were in, as did every
member of the legal firm she worked for.

Dee cut into his thoughts. 'I'm sorry,
Derrick, I don't mean to be a wet blanket,
but I'm afraid to start feeling too optimistic.
We've been knocked back so many times. By
the way, you mentioned that you'd agreed
for us to go to Brighton this afternoon. Is
another visit to Mr Wilbourne really necessary?'

'Of course another visit is important. We
don't know what that detective has come up
with, but every scrap of information we can
gather about Chloe Warburg has to be to
our advantage. But hang on just a minute.
Who was it that came up with the idea of
going to visit a private detective in the first
place? It wasn't me; it was you, Dee, and
your father encouraged you, before either of
you said a word to me. I went along with
you both to please you, and now, well...' He
shook his head. 'I just can't fathom you out
today.'

Dee tried her best to calm down, but her
mind was in turmoil. She hated that woman

ly she felt she could cheerfully kill her. only for the suffering she had brought to rick and herself but for what she had ne to their daughter. How would any adult nanage if they were locked away in an institution and had no idea why or how they had got there? The visits to the children's home continued to be pure purgatory: coaxing, enticing with fruit and sweets, wheedling, sweet-talking; nothing worked. Ann never made any response. She had not spoken one word during the whole time she had been shut away. It broke their hearts that she shrank away from them.

Every time they visited the home, they pleaded in vain with the staff to allow them a little time on their own with Ann. They asked how she acted when they weren't there. Did she speak to other people? Did she cry at night when they put her to bed? Did she ask for her mummy and daddy?

They never got an answer.

Would a little bit of cooperation have hurt? Were the staff who worked in these places totally devoid of feelings?

But going over and over all these wrongs was never going to put them right.

'Ah well,' Dee said at last, smiling at Derrick, 'let's hope the news turns out as well as you seem to think it will. I'll clear up here and then I'll get myself ready to go with you to Brighton.'

Having washed up the breakfast dishes tidied the kitchen, Dee went upstairs to t. bedroom, unlocked the French doors a. stepped out on to the balcony. She leant he arms on the iron balustrade and looked down over the garden and beyond to the sea. It was a very dark blue, choppy and threatening, and the sky above was cloudy and grey. As she watched, a huge wave rolled in and crashed against the cliffs to the right of where she was standing. Dee allowed herself a timid laugh as the tail end of the spray hit the balcony and her face caught the sting of the cold seawater.

She hoped all this darkness wasn't an omen. Derrick had seemed so hopeful since he had taken Jane Clarkson's telephone call, and she would hate for him to be knocked back again. She sighed under her breath, pushing away her sadness as she thought about her two wonderful grown-up sons. Both Martin and Michael loved their father dearly, a fact that she was always eternally grateful for. Often she had thought how heartbreaking it would have been if they had treated him differently after his accident, as sometimes happened when folk were embarrassed to look at Derrick's scarred face and his artificial arm. Both lads were protective of their dad, as were his nephews and nieces and every other member of their large family.

how she counted her blessings, know-
, how much she loved them all and was
ved in return. It was, at times, a love that
vas heart-stopping.

It was half past two when Derrick and Delia
walked into the offices of Discretion Foremost. Miss Baldwin was seated behind her
desk, still elegantly attired, but her attitude,
as she looked up and took notice of Mr and
Mrs Underwood, was a whole lot more
amiable than it had previously been.

'Good afternoon,' she said pleasantly. 'I'll
let Mr Wilbourne know that you are here.'

Within five minutes they were once again
entering Anthony Wilbourne's exclusive
office. Mr Wilbourne was standing in the
centre of the room, his hand outstretched
and a welcoming smile on his face. He made
sure that both clients were comfortably
seated before he sat in his own office chair,
laid his hands flat on his polished desk and
began his report.

'I drew nothing but a blank here in England. I did try the London Metropolitan
Archives for Crown Court records, but they
are held closed for seventy-five years. I also
tried the British Library and back copies of
the *Times*. I knew then that I was searching in
the wrong place, so I took myself over to
Belgium. Luckily enough, I have a few
friends who live there and are associated with

the world of journalism. To begin w...
combed the provincial dailies. I discov...
that Miss Warburg – and incidentally tha...
not her legal name – has a colourful past. ...
have unearthed proof that she was married a...
the age of seventeen to a very elderly gentleman who apparently promised to leave her
his large fortune. After the marriage cere-
mony the husband lived for only five months.
He died leaving no will, but his five children
and numerous grandchildren very quickly
made sure that his new wife would get nothing. At the age of twenty this same young lady
was hospitalised and underwent an abortion.
At twenty-two years old she was heavily fined
and served a three-month prison sentence for
attacking a male client.'

Mr Wilbourne paused and smiled broadly.
'I didn't bother with any further searches.
Now, before we start on how we go about
the legalities of using this information, how
about drinks all round? A glass of wine, Mrs
Underwood?'

Dee didn't know whether to laugh or to
cry. 'I'd rather have a cup of coffee, please,'
she said. It was a struggle for her to remain
silent; there were so many questions she
would have liked to ask.

Miss Baldwin brought in a tray, and Delia
helped herself to coffee. As she did so, the
shrill ringtone of Derrick's mobile phone
was heard, and he quickly took it from his

t saying, 'I do apologise for this inter-
ion.'

Not at all. Please, take the call in my
oakroom; the signal from in there is not
oo bad.'

It was a few minutes before Derrick came
back into the office, and Delia needed no
telling that he had received bad news. The
colour had drained from his face and he was
completely lost for words. He picked up his
glass and tossed back the remains of the
whisky that Anthony Wilbourne had poured
him. Finally the words came tumbling out.
'Mr Wilbourne, I cannot begin to tell you
how much my wife and I value the help you
have given us, but I am afraid we must cut
this visit short. That was my brother on the
phone,' he said, avoiding eye contact with
Delia. 'We saw on the news last night and
again this morning that there has been an
explosion down in the London underground and many people have been killed
and injured.' Now Derrick forced himself to
turn and face his wife, and in a quiet voice
that was filled with sadness he told her,
'God knows why, but Jodie was travelling on
that train.'

Anthony immediately took charge. 'Have
you been told where she is now?'

'Yes, John said it was after midnight before
they got her out; they took her straight to St
Thomas's Hospital.'

'In that case, the quickest way for you get up to Westminster will be to catch direct train from Brighton to Victoria and then a cab to St Thomas's. You can leave your car here. I'll call you a taxi and tonight one of my colleagues will drive your car back to your house.'

It was as if time stood still as the efficient Miss Baldwin and Anthony Wilbourne did everything possible to ease their journey.

The trains from Brighton station were frequent and reliable, and as they travelled, Derrick's right hand and Delia's left were clasped tightly together and their lips moved as they prayed soundlessly for Jodie's safety and for all the numerous victims of this ghastly calamity.

# Chapter 22

Within half an hour of the police having made contact with John, he had rung both Reg and Lenny. The two young men were distraught when told of what had happened to their mother.

John himself was half out of his mind. What the hell was his wife doing travelling on the underground, especially in the busy peak hour? It didn't make sense. And why did this have to happen now? For years he had been aware that he had thrown a good life away when he and Jodie had split up. Month after month, year after year, he had watched her prosper. Too big-headed and self-centred to admit how much he had been at fault, he had outwardly led the life of Jack-the-lad, giving the impression that he hadn't a care in the world.

These last few weeks had been unbelievably good. John knew that he could put the change in his own character down to the shock and dismay he had felt when his good friend Wally Rittman had slit his wrists with a razor blade because he hadn't enough money to keep himself supplied with the drugs he had come to be so dependent

278

upon. Fortunately it hadn't been fatal.

Wally had been down and out, living absolute squalor. Once his father had learnt that his son was using drugs, he had refused to give him any more money and had washed his hands of him entirely. The night John had found him, Wally really had reached rock bottom. John himself would readily admit that he himself was no saint, but the sight of the state that Wally was in had brought him rapidly back to his senses. With a great deal of help from their mates, he and Wally had boarded the midnight express to Edinburgh, and there they had remained hidden for eight long months, during which they had shared horrific nightmares before Wally was finally off the drugs for good.

They had both been pleased that Isaac Rittman had lived long enough to see the change in his son, and in his Will he had truly shown his appreciation for the help that John had given Wally.

Reg was driving the car, and his father, in the passenger seat, was in a right state, clenching his fists until the knuckles showed white and tapping his feet with impatience because they were held up at traffic lights that seemed as if they were stuck on red.

'For God's sake get a grip on yourself, Dad,' Reg pleaded, but his voice was low and husky. Like his dad, he couldn't bring

elf to believe that his mother had been
ght up in this terrible tragedy. Jodie was
independent, hardly ever asking for help
or herself, she was always too busy working
or taking care of the older members of the
family. Christ almighty! Whatever must it
have felt like to be trapped in darkness deep
down in a tunnel? And she had been there
for hours before she had been rescued.

'At least she is still alive; we must be
thankful for that,' Reg reminded his father.

The lights changed and Reg drove on towards Westminster. He was longing to see his
mother and yet dreading having to face her.
Would she be badly injured? He hoped to
God that she hadn't been burnt, especially
not her face. They knew all too well the
terrible scars that burns could leave.

It had seemed an endless journey, but
finally Reg was driving into the car park of
St Thomas's. As they walked towards the
main entrance, they spotted Lenny standing
at the foot of the stone steps smoking a
cigarette. As soon as he saw his father and
brother, he dropped the cigarette and
ground it out with the tip of his shoe. Then
he threw his arms around Reggie's shoulders and drew his brother close; it was an
action that said it all. Turning to his father
next, he clasped him in his arms and held
him tight. John was six foot three, and his
sons were both a good inch shorter than

him, but today it didn't seem like that. John appeared to have shrunk as he allc his sons to lead him up the steps and 1 the busy hospital.

From his inside coat pocket Len drew out ⌐ sheet of paper and a small card. 'This paper shows all the information that the doctors are able to give us at the moment, and the card is a visiting pass; on the top is Mum's hospital number, which we have to quote whenever we telephone. Mum has been taken downstairs to the operating theatre. The doctor told me that at this point it is mainly so that they can ascertain exactly what injuries she has suffered. The nurse suggested that I should take you both to the canteen and she will come and find us as soon as Mum is brought back up to the ward.'

John looked up from studying the paper Reg had passed to him. 'I couldn't eat a thing, but I would like a cup of coffee.'

'So would I,' Reg wearily admitted, as Lenny led the way.

Their coats off and laid over a chair, John and his two sons were seated around a table, each with a big mug of coffee in front of them.

The whole hospital was humming with activity: dozens of anxious-looking relatives, and numerous workers in many different uniforms. The emergency services were

ed to the limit, with every division strug-
g to cope.

he shrieking of sirens from ambulances
they continued to arrive repeatedly broke
hrough the general hubbub, and over the
whole hospital there hung a pervasive smell
of smoke. Questions were being asked in all
quarters as to what had exactly happened
and who was going to be held responsible.

Coffee all drunk, the waiting seemed endless. John took his elbows off the table and
raised his head. 'I'm going to let you in on a
big secret,' he said. 'What you will make of
the irony of it all ... well, I just don't know!'

'Neither will we, unless you tell us,' Reg
said, raising his eyebrows in question at his
brother.

'Here goes then,' John declared. 'Both of
you are aware that your mother and I have
been getting on well these past few months,
and this last week has brought matters to
such a head as I wouldn't have thought possible.' There was a lump in his throat and he
was almost overcome with emotion. This
was so different to what he had planned, but
he had to carry on.

'Yesterday your mother and I made a decision: we are going to buy a house together
and take up our married life that we cast
aside all those years ago.'

Reg and Lenny looked at each other. If
they had been anywhere else other than in a

hospital, they would have been on their feet and cheering.

In their opinion, this was long overdue.

When neither of his sons made a comment, John decided to press on. 'Yesterday I took your mother to Hatton Garden and bought her an engagement ring, and when you see her, you will notice that she has her wedding ring back on her finger.' Again his emotions got the better of him and he paused.

'It was never meant to be like this,' he murmured. He was trembling and his eyes were clouded by tears, but he pressed on. 'We were going to organise a family do, tell everyone at the same time and have a really good celebration. What the sodding hell was your mother doing down in the under-ground? Why now? It is all so bloody unfair. But I'll tell you this, I'll get the best doctors in the country; and she will get well. We've a helluva lot of time to make up for and I'm not going to lose her again. Not this time.'

'Dad, calm down. It'll be all right.'

The three of them hugged, and then it was the two lads who gave way to emotion and their father who had to comfort them.

When John had picked up the empty mugs and gone to join the queue for fresh coffee, Reg and Len looked at each other and smiled. It was the first time since they'd heard the bad news about their mother that they'd seen their father assert himself. As far

as they were concerned it was a great outcome. They really might get back to being a
happy family. All they needed now was for
God to be merciful and let their mother get
well.

It was late before the nurse came to say that
it would be possible for them to see Mrs
Underwood now. They had been waiting for
hours, and still the hospital resembled a
busy airport. The doctors and nurses were
run off their feet.

The three men followed the nurse down a
long, broad, white-walled corridor off which
were a number of side wards. At the far end
of the corridor she pushed open a door and
ushered them into a fair-sized room. In it
was a wheeled bed with side bars, and lying
in the bed was what looked to be a mummy,
except for two eyes that were clear of covering. The arms that lay outside the bedclothes were both well wrapped in bandages
too.

A doctor turned from a table in the corner
of the room and the nurse said to him, 'This
is Mrs Underwood's husband and her two
sons.'

The doctor said, 'Good evening,' and held
out his hand.

John muttered something in greeting; he
wasn't quite sure what, for his whole attention was on the body in the bed. The nurse

went out of the room, then the doctor brought a chair forward and John sat down, his two sons on either side of him.

Looking at the eyes that were by now staring at him, he gasped, 'Jodie. Jodie my darling, it's me, and I've got both of our boys with me.' He was about to ask what had happened and how did she feel when a voice in his head screamed at him not to be such a bloody fool.

He got a response, but it was muffled, and he stood up and put his head as near to the bandaged face as he dared. He couldn't work out what Jodie had said but he was breathless as relief flooded through him. She was alive! He hadn't just planned a future with his Jodie only to lose her again. She was alive and breathing. Thank God!

The bandages round the mouth moved, and a sound that had no connection with Jodie's normal voice uttered his name: 'John.'

The silence that followed was almost unbearable, then the muffled voice came again, and one arm was raised slightly from the bed. 'Reg, Lenny?'

John nodded, but the two brothers called out, 'Yes, Mum, we're here.'

Then the doctor was saying, 'If you'd like to step outside, Mr Underwood, I will be able to give you a report.' Turning his head he said, 'You two young men may stay a while, and then as soon as I have spoken with your father, you'll all have to leave.'

Outside in the corridor, the doctor introduced himself as Dr Jackson and got straight down to business.

'We have patched your wife up temporarily, but she will need to have her right leg set in plaster. The difficulty is that it has been badly burnt and she has broken her ankle. Like every patient that has been brought in, she is suffering badly from smoke inhalation, which is causing difficulty with her breathing. Her face and arms have also suffered burns, but nowhere near as badly as we first thought. You will appreciate that it will take us a day or two to get into a steady routine, but luckily other hospitals all over the country have come to our aid. Many patients who do not live anywhere near London are being transferred, and more doctors are being drafted in to help. As soon as you and your sons leave, we shall sedate your wife to ensure that she has a good night's rest, and tomorrow we shall see to her every need.'

John murmured his thanks. There was much more he would like to say and questions he'd like to ask, but he fully realised what a great deal of stress the whole hospital staff were working under, and for the moment he felt the least said the better.

'May I stay a while with my wife now?' he asked quietly.

'Ten minutes only, I'm sorry, but please,

telephone early tomorrow morning and whoever is on the desk will tell you the best time for you to visit.'

The doctor smiled at him as he took his leave, but it was an effort for John to smile back. He turned to go back into Jodie's room, only to find that his legs were shaking and his heart was beating far too fast.

He thanked God that Jodie didn't appear to have any life-threatening injuries, yet all the same, it seemed grossly unfair that at this point in their lives, when everything had been going so well, she was being made to suffer just because she'd been in the wrong place at the wrong time.

Like almost everyone in the country today, he couldn't help wondering what had caused the explosion. The after-effects had ruined so many lives.

'It is a sad day, so very sad for so many people,' he murmured, shaking his head.

He was a thoughtful man as he entered the room in which his wife was lying in bed, his two sons sitting by her side.

There was one blessing. They were now, or very soon would be, a properly united family once more.

# Chapter 23

The news had spread through the family like wildfire. Everyone had been stupefied with horror to learn that Jodie had been caught up in the underground explosion that was by now front-page news in all the newspapers and on every news bulletin that the TV broadcast.

Why the hell had she been on the underground in the first place? the rest of the family asked, which was exactly the question John and his sons had wanted an answer to.

The whole family were delighted to hear that Jodie and John were now both wearing wedding rings and planning to buy a house in which they would live together. Mrs Underwood senior in particular was thrilled to bits. Her one dread had been that Jodie would suddenly demand a divorce and marry someone else. She had been Marian's lifeline during the period when John had been living his life with thoughts for no one but himself.

Jodie's two sisters-in-law were also overjoyed. Three Mrs Underwoods had always been a force to be reckoned with.

Derrick had been appalled at the knowledge that Jodie had been caught up in an explosion, and his heart ached for her. No one on this earth had more comprehension of what she must be suffering. His memories of the explosion on the oil tanker were often still a living nightmare. On the other hand, he wished both Jodie and his brother the very best of luck in setting up a new house and spending the rest of their lives together.

The telephone never stopped ringing. Every member of the family, male and female, old and young alike, wanted to know when they would be allowed to visit Jodie.

John had returned home from spending all day at the hospital, yet he had only been able to see his wife for about half an hour, and even then she had scarcely been conscious. Hardly had he set foot inside the door than Laraine was on the phone. He felt sorry for her – he knew how close she had always been to Jodie – but he felt too ragged and tired to cope with her feelings.

'I'll let you know the minute the doctors say that Jodie is up to receiving people, but for the minute they seem to think it best if I am the only one allowed,' he told her. 'The hospital is filled to overflowing and the out-patients' department is packed to the doors, so they've had to restrict the number of visitors. The place is still bedlam. If you could be patient for a little while, I will phone you the minute they lift the visiting ban. You do understand, don't you?'

'Yes, yes, of course I understand. But John, can I ask you a couple more things?'

John sighed, but said brightly, 'Of course, anything.'

'How badly is her face burnt? And how is her mental outlook? After all, she was trapped down in that inferno for a long, long time.'

It took John a while to form an answer. He knew that Jodie would have to face a lot of pain before she could put this ordeal behind her, but as for losing her marbles, never! His Jodie was made of stronger stuff than that.

'I'll ask the doctor if you and Delia may visit at the weekend. I'll explain how close the three of you are and tell him that I am sure just seeing both of you will do Jodie the world of good. Now I'm dead beat, so I am going to ring off. Good night, Laraine, love you lots, see you soon.'

He replaced the receiver and wearily climbed the stairs of his rented house. The place held no appeal for him and no memories. Soon, really soon, he hoped, he and Jodie would be able to go house-hunting. Right now what he needed was a good night's sleep, then first thing in the morning he was going to Newhaven to see Derrick and Delia. God knows those two had gone through the mill one way and another dur-

ing their married life, and they were :
suffering heartache over whether the cour
would make the decision to return the:
little girl to them. Last time he had spoken
to his brother, over a week ago, Derrick had
declared that if he ever learnt that his
daughter had been interfered with during
the time she had been missing, he would go
after those responsible and kill the bastards.
And who would blame him?

As he took his clothes off and reached for
his pyjamas, John's mind was once again full
of Jodie. There was no way that either of
them could turn the clock back, but they
were going to put the past behind them and
live their lives to the full. This disaster wasn't
going to stop them. Jodie was going to get fit
and well again; he hoped and prayed that she
would, because he knew he wouldn't be able
to face life without her.

It had only just turned ten o'clock when
John walked in through the back door of
Derrick's house in Newhaven the next
morning. Delia was sitting at the kitchen
table reading the *Daily Mail*.

'Oh John, it's so good to see you. I was just
reading about the underground disaster.
None of us can believe that Jodie was caught
up in it. It beggars belief, it really does. Look!
Look!' She pointed to a column on the
folded sheet of newspaper, and John, taking

paper from her, read the numbers of injured and those that had died. According to the headline, bodies were still being recovered.

Silence hung heavily between them for a couple of minutes until Dee said, 'Derrick is devastated by the fact that Jodie has suffered burns. He will be so relieved to see you and get a first-hand report of how she is. Sit yourself down. Will you have tea or coffee?'

'I don't mind either, whatever you're having,' John told her.

At that moment Derrick came into the kitchen and John was more than pleased to see his brother. He got to his feet and the two men clasped each other closely. It was unusual for the Underwood men to show their feelings, but these were abnormal times.

It was some time before they separated, but when they did, John felt that some of his brother's determination and willpower had been transferred to him and he felt a whole lot better because of it. Derrick was living proof that disaster could strike but the outcome didn't always have to be catastrophic.

'So, what is the latest bulletin on our Jodie?' Derrick asked as the two brothers seated themselves at the table.

'I phoned about eight this morning, bit early I think, because all I got was that she had had a fairly comfortable night and they would be able to tell me more after doctors had done their rounds.'

'Thank God Jodie's life was spared, Derrick said, sighing softly. 'She is such a lovely girl. Everybody loves her because she is so straightforward. She's a good listener and with her there is always a hug and a cup of tea at the ready.'

John laughed as he said, 'I suppose the news that she and I are going to give our marriage another go has reached you two.'

'Yes, we heard,' it was Dee that answered, 'and we couldn't be more pleased. Reg rang and told me, and when he commented that he and Lenny thought it was long overdue, I agreed with him wholeheartedly.'

'Thanks, Dee, bless you. How about you, Derrick?'

'I've always looked on Jodie as a sister, and the two of you coming to your senses couldn't please me more. I'm glad you sorted it out before this wretched accident; makes you realise what a lot you might have lost. Go for it, bruv, make the most of this God-given second chance. Dee and I did, and there is no reason why you two shouldn't.'

John put out his hand and touched Dee's arm, saying in a low voice, 'Jodie will be looking forward to seeing you. She'll be grateful for your company, and so am I.'

Derrick picked up on the sadness in his brother's voice and said gently, 'Stay here d have a bit of lunch with us, then if the ospital say it is all right to visit, I'll come with you. I know they won't allow me to see Jodie, but I'll be company for you on the journey.' He turned to Dee and said, 'Would you like to come along for the ride?'

'Why not?' Dee said, smiling quickly. 'The fresh air will do me good.'

While Dee made lunch and Derrick went upstairs to change, John took the newspaper and settled himself down in the lounge. The news was so dreary, he let the paper drop and his mind began to wander. Oh how thankful he was that Jodie's injuries were not life-threatening. Having been given a glimpse of a new life with her, he was counting his blessings, and by Jesus he had a lot to be thankful for. They really had been two mad youngsters when they had got married, and he had treated her so badly. He would freely admit that it hadn't taken him long to realise that he missed her like hell, but he'd always been too arrogant and pig-headed to confess it. Now, with age, he had mellowed enough to admit that he was in the wrong.

The last couple of days had been hell on earth for him, but he vowed to himself that when Jodie came home, he would make sure that both of them made the most of what must certainly be a heaven-sent second chance.

# Chapter 24

It was Sunday morning. The past two weeks had been nothing but worry, and none of the family had been able to get much sleep. Delia's face was flushed from cooking as she placed a pot of coffee on the table. 'You two can help yourselves,' she said, smiling at Michael Connelly and his partner Danny Spencer.

'Oh, I've done enough baking for now,' she added. She sat down and drained her tea, which had gone cold. 'My heart has been aching wondering how poor Jodie is coming along, and I haven't been able to put my mind to much else.'

Michael reached over and brushed his hand over her cheek. 'It's been the same for everyone. There isn't a soul that doesn't love Jodie.' His smile remained bright but his eyes dimmed a little.

Danny waited a minute before he covered Michael's hand with his own. Then, looking at Dee, he said, 'We've just popped in to see if it has been decided who is going to visit Jodie today.'

Dee smiled. 'If John had his way, he would have taken up residence in that hospital and

ver leave her bedside, but even he has to
st sometimes. It's been so difficult for him
o cope with this disaster; the feeling that
Jodie could so easily have been killed has hit
him hard. More so because they'd settled all
their differences and were looking forward
to having a good future together. Anyway,
Derrick has sorted out a rota for today.
Laraine and I are going in this afternoon
and Derrick with John this evening. Oh, and
I think Derrick said something about Alan
Morris wanting to go with the men.'

'Michael and I will buy some flowers and
just leave them at the desk. I rather fancy we
shall have to wait until Jodie is discharged
from hospital before we get to see her. But
Dee, you will be sure to tell her just how
much we both love her, and that we have
been asking after her.'

'Of course I will, and she'll want to send
her love to both of you. We all appreciate
what good solid friends we have in you two.'

Danny patted the back of her hand and
went quiet.

Michael was brooding. 'It must have been a
terrifying nightmare for her, trapped underground with fires raging all around her.'

'Obviously,' Danny muttered. 'All the
more reason for being thankful that she was
brought out alive. What did you and Derrick
think about Jodie and John's other news?'

'How about the pot of gold at the end of

the rainbow? There's always that wa_
looking at it.' It was Derrick, who, hav_
just walked into the room, had voiced the
profound words.

Michael and Danny stood up and shook
his hand. Derrick smelt of fresh air and
brisk breezes. He had been walking over the
Downs and had come up with the idea that
he might buy a puppy for Ann when she
came home – it might help her to talk again
– though he would keep the idea to himself
for now.

Michael turned to Delia. 'Are you happy
with the fact that Jodie and John are going
to give married life another try?'

Dee looked thoughtful. 'I think that John
has dreamed of this happening for a lot
longer than he would care to admit. He's
always been full of schemes but never had
the sense or the luck to make them work. So
my answer is yes, I am really happy for both
of them,' she said simply.

Derrick's face softened. He was proud of
his wife. Dee almost always chose to see the
best in everyone. 'I think the whole family
feel the same way. All we need now is for this
wretched custody case to come to court, and
then perhaps we can all get on with living
our lives to the full again.'

'Have you been given a date for the hearing yet?' Michael quietly asked Derrick.

'Well, we received two letters yesterday

ning; they would have to arrive on a
urday, when there is nothing we can
oceed with. We can't even ask for more
details until the various offices open on
Monday morning. We'll just have to go on
showing patience, though both of us are
getting a little short of that.'

'What time does visiting start at the
hospital this afternoon?' Danny asked.

'Two o'clock,' Dee answered. 'Derrick is
going to drive me over to Laraine, and we'll
go on from there in her car. Then later
Laraine will bring me back here and she will
stay the night with us.'

Everything had worked out as planned.
Laraine had given Dee and Derrick an early
lunch, and now Laraine was at the wheel
and Delia was sitting back letting her
thoughts run wild. If at times during the
journey she became frustrated or restless,
she only had to remind herself that Derrick
had promised they would sort those two
letters out tonight when they were alone.

On this early July afternoon, the sun was
shining, which made a nice change. Up until
now the summer had mostly been a washout,
with rain and high winds day in day out. Sun-
shine certainly did make a difference. London looked a picture as they approached.
There could be no city in the world that had
more to offer, thought Delia, as she gazed

across the sparkling river Thames at Houses of Parliament opposite.

With the car parked safely, Laraine and Delia walked through the busy entrance hall of St Thomas's feeling apprehensive about how they would cope on seeing Jodie. Immediately the sterile hospital scent filled their nostrils.

Jodie was still in the side ward that held only the one patient. Laraine pushed open the door, and both she and Delia were surprised to see John and his two sons sitting beside the bed.

'Sorry, we don't mean to intrude. We were told you men were coming in this evening,' Laraine hastened to explain, as she and Dee hurriedly backed out of the room.

John was on his feet in next to no time, 'Come on in, please, the pair of you. I spend most of my days in this hospital, and when my lads put their heads round the door, I told them they could stay until you arrived. They've seen their mother every day so it won't hurt them to go now. Besides, Jodie is longing to see you two. Please come in, see for yourselves that she is getting better.'

Before any of them could move, Reg and Lenny had come out of the room and were assuring their aunts that they had just been leaving.

'Honestly, the first week was awful, but this last seven days have seen such a difference.

ither of us can believe that Mum has come out of this ordeal as well as she has,' Reg was happy to tell them before adding, 'We're going to get off now, but we'll take Dad to the cafeteria first, give you a little while on your own with Mum.' The two young men kissed and hugged Laraine and Dee before leaving.

One look at Jodie's face, still heavily bandaged, and both Laraine and Delia had to swallow back the lumps in their throats as they each in turn leant across the bed and kissed the top of her head. The next three quarters of an hour was the most difficult time that either of the visitors had ever had to sit through. Jodie could just about speak, but only very slowly and with great difficulty. They had no way of telling if her face was showing any emotion.

It was Dee who suddenly picked up that Jodie wanted them to look at her left hand where it lay on top of the white counterpane. Standing up, she very carefully raised the hand, smoothing the skin with her thumb and nodding to Laraine to take notice. Both Dee and Laraine were smiling, but their eyes were brimming with tears as they stared at the three rings that Jodie was now wearing: a plain gold wedding ring, against which lay a thin gold band with a scroll pattern engraved around it, and finally a diamond ring that glittered and sparkled, saying much more than any amount of words could have done.

'Proper married woman now,' Laraine remarked happily.

'Everybody wishes you and John a real happy future,' Dee whispered softly, holding her own face close to Jodie's bandages.

It the truth were told, relief flooded through both Laraine and Delia as John put his head around the door and told them the bell was ringing to signify that afternoon visiting was now over.

So badly had they wanted to hug and hold their sister-in-law. To encourage her to believe that her face would mend without a trace of a single scar. But that hadn't been possible and probably wouldn't have been the truth. They were not sorry it was time to leave. If they had stayed any longer, they would not have been able to hold back their tears.

John said he would just say his own goodbye to Jodie and then he would meet them in the car park.

It was a good twenty minutes before he came to sit in the back of Laraine's car. 'I just wanted to bring you both up to date as far as the doctors have briefed me,' he said, trying hard to show a confidence he was far from feeling.

Both Dee and Laraine were astonished to discover the depth of John's feelings; everything he had ever felt for Jodie was showing clearly in his eyes. They were more used to

...rding him as a hail-fellow-well-met type ...nan. Today, however, they both sensed his notion and discreetly they remained silent.

It seemed ages before John uttered another word, and even then he first had to hastily brush away the tears that were almost brimming over.

'First off, she has fractured her elbow. As you could see, that arm is in plaster. Both of her legs are really badly burnt and she has chipped a bone in her ankle, so one way or another it will be very painful for her to walk for some time to come. The main problem is her face, the right side of which apparently still has glass embedded in it. She was taken off the respirator after just three days and her breathing is much better. Thank God her lungs were not too badly affected.'

Having given them all the main facts, John suddenly succumbed to his own fears. He buried his face in his hands and started to cry as if he were a small boy, pouring out all the emotion that he had, up until now, held in check.

'Oh Dee, oh Laraine, I've been a right bastard and a mad one into the bargain. In spite of all the years we've been separated, and everything that happened during that time, she never once turned on me. I know I'm not worthy of her. Never have been, but I do love her.'

'Hey, hey, you just listen to me.' Laraine's

voice rang with strength. 'You're co.
back to Dee's house with us. Your bro.
will know just what to say to you, 'cos th.
isn't one amongst us who wouldn't wri.
some pages of their life very differently i.
given the chance.'

'I can't do that, I've got my own car here,'
he protested feebly.

'Yes, and you've got two sons who will be
back here later. One of them will drive your
car home.'

'John, have you finished telling us all that
the doctors told you?' Dee was doing her
best to encourage John to gather his wits
together before they started on the journey
back to Newhaven. She was also reminding
herself to phone Derrick and tell him they
were bringing his brother home with them.

'I think I have, Dee. All the doctors were
most kind, especially so considering the
number of patients they are caring for. Dr
Jackson was astounded at how lucky Jodie
has been. Forty-one people have been seriously hurt and nineteen have died. He also
said that inevitably she will need plastic
surgery on her face, sometime in the future.
So far she has been mentally strong, but be
warned that it is still early days.'

Dee sighed softly before she whispered
something to Laraine. Having received a nod
of approval, she twisted round in her seat to
face John. 'You are not alone in this, you

v. It does seem as if each of us has a great deal to be thankful for. Now I am going to make a suggestion. Why don't we go back into the hospital, and grab a hot drink and a sandwich before we set off home. Meanwhile we can all use our phones. John, you speak to Reg and Lenny and ask them to visit their mother this evening. All the rest of the men, yourself included, can bunk down at our house tonight. Derrick will cook dinner and then maybe we'll all get a good night's sleep, God alone knows, each and every one of us could use one.'

'But I'll miss seeing Jodie!' John exclaimed.

'Better that than you go to pieces altogether. Reg and Lenny won't mind, and they'll be able to fetch your car back. Also, if you do manage to get a good night's kip at our house, you'll be so much better able to cope in the morning. So come on, John, agreed, yes?'

Dee could see the relief on his face as he murmured, 'All right and thanks.'

'No thanks necessary, John. You were there when Derrick and I needed you; still are, aren't you? So slate equal, yes?'

John leaned forward, Dee leaned into the back of the car, and somehow the two of them managed a hug.

Seated with a coffee in front of each of them, Laraine studied John's face: the sharp,

stubborn chin that all the Underwood
had, and the eyes, as dark and restless as
sea that they all loved and lived by. H
words came out of the blue as she spoke t
him.

'You're a strong one, John. Tough and
strong, with a true heart beneath what you
pretend is a steel coating. God knows you're
smart when you want to be. I can't begin to
understand how you let the good things in
your life go so wrong. It's not everybody
that gets a second chance, but someone up
there must surely be putting you and Jodie
back on the right track. I and all the rest of
the family want you, the both of you, to
follow the plans you've begun to draw up
and start to live life to the full.'

There was no answer to that outburst, but
John did manage a flicker of a smile.

A quick wash and brush-up in the toilets
and the three of them were back in Laraine's
car heading for home.

It was just after six thirty when she pulled
up at the seafront in Newhaven As they
walked into the house, the delicious smell of
roasting meat was coming from the kitchen.
The place seemed to be alive with men.
Michael and Danny had been invited to stay
for the evening now that arrangements had
been altered. Laraine had invited Alan
Morris, and her twin girls had been spoken
to on the phone but had declined the offer

join the party. They had arrangements of their own. Martin and Michael, too, were otherwise engaged. That still left five men to sit down to dinner with Laraine and Delia. It was a most enjoyable meal even though there lay between them the knowledge that Jodie was lying in a London hospital.

The offer to stay the night had been extended to everyone. As it turned out, the only visitor still in the house at half past ten as Dee and Derrick climbed the stairs to their bedroom was John. The others had all chosen to go to their own homes.

Dee had made sure that John was comfortable, giving him one of the big front bedrooms, and Derrick had insisted that his brother should knock back a good measure of whisky before he tried to sleep.

Delia lay with Derrick's arm behind her shoulders and her head resting in the hollow of his neck. She had thought about asking him not to discuss the two letters that they had received the previous day, but after considering the matter, she decided it was best they get it over and done with.

The first one was from Jane Clarkson, confirming the altered venue for the custody hearing. Neither of them had any point they wished to make except to agree that in all probability these new arrangements would work in their favour.

306

The second letter was from the p[...] headquarters at Dover Harbour, and e[...] as Derrick glanced at it, Dee knew strai[...] off that the contents had infuriated him.

'Derrick, I don't need to listen to all the legal jargon. Why don't you just tell me the gist of the letter?'

She didn't think it was her imagination when she heard Derrick sigh softly, as if in relief.

'Right,' he said forcefully as he straightened out the two pages of the letter and began to silently read them. A few minutes passed before he put down the typewritten pages and turned to look down at her. First he gently laid his lips on hers in that sweet, soft way of his that always had her longing for more. Then, brushing strands of hair from her forehead, he said, 'Sit up, Dee – here, let me put another pillow behind your head. You're not going to like what this bloke has to say any more than I bloody well do.'

Once Delia was settled she said grimly, 'I don't really give a damn about what the harbourmaster or police chief or whatever else he wants to call himself has to say. We've only to wait now to be given the exact date for the final hearing, then once we get our Ann back home here with us, I shall start to think about settling some of these rotten scores that have been notched up against us.'

e harsh tone of his wife's voice had
rick raising his eyebrows.

'Delia! I know even a worm can turn, but
his coming from you is hardly believable.'

'Not before time, I reckon. I've swallowed
my pride for so long it has begun to choke
me. We, both of us, should have been far
more aggressive from the very beginning. I
have nightmares, and so do you, Derrick, if
you own up to the truth. Months we've let
strangers take control of Ann. You could
have produced papers proving that you are
her legal father, never mind about me, never
mind if the truth had come out that her
mother was a prostitute. We should have
gone to the newspapers.'

Derrick picked up the letter again, asking
himself how he could possibly hold this
show of temper against his soft-hearted
Delia when there had been times while visiting their daughter in that institution when he
could cheerfully have murdered her so-
called carers.

'Shall I go on with this?' he asked, trying
not to grin as he waved the two sheets of
paper.

Delia was by now laughing outright because of her own outburst. It had been worth
it just to see the look on her husband's face.
'Get on with it,' she told him.

'In the main it is about the man who was
arrested while attempting to board a ferry

with Ann. He has never been charged
any offence. Why? Because Miss Chloe W
burg came forward and stated that he mo
certainly was not abducting the child. Sh
signed a written statement in which she declared she was the child's mother and that
the man the police had arrested was her
brother, uncle to the child. Therefore no
action against the man in question has been
taken. Doesn't it make your blood boil? I
want some bloody answers,' Derrick
stormed.

Dee supposed that it was all right for
Derrick to have his turn at being mad. But
as much as she fully agreed with him, she
didn't want him to get too upset.

'Please, Derrick, calm down and carry on.'
It took a while before he did.

'Well the long and the short of it is that the
police have their own theory and they are
playing a waiting game. They are claiming
that as a custody case is pending they have no
way of telling right from wrong. The council
or child welfare people, whatever, decided to
jump on the bandwagon; in other words they
needed to be seen to be doing some good for
the child. And their definition of good was to
place our daughter in a children's home and
leave her there amongst strangers. There is a
bad smell about this whole affair. One bloody
letter is supposed to satisfy all of our questions! Well, it goes nowhere near being able to

lify me!'

Derrick had to pause and take a deep breath.

'No, Dee, it just is not good enough! There has been a cloud of secrecy over the whole matter from start to finish, and if we don't get some answers soon, I will do as you've just suggested: I will tell our side of the story to the press. Bugger whether it embarrasses me, or you even. I'll let the reporters know every single detail.'

By now Dee was really frightened. The repercussions for Ann if Derrick were to do what he was threatening didn't bear thinking about, and what was making the whole matter worse was the fact that she herself had made the suggestion in the first place.

She wriggled to the side of the bed and flung the bedclothes clear from her body before swinging her legs to the floor.

'Where d'you think you're going?' Derrick asked, laughing. He had suddenly seen the funny side of this matter. For months on end they had suffered insults and accusations from many quarters, all the while doing their best to remain calm and collected. Now they had both blown their top!

Dee burst out laughing too.

'I'm going downstairs to make a pot of tea,' she told him, still grinning. 'You tidy the bed and I'll bring a tray up.'

'Best idea you've had all night,' Derrick

told her. He too was still smiling but hi
were shining with unshed tears which i.
way disguised the love he felt for his w.
He had loved Delia ever since they had fii
met, many years ago, but never more than
he did at this moment.

# Chapter 25

Jodie had woken up in the dark. The one thing she was certain of in those first groggy moments was that she wasn't in the hospital; she wasn't even in a proper bed. Thoughts were buzzing around in her head and she had to get them all in the proper order.

Her last clear memory was of John talking to Dr Jackson and doing his best to assure him that if his wife was discharged from the hospital she could be certain of adequate care and attention at all times. Yes, he would employ a nurse to bath and dress his wife. No, they didn't have a bedroom on the ground floor, but he would make certain that their lounge was made over into a bedroom for Jodie's immediate use. Yes, he would be at home with her twenty-four hours a day.

She had listened to this conversation and her heart had been singing. John seemed to delight in referring to her as his wife, and the house he was talking about was her house. Maybe for the time being he was thinking of taking up residence.

What came next had been a bit of a blur. Derrick had been there with John; hospital

312

staff had wrapped her in blankets and wheeled her out to John's car, where they had gently laid her down along the back seat, propping two pillows beneath her head. Wonderful to have come home. Sleeping on and off and then feeling so much more rested. Dear friends popping in and out, the fragrance of flowers everywhere. A cup of tea that had been so enjoyable because it didn't smell of hospital disinfectant, and oh what she wouldn't give for one right now.

If she had been tempting the angels to come and wait on her, she couldn't have done better.

Slowly the door of the lounge was eased open and John's face appeared. 'Good morning, sleepy-head, just coming to enquire if my wife would prefer a cup or tea or coffee?' He was smiling as he drew the curtains.

Jodie let out a sigh of sheer contentment. Having spent four weeks in hospital, the last week in a long open ward that had held thirty-six patients, this morning she was being given a glimpse of sheer heaven.

John had by now come to her side and was down on his knees and leaning across to gently kiss her. 'I won't break, you know,' she told him, flinging her arms around his neck.

'I was worried as to what kind of a night you would have sleeping on this sofa bed. They're not exactly known for being comfortable. I did check on you almost every hour and you were well away. The cage that the hospital insisted you bring home with you to keep the bedclothes from touching your legs stayed in place pretty well. Anyway, my darling, your new bed will be arriving this morning and the nurse said she'll make it up while she's here.'

Jodie had to hide a smile. She almost asked if he had ordered a single or a double bed, but thought perhaps it was a little early in the order of things to be asking questions such as that. During her stay in hospital she'd got used to folk referring to her as John's wife, but all the same she felt a little cheated. She had the rings on her finger that proved to her that that night hadn't been a dream. It had been, and still was, absolute reality. John had spent the night with her in this house and the next morning he had proposed to her all over again. All very theatrical, but wonderful!

If only her car hadn't packed up, she wouldn't have been a passenger on that underground train. *If*: such a little word, but little or not, it could certainly carry weight.

During the period following Jodie's homecoming, those taking care of her had fallen into a steady routine, while Jodie herself slept many of the hours away. Towards the end of the second week, an ambulance came to the house to collect her and take her to the same hospital in East Grinstead that had previously treated Derrick's horrific burns. John had gone along with her. Relief had flooded through each of them to hear that the treatment on offer would be of enormous help, and although it would take time, eventually new skin would cover her badly burnt legs. Meanwhile the hospital was offering Jodie the use of a wheelchair.

On that very first visit Jodie was also examined by a second doctor, who was amazingly cheerful, assuring her that he was going to remove the lingering fragments of glass from her cheek that very same afternoon.

'It will be all to the good,' declared the remarkably handsome Dr Morley, who Jodie was thinking was young enough to be her son. 'Because then, Mrs Underwood, you will be coming back to see us again, and I and my colleagues will together continue repairing the damage. When our work is finally complete, we want to be able to listen to folk telling you that you are even more beautiful than you were previously.'

'And just where did you originate from?' Jodie asked, doing her best to smile, while her insides were turning over. She'd been in the beauty business long enough to know that plastic surgery didn't always turn out well.

'Oh, so you'll be assuming that my grandparents were from Ireland and that the little green folk blessed me the day I was born?' Every word that Dr Morley uttered was lit by a smile.

'I'd go further and say you brought a piece of the Blarney Stone with you,' Jodie quickly retorted.

'Sure and why wouldn't I? And I'll make you a promise: the day we operate on your sweet face, I shall allow you to hold my piece of the blessed stone in your hand.'

'You, Doctor, are enough to make the saints smile,' she told him, but the funny thing was that she really meant it.

John pushed her wheelchair into a corner of the waiting room and left her while he went to the reception desk to make her next appointment. Standing in the queue, John was smiling. He had heard every bit of the banter that had passed between Jodie and the young doctor. He stared across at her, thinking how brave she had been, right from day one. Never once had she complained, only been thankful that she was still amongst the living. He knew full well that Jodie was unpredictable, more impulsive and forthcoming than any woman had a right to be. She was a law unto herself.

All that set aside, he loved her, desperately so. It had taken him years to admit it, and now he had such a lot of time to make up for. At least he was under no illusion. When first they had been married he had treated

Jodie abominably, and over the years he'd been a bare-faced rotter. There had been times when he had been eaten up with envy that every business project Jodie had entered into had turned out successfully. He had also been jealous that she went out with other men, and hated the admiring glances that so often were cast her way. Now once again she had promised to be his wife.

Dear Jesus! It was unbelievable and so much more than he deserved. He was going to have to work hard to prove that he had altered, that he loved her sincerely and with all of his heart.

Safely back home again, John decided to make sure that Jodie rested for the next couple of days, but come Thursday morning he couldn't keep the surprise to himself any longer.

With Jodie in the back seat of the car so that her legs could be stretched out along the seat, and her wheelchair in the boot, John drove her through Eastbourne and over the Downs to the small, picturesque village of Alfriston, explaining on the way that he wanted her to look at an old house with him.

'It's a house I've always liked,' he said. 'My only worry is it has been on the market for quite some time and you might think it is a bit ramshackle and needs too much work.

But we can look it over, see how we feel about it, can't we? As long as you tell me when you get tired. Don't want you doing too much too quickly. Actually, it won't be much bother for you: most of the rooms are on the ground floor, so you'll be able to use your wheelchair.'

Jodie agreed, though she was surprised that John was even thinking about a house when he was still paying rent on the place in Brighton. However, the idea of a detached house surrounded by fields, woods and green countryside really did appeal to her, as long as it had at least three bedrooms. Jodie was still hoping for grandchildren.

During the drive over, Jodie had learned that a friend of John's mother had lived there. As a boy, he and his brothers had many times been taken to visit Dorothy James and have tea with her and her husband, James. When James had died, Dorothy had gone to South Africa to live with her daughter and son-in-law and the house had been put on the market.

John was laughing because of the look on Jodie's face.

'You think it funny that Dorothy's husband's name was James James? Mostly he was called Jimmy James, and our mum always referred to him as Sir James. For some unknown reason no buyer has been found for the house. It's been empty for almost two years. It was Derrick who told me it had been put back on the market at a lower asking price,' he told her as he pulled up outside a long bungalow standing in its own grounds behind a stone wall.

'Derrick said we shouldn't worry too much if the inside is in a bad state, just as long as the outside is structurally sound. Anyway, come on, darling, let's get you into your wheelchair. I have the keys from the estate agent and it won't cost anything for us to look over the place.'

John got out of the car and ran around to the boot to fetch the wheelchair. It took a bit of manoeuvring to get Jodie out of the car. When she was settled in the chair, blanket tucked around her legs, he patted the top of her head and asked, 'All set comfortably?' When she turned her head and smiled, he said, 'Right, we're off then.'

Skilfully he steered her towards the big iron gate set in the ancient stone wall. It was quite a high wall, with moss growing between the stones, and many tall trees were visible above it.

'Swan House,' Jodie read as they stopped in front of the gate. 'Nice name, but I fail to see the significance,' she murmured.

John grinned. 'You soon would if we came to live here. There's a river here, behind those trees. I remember Dorothy giving us boys food to feed the swans and their young, and once when I was here two enormous great swans came knocking on the windows of the house with their beaks. Dorothy said they often did that, just to remind her that they would like to be fed.'

John left her for a moment and went forward to open the gate. He was soon pushing her chair along a lengthy winding path.

The minute the house came properly into view, Jodie asked John to stand still for a minute. She was feeling utterly spellbound. Long and rambling, made of stone, it had tall chimneys, leaded windows and a huge studded front door. And when John put the big old key into the lock, Jodie's excitement grew and she couldn't wait for John to wheel her inside.

She wasn't disappointed; despite the cobwebs and the dust, she was thrilled, filled with a wonderful sense of happiness. She had become a dab hand at wheeling herself about her own home in the few days since she had acquired this chair, and here, in this long bungalow that had no furniture to restrict her, she was having a grand time. She had lost count of the number of rooms she had looked into, and the further she explored, the more excited she became.

The kitchen had her calling out in sheer disbelief. It was enormous and old-fashioned, with dark-wood ceiling beams and a huge stone hearth. Jodie giggled as she pictured a whole hog being roasted on a spit. Then, wonder upon wonder, she turned around to find that where the original cooking range must have been there now stood an enormous gas stove. It beggared belief! Surely Dorothy James had never had it installed?

The two main rooms were spacious and well proportioned: both lounge and dining room had deep fireplaces, while the views from every window were a joy to behold.

There were two flights of wooden stairs, one each end of the long hall. Jodie realised she would never be able to climb them. Suddenly she felt tired, and she ached all over, but she felt loath to say so.

As she faltered, John was beside her. 'That's enough for one session,' he declared, reaching out and putting the brakes on her chair, before sitting down on the floor beside her.

'Are there rooms upstairs?' Jodie asked, when she'd got her breath back.

'Yes and no,' came his comical answer. 'The story goes that when building first started on this house, the idea of the two flights of stairs, one at each end of the long gallery, was to make ascending and descending easier depending on which bedroom one was occupying. Apparently the builders ran out of money, and the Jameses never felt the urge to add more rooms to the property. All the floors and ceilings were reinforced, though, and according to the estate agent, there is still planning permission for upstairs rooms.'

A nice friendly silence settled between then as they sat in the empty shell of what had once been such a happy house.

John broke it by saying, 'Shall we think about buying this property?'

His question made Jodie realise just how serious he was.

'Let's not make a hasty decision,' she answered wisely. 'I think you should get a good surveyor in to go over the whole place, get a detailed report before you decide.'

John sighed, yet he was gently smiling as he said, 'Jodie, we are man and wife; we have already decided that we want a home that belongs to us, that will be referred to amongst the family as our home. Please, my darling, will you stop talking as if I were the only one concerned with the purchase of this or any other property we should decide to view?'

His words were lost on Jodie. Her head had slumped forward, her chin was resting on her chest and her eyes were closed. This peaceful picture of her was a joy, but the reality of her being in that wheelchair had him breathing a heavy sigh. How close he had come to losing her didn't bear thinking about. For now, it was time to take her home. No decisions would be made on the spur of the moment; a lot of thinking had to be done if they were to accomplish the best result.

None of the Underwoods would dispute the fact that a bush telegraph system existed between the members of the family. It was said locally that news travelled faster than fire or water where the Underwoods were concerned.

It was only just coming up to two o'clock as John parked the car in the drive of Jodie's house in Epsom. Her nurse took over and without delay had Jodie undressed and lying on her bed. Nurse Watkins smiled at her patient, drew in a long breath then turned her gaze on Jodie again and said, 'You're not ready to sit in the wheelchair for long periods; you do need to keep those legs out-stretched. I'm not going to replace the bandages just yet; I'll use the soothing lotion, give it time to soak in while you have a sleep, and then later on I'll put fresh bandages on both legs.'

Although John had been assured that Jodie was fine, he still had to pop his head round the door to see for himself that she was sleeping peacefully. Satisfied that she was comfortable, he made a beeline for the telephone.

He dialled the number. Three rings, then a distinctive deep voice said, 'Hello.'

'Derrick, it's me, and mate, have I got a lot to thank you for. Jodie's more than half in love with Swan House, even though she saw the state the property is in.'

'I'm glad for you, bruv, didn't think it would be a wasted journey. On the other hand, don't jump in with both feet until you get yourselves a surveyor's report. By the way, what are you doing this evening?'

'Nothing much. The short time we were out has been more than enough for Jodie. I was glad the nurse was still here when we got home; she saw to Jodie straight away and she's sleeping now.'

'Tell you what, I'll give it a couple of hours and then I'll bring Dee over. She's been on and on about not seeing much of Jodie. What say I give Laraine a ring and pick her up on the way over? Don't want her feeling she's being left out of things, do we?'

'That would be great. Say about half past four? Jodie will be awake by then and seeing the girls will be a good tonic for her. Thanks again, Derrick, see all of you later.'

Jodie was awake soon after three. Nurse gave her a refreshing blanket bath, then attended to her legs and the side of her face. There wasn't much she could do for her arm; the elbow had been set and the whole arm was in plaster. After a refreshing cup of tea, John told her that some of the family were coming to visit. That put new life into her. John was ordered to go upstairs bring down a selection of light dresses her to choose from. 'I am not sitting arou in a dressing gown looking like a casualty she declared.

John had rung their two boys and of course they wanted to be there. When Derrick had phoned Laraine, Alan Morris had been with her and they had said they'd be delighted to come over too.

Before leaving, Laraine said to Alan, 'I'll just make a quick call to Adele and Annabel, let them know we're going out.'

'Oh, we'll come too,' Adele said cheerfully. 'We'll meet you there.'

When Laraine put the receiver down and told Alan that the two girls were meeting them at Jodie's house, his face dropped.

'Have they been giving you headaches, then?' Laraine asked, grinning.

Alan had the grace to look sheepish. 'I ought to be used to it by now. I don't mind it so much. Most times I think I give it back in fair measure.'

When Laraine didn't break the silence, he said, 'I suppose you told them your side of the story.' Still she didn't answer him.

Alan sighed heavily before saying, 'Well, I've had more than enough time to think things over. I know one thing for certain: you worked yourself up into a terrible temper. Thinking back, I suppose I didn't propose to in a very successful way. Didn't say the ~~rds~~ you needed to hear. I realise that now. ~~.ave~~ you never felt you would like to ~~:econsider?'~~

Laraine's fists were balled so tightly her fingernails were digging into her hands, and she could feel her temper rising. She couldn't hold back. She shot a look at Alan that was designed to wither any man. 'If you're apologising for offering me a job as your housekeeper, you can save your breath.'

Alan's lips came together and his mouth closed up like a clam. Now he was angry too, but he had the sense to know that it wouldn't do to let it show.

Laraine, however, couldn't keep quiet. 'Come on, Alan, you're asking me to reconsider your proposal. Does it differ in any way from the original one? Maybe this time there is a sprinkling of love in there somewhere.'

'Oh, Laraine, you must know how I feel about you.'

'No, Alan, I don't. I am not a mind-reader. I do know you enjoy having sex with me, but even that is always at my house or on the odd occasion at Dee's, but never at yours. Wouldn't do to sleep with someone there, not in the same bed that you slept in with your wife. You hardly ever invite me to step over your doorstep; are you afraid I might disrupt all that tidiness or intrude on your

memories? Alan, there has to come a po.
when we all move on. You have to make
choice: cling to the past, live on just memories; or start a new life. Which doesn't
mean you forget the past – you learn to
recall incidents and events with love, sometimes love that almost breaks your heart –
but you cannot allow the past to rule your
future or you'll end up with a lonely life that
is not worth living.'

Laraine had to stop talking. Unshed tears
were almost choking her.

'Why the hell didn't you tell me all this
before? You can change my house around,
have the furniture just as you want it. Honestly, I wouldn't be offended.'

'Oh for heaven's sake, Alan! You still don't
get it, do you?'

If Laraine had struck him, Alan couldn't
have been more amazed.

'Right.' She shot the one word at him.
'You might be a bigwig up in Westminster,
but when it comes down to rock bottom,
you haven't a clue how the other half get by.
So, win or lose, I am about to spell it out for
you. I don't want to live in your house and I
never shall. If there is any hope of us getting
together and spending the rest of our lives
as a couple, it has to be somewhere else.'

There, she had said it. The matter was out
in the open now.

There was no bitterness in Alan's eyes, just

...dness. And Laraine thought she saw a pain-
...ul kind of longing. Oh why the hell couldn't
...e speak from the heart, lay it out straight,
then they could maybe have a good life
together. For herself, she knew damn well it
could never come close to what she'd had
with Richard, but loneliness made queer
bedfellows. For Alan, if what he'd told her
had been the truth, anything that came even
close to a loving relationship had to be a
hundred per cent better than what he'd lived
through. Trouble was, he never spoke much
about his previous marriage. At this moment
he looked so woeful Laraine almost gave in.
She was saved from saying something she'd
surely regret by Alan finding his voice again.

'You may be right about the house,' he
admitted timidly, 'but wouldn't it be best to
give it a bit of a try? Get married, live there
for a while, see what you think, before
jumping head first into a new property?'

'No! Alan, I am not going to even consider
going down that road. In that house you
have created a museum, a showpiece, and if
that is what you want out of life then that's
up to you. But, and it is a big but, Alan, if
the two of us are to have a happy life, it has
to be somewhere we have chosen together.
We shall live there, make it a home for my
girls, until such time as they decide they
want places of their own. It has to be a home
where our friends will be sure of a welcome.

But first and foremost you have to be convinced that it is what you really want.'

Alan sighed softly. He and his wife had never had children. He did think that Adele and Annabel were lovely, well-mannered young ladies, but he also knew that they looked upon him as an old fuddy-duddy.

Taking a deep breath he said quietly, 'I want to be with you, Laraine, for always, I really do. I never thought, not for one moment, that I would be lucky enough to have someone like you who would care for me.'

'There you go again, Alan Morris!' Laraine yelled at him. 'I am not the motherly type. I am not a nurse. I am not a social worker. Take your pick from that trio if it's someone to care for you that you're looking for. How many times do I have to spell it out? I do not care for you, I love you, and I do believe we could have a good, happy future together, but only if you can bring yourself to say that you love me too.'

'Laraine, dear, you know I do.'

'No! How many times, that is not enough, Alan.'

'All right, all right.' Alan was up on his feet. Quite roughly he pulled Laraine to him, and when he had her close in his arms he lowered his head and began to kiss her. Sweetly and softly to begin with, and then the passion in him was let loose.

It was a good few minutes later when Alan released his hold. He remained silent but his eyes were sparkling as they never had before.

Laraine shook herself before she burst out laughing.

When she had regained her composure she said calmly, 'I damn well knew you had it in you. Alan Morris, I will marry you, and once I have finished thawing you out, we'll have a great life together.'

# Chapter 26

Not a soul had anticipated such a gathering as there now was in Jodie's house.

As soon as everyone had greeted each other, refreshments and drinks were handed round and Jodie's terrible experience was discussed to the full. Jodie was stretched out comfortably on her new bed, while the ladies found seats and the men stood in groups.

The main topic of conversation then became the house in Alfriston that John had taken Jodie to view that morning. Even their sons, Reg and Lenny, and the cousins – Laraine's girls and Delia's boys – seemed to be showing a great deal of interest in the property. Somehow it didn't seem possible that they were all grown up, making their own way through life. Each and every one of these young people would have given their right arm to have Ann here with them today. Jodie's accident had scared every member of this loving family, but at least they were able to be there for her, see that she got the best care possible. But Ann! The very mention of the youngest member of the family could bring tears to everyone's eyes. It was days like this when everyone got together that they felt so utterly useless. Each individual had the same thoughts. What on earth must be going through Ann's mind? Had anyone at the children's home tried to explain to the little girl what had happened to her? It would take a clever person to persuade her that she hadn't been abandoned. Or indeed to convince her that she meant the world to her family and that everyone still loved her. Sweet Jesus, they'd all have to work damned hard when they did bring her home; there was so much heartbreak that the whole family would have to try to make up for.

Derrick was helping John to be the perfect host. Although Derrick had a smile on his face, he looked tired, but these days he always did. Delia hardly took her eyes off him. How she wished that this business of getting their daughter back could be over and done with. Half the time she felt she was being selfish, thinking only of herself and how very much she missed their little girl. When all was said and done, Derrick was Ann's father, and by God he had been made to pay for that indiscretion. Very soon his hair would be completely grey, and the creases in his cheeks, blemishes left from when he had been so badly burnt, were getting deeper and deeper. Just looking at him made her heart ache, yet she loved him every bit as much as she had on the day they had first met.

Delia could hear her two sisters-in-discussing the house that John had tak Jodie to look at. Laraine in particular wa being very inquisitive; in fact, after the set-to she had had with Alan that morning, she was laughing to herself.

'It's ironic,' she said sharply, as Delia drew up another chair and joined her beside Jodie.

'What is?' Dee and Jodie asked in unison.

'There's me, almost having to plead with Alan for us both to sell our houses and buy one that could become a happy family home. But John takes Jodie, wheelchair an' all, to see just one property and by all accounts he's got her practically moving in.'

Jodie took hold of Laraine's hand and squeezed it. She felt great pity for her sister-in-law. Richard had been so young when he had died, without any warning. Laraine had done such a good job of bringing up Adele and Annabel; both girls were lovely, a credit to their mother. The trouble was, Laraine was never going to find another man like Richard.

'You liked the look of that house?' Dee asked, as Jodie wriggled her shoulders to get comfortable against the pile of pillows John had brought down from upstairs.

Jodie's face split into a dazzling smile. 'Honestly, Dee, you have to see it to believe it. Before John had even opened the front

or I was in love with the grounds. Every
ngle shrub, bush and tree is overgrown, yet
owers are blooming everywhere and the
roses are miraculous.'

'Lovely red ones, yes?' Laraine asked.

'Yes, and pink, and some were a gorgeous
creamy colour. It just goes to show how
reluctant nature is to give up.' Jodie went
on, 'There's a river nearby with swans on it,
and a weeping willow tree.'

'What about the inside of the house? Did
John manage to get you in?'

'Yes, he struggled a bit at first with the
wheelchair, but I saw enough to know that if
the surveyor's report is all right, that is the
house where John and I stand a good chance
of making a go of our second attempt at
married life.'

'How did John feel about it?' Laraine asked.

Jodie looked at her, and a flash of under-
standing passed between them.

'He would have written a cheque there and
then if he'd had his way. It's a good job that
Derrick is a bit more cautious. If only half of
John's plans come to fruition, then the hard
work will have been well worthwhile.'

'Typical,' Laraine said, grinning. 'John
buys a higgledy-piggledy run-down old place
that has been empty for years, and before we
know it you'll be living in a house that will be
the envy of all of us.'

Suddenly there was a knock on the front

door – not just an ordinary knock, mc
loud hammering. John put his glass dc
on the table and hurriedly went to answer

'Hello, son,' Marian Underwood sai
cheerfully. 'I rang around all the family and
got no answer, so I went next door and Jack
suggested that he bring us over in his car to
see Jodie.'

'Well, where are Mary and Jack now?'

'They're just coming, Jack had to park well
up the street.'

Delia had heard her mother-in-law's voice
and appeared in the doorway. 'Why are you
standing out there, Marian?'

'I'm waiting for your mum and dad. We've
all come over to see Jodie. Sounds as if the
whole blooming clan are here.'

Dee's heart sank. She knew exactly what
her mother-in-law was thinking: that there
was a party going on and the older gener-
ation hadn't been invited. But it wasn't like
that. It had been a spur-of-the-moment
kind of thing.

As her mum and dad reached the gate,
Marian called out to them, 'You're never
gonna believe it. Jodie was in that terrible accident and the whole family are here having
a bloody party. I knew something was going
on when I saw all the cars parked out here.'

'It isn't a party,' Dee's voice shook ever so
slightly, 'but I know Jodie will be really
pleased to see all of you. John, you take their

s and things. I'll go through and put the tle on.'

On hearing of the latest arrivals, Jodie ighed. 'I do feel a bit guilty,' she murmured. 'So much has happened between me and John lately and I have rather neglected his mother. Poor Marian, I hope she isn't in a bad mood. I'm trying to think of how to explain why everyone has turned up here today. Perhaps it would be best if I didn't say anything.'

'Hello, Ma-in-law,' Laraine called out cheerfully. 'It's great you've turned up with Dee's parents; these unplanned gatherings always work well.'

Jack Hartfield pushed past all the women, leant down over Jodie and softly kissed her forehead. 'How are you feeling?' he asked gently.

'Strange but true, Jack: today, for the first time, I am completely relaxed. I really am pleased that you have all come to see me today. When I was lying underground in the dark, with fires roaring around me, I wondered if I would ever see any of you again.'

Jack took hold of Jodie's right hand and enclosed it in both of his.

'Mary and I thanked God when we heard you had been brought out safe and taken to hospital. It's amazing how someone's life can change so drastically in the space of just a short time.'

No arguments: it was a joint decision. J[...] and Jodie were going ahead with the p[...] chase of Swan House.

A London architect was engaged. Mauric[...] Hayward was the best there was. Even before the plans were drawn up, the whole site out at Alfriston had become a hive of activity. A local sweep had been discovered and he had spent three days sweeping the chimneys. The same thing with the windows; a local man had laughed when first approached, but he soon accepted the job when John proved that he and his wife were the new owners of Swan House. Two young men from the local garden centre had started to clear the rubbish from the grounds before any attempt was made to start cutting back the undergrowth and the very tall trees.

The main structural alteration was that the roof was to be raised, allowing for two bedrooms to be positioned on the first floor.

What seemed like an army of carpenters were working on restoring the wooden floors, all the doors and cupboards. Discussions with a team of plumbers had led to plans being submitted for two bathrooms to be installed, one on the ground floor and one on the first floor, as well as two separate toilets. So many renovations.

So far nothing had been done about the huge kitchen. John was adamant that that

Jodie's department, but he kept a beady on her, not allowing her to get over-ed, and whenever she had a hospital or octor's appointment he always insisted that he himself took her by car.

Truth be told, Jodie was having a whale of a time, though she did tire very easily and there were bad days when terrifying memories would recur and catch her unawares.

However, Laraine and Delia kept her up to date by bringing her samples of material for the making of curtains and cushions, telling her she had to get well and become mobile again because she had to be at the house to supervise things. Jodie thought that was jumping the gun a bit. Michael Connelly and Danny Spencer also came into their own. They were both so sophisticated and stylish. Already they had bought Jodie and John a house-warming present of beautiful table linen. 'To be used when you have dinner parties,' they had said.

They were not the only ones. Word had spread, and it really was as if Jodie and John had just got married for the first time. Neighbours as well as Jodie's customers and clients flocked to her house, bringing gifts.

Jodie and John were hardly able to believe they were getting on so well, that they were back together as man and wife at long last. They were still having to get to really know each other all over again, but Jodie felt they

had both learnt so much and wou
better people because of that knowl
Reg and Lenny were over the moon; the
that their parents were living under t
same roof was fantastic.

Now Jodie was impatient to move to Swan
House.

She supposed it was inevitable that delays
would happen during the restoration, but she
hoped and prayed that it wouldn't be too
long before they were giving their new address in Alfriston to their friends and relatives.

# Chapter 27

The time was drawing nigh. Five more days and it would be the first of September, and once more Derrick and Delia would be appearing in court defending an action brought by Miss Chloe Warburg. The petition was a request that the custodianship of Ann Underwood should be removed from Mr and Mrs Underwood and that full custody should be granted to the woman who had actually given birth to the child.

With only a short time to go, the situation between Derrick and Delia was becoming strained. It wasn't helping that Dee absolutely refused to meet Chloe Warburg – or 'that woman', as she had taken to calling her. At times she had also called her several other names, which didn't help matters.

'Bloody cheeky bitch,' she had been known to exclaim. What right had the woman to turn up almost six years after she had abandoned Ann? 'I'd like to kill her!'

Derrick knew she didn't mean it. Delia could never be violent. He didn't think she was weak, but where Ann was concerned she was very vulnerable. At times he also thought she was in some kind of shock. She had been absolutely dazed by the dis that there might be a chance that would be taken away from them. If she herself given birth to that child she could have loved her more or been a better moth than she had been over the years.

He wished there was something he could do for his wife. Something to heal or soothe her. He owed her so much, and he loved her more than words could say. During that terrible period when he had undergone so many operations, she had always been there for him, helping him through his pain and his nightmares. Loving him unconditionally.

'I know it is up to me,' he declared out loud. 'We have to keep our daughter, but what more can we do to prove that we are good parents? We have to fight when we have our day in court. Prove to the best of our ability that Ann Underwood is our little girl, our daughter.'

Much the same thoughts were going through Delia's head. She was so glad that at last the date of the final hearing was almost here.

Jane Clarkson had been so encouraging, but there was always a chance that this panel of magistrates would consider that Ann should be brought up by the woman who had given birth to her.

The very thought had Dee gasping for

n. How the hell did you tell a six-year-
that you were not and never had been
mother, and that she must go to a
reign country to live with strangers?

'I just wouldn't be able to do it,' yelled
Dee, smacking the tabletop with the flat of
her hand.

Folk were fond of saying that you got over
grief eventually. But Dee knew that if Ann
was taken away from her she wouldn't get
over it, not now, not for as long as she lived.

Without warning she found herself
wishing that she had a film of their lives over
the past six years, when she and Derrick had
been the only parents Ann had ever known.
It would serve to show Chloe Warburg and
those magistrates and judges that there was
a whole lot more to bringing up a child than
they could imagine, and that no child was
ever loved more than Ann was. Yes, it should
be made compulsory for that woman to sit
and watch Ann as she opened her presents
on Christmas morning, and as she blew out
the candles on her birthday cake and played
games with all her little school friends. That
was what had happened each and every year
since she was born. Until now!

If they had to lose her, Dee thought, she
would rather have known from the very
beginning, then she would have taken each
day and held on to it, kept a recording of
their time together. Instead of assuming that

they would have a future where Ann
grow up, go to college, bring her boyfri
home, and the day that would dawn w.
her father walked her down the aisle.

Suddenly Dee wished she could confror.
Chloe Warburg face to face and tell her to
go to hell. And if the woman was granted
custody of Ann, wherever she chose to live it
had better be a long way from any of the
Underwood family.

Delia came into the small courtroom looking pale and tight-lipped. She and Derrick
were about to slip into seats at the back of
the room at almost exactly the same time as
Jane Clarkson and her secretary filed in.
Jane beckoned to them to come down to the
front of the court, explaining that they were
to sit at a table with her.

They had both been taken by surprise by
the number of journalists and photographers
waiting outside. They were well aware of the
public interest ever since Ann had been
abducted, and the sympathy mail they had
received from well-wishers had given them
encouragement. However, all that had been a
long time ago, and they had presumed that
interest in their case had lessened.
Apparently that was not so.

It was a sunny September day. The courtroom had bare brick walls, a high ceiling
and narrow windows set high in the roof.

lifted her head and watched the par-
ticles of dust dance madly in the sunbeams
that slanted across the room. She soon
realised that the place was getting crowded,
but she hadn't the courage to turn her head
and look around.

Jane put her hand on Delia's leg, because
she was jiggling it about nervously without
even knowing she was doing it. Then, seeing
how nervous Delia was, she took hold of her
hand, gave it a small squeeze, and instantly
released it. Smiling now she said, 'You look
fine, Delia.' She was glancing at her smart
navy blue suit and tailored white blouse.

'Thank you,' Delia murmured. 'You did
say to dress simply.'

Derrick wasn't doing too well. His mind
was racing, seeking answers. Would today's
verdict be the one he and Dee had been
wishing so hard for? But if wishes were
horses, then beggars would ride, he thought,
sighing sadly.

He must stay calm, he chided himself.

'Everything is going to be settled once and
for all,' Jane told him, her voice strong and
confident. 'Let's not dwell on the worst, but
think of the best outcome. You're not going
to lose your daughter: just hold on to that
thought.'

Derrick made no attempt to answer and a
silence developed between them.

Delia had her head bent and was now fret-

fully twisting a handkerchief in her ha
continually asking herself what they wo
do if the court's decision went against the.
Her nerves were taut, and she was filled wit
apprehension; so much so that she almost fel
off her seat as the bailiff requested that
everyone rise for the judge, Mr Matthew
Rickworth, and his associate magistrates.

Two ladies and two gentlemen filed in
with the judge and each placed a wooden
rack displaying their name at the front of the
bench where they were sitting. The two lady
magistrates were Edna Carrington and
Eugene Gillingham. The gentlemen were
Laurence McDonald and Russell Harwood.
Both men were barristers.

Derrick and Delia had met Russell Harwood on more than one occasion and were
well aware that he had been a member of
the Law Society specialist family panel for a
great many years. He was a good-looking
man, whose appearance spoke of him coming from the aristocracy, but neither Derrick
nor Delia was fooled by his looks. His voice
was always loud and booming, and they
both knew that there was no way this man
could be persuaded to do anything he didn't
agree with. Laurence McDonald was in his
early fifties; he too was a distinguished-
looking man, with deep-set brown eyes, and
dark hair sprinkled with grey.

The two women were the matronly type.

a Carrington wore a charcoal-grey suit
in the very palest of blue blouses and a
vy blue scarf that had a gold crest em-
roidered on it. Eugene Gillingham looked
as if she had just had a holiday abroad. Her
face was brown from the sun. The expensive-
looking beige suit she wore was simplicity
personified, and her brown silk blouse complemented it perfectly.

When all the shuffling had stopped and
everyone was seated, Judge Rickworth made
ready to deliver his opening comments.
Having cleared his throat, pushed his rim-
less glasses further up his nose and run his
hand over his thinning grey hair, he began
to speak.

'The session being held here today is
known as a family court. Men and women
who work within the legal profession know
better than to become emotionally and personally involved with their clients, but that
doesn't mean that it doesn't happen. Many
people in this country have come to know
and to care about Ann Underwood. No one,
myself included, will dispute that the circumstances surrounding this case are heart-
rending and very distressing.

'As a panel, however, we shall listen to the
facts, taking into account that this case has
been brought for lawful decisions to be
made. It is not about compassion or sympathy; it is the rightful law we are here to

346

consider, and it will be the law th
stipulate the outcome. We shall adjuc
as a team, which means our conclusion
be accepted by both sides. Our verdict
be final.'

The silence that followed had Delia
shaking nervously.

Judge Rickworth nodded towards Jane and
in a softer voice said, 'Miss Clarkson, how do
you intend to open the proceedings?'

'I'd like to go back to the beginning, if it
pleases your honour. To when Captain Derrick Underwood was in command of an oil
tanker on which there was an explosion
while at sea. I would like to put Mr Robert
Patterson on the stand.'

Derrick and Delia had been totally un-
aware that Bob had been roped into their
troubles, or even as to when and where he
had been contacted.

As a serving member of the Merchant
Navy, he looked immaculate in his uniform
as he walked to the front of the court. Once
he had been sworn in the judge said, 'Take
your time, Mr Patterson. In your own words,
can you tell us how the two main participants
in this case came to know each other?'

Bob cleared his throat. 'I wasn't on board
the tanker when the explosion occurred, a
tragedy in which Captain Underwood was
injured so very badly. He was flown to a
base owned by the shipping line to have his

peration, and I stayed with him until
as finally discharged in England. In all,
tended to the captain for two years.' He
used, but was encouraged to continue as
ach member of the judging panel nodded
their heads.

'By the time the captain was brought to a
specialist burns unit in Belgium, he was still
suffering from horrific wounds and was facing a great many more operations. However,
there were times when it was his mental
state that caused the greatest worry; not
only to his medical advisers but to myself
too.'

'Oh no!' Delia was heard to mutter.

A nod from the judge told Bob to continue.

'Captain Underwood had made it known
from the very beginning that members of his
family were not to be made aware of what
had happened to him or notified of his
whereabouts. There was one exception; his
eldest brother came twice, maybe three times
to visit, mainly because the captain had given
him power over his legal affairs. He had to
make sure that his wife and sons were finan-
cially taken care of. Other than that, the
captain didn't think much of the prospect of
a life in the future. He was already well aware
that people turned away from looking at him.
The worst part was when folk let him know
how sorry they felt for him. He hated that.

Got very low, he did. That's when he
times lost his temper, or even worse, h
the will to carry on.

'Then one day, when he was well bei
par, I had what I thought was a brainwav
Having got approval from the doctors who
were treating the captain, I arranged for
Miss Warburg to spend some time with him.
At the time, everyone concerned was under
the impression that things had gone well. If
nothing else, it had allowed the captain to
feel he was still a man.'

As Bob finished speaking, his shoulders
dropped and he was heard to sigh heavily.

The judge turned to his associates. 'Have
any of you a question you'd like to put to Mr
Patterson?'

Edna Carrington raised a hand. 'Have you
been in touch with Mr and Mrs Underwood
since that time in Belgium?'

'I have never lost touch, madam. I attended
to the captain before and after every operation in all of the various hospitals in several
countries. When I heard about Miss Warburg
coming to London to give birth to the baby
girl she abandoned the very next day,
Captain Underwood was receiving treatment
in East Grinstead. That was the first time I
was introduced to Mrs Underwood. Until
then the captain had kept his injuries a secret
from his family.'

Bob paused for a moment and cleared his

Aware that the magistrates and the were expecting more, he continued.

well remember when finally Mrs Under- od was allowed in to see her husband. Did e recoil or walk away? No, she did not. She was naturally terrified at the sight of him, but also hurt that she hadn't been with him right from the beginning. What she did do was pull herself together and tell him that no matter what had happened to him, he was still her husband, still the same loving man inside.

'I can tell you now, he shouted and hollered at her, said he didn't want her near him. Declared himself to be a freak. Still she wasn't put off. From that day onwards she visited him in each and every hospital until he was allowed home, even though she spent much of the time sitting in lonely waiting rooms. Just think about it. Eighteen months is a long time to sit on and off in a waiting room.'

'Thank you, Mr Patterson,' Mrs Carrington said softly.

'You may stand down,' the judge said, nodding at Bob.

'I have been given to understand that Miss Warburg has no counsel acting for her, is that right?' The judge raised his head so that his eyes could meet Chloe's.

Chloe stood up. 'Yes, your honour, I don't need anyone to speak for me. I will tell the truth.'

'Miss Warburg, did you realise th[...] present your own case you have the r[...] ask questions of the witnesses? Do you[...] to have Mr Patterson recalled?'

'No thank you, sir.'

'In that case, the bailiff will advise you.'

Chloe was sworn in. She pushed her chest out and made her hands into tight fists before she started to speak.

'This baby girl that all this discussion is about belongs to me. She is my flesh and blood. Not hers.' She pointed a finger at where Delia was sitting. 'I gave birth to her and yes, I had to go home and leave her behind because I had no money. Things are different now. I am going to be married to a wealthy man who will care and provide for both of us. My baby does not need to live with strangers any longer.'

Chloe fell silent and Laurence McDonald shot out a question. 'Why the change of heart?'

Chloe tried hard not to be daunted by him. 'Circumstances do change, you know,' she said, glaring at him.

Silence hung heavily until the judge asked, 'Miss Warburg, have you no more to say?'

'No, sir. I said I would tell the truth, and I have.'

'Miss Clarkson?' Judge Rickworth raised his eyebrows in question and Jane got to her feet.

honour, so many horrific incidents
ιken place since the child in question
aken into safe custody that Mr Under-
.d has been driven to retaliate. Recently
sought advice from a reputable firm of
rivate detectives. Would the court deem it
ιn order for Anthony Wilbourne, a partner
in the firm Discretion Foremost, to present
his findings?'

There were a few minutes of quiet whis-
pering amongst the members of the panel.
Eventually the judge spoke.

'Miss Clarkson, we have decided to call a
recess in order that we may discuss your request. This court will resume at two o'clock.'

'All rise,' the bailiff called, but Jane Clarkson and her secretary were already steering
Derrick and Delia out through a side entrance. The last thing they wanted was a con-
frontation with Chloe Warburg.

# Chapter 28

At one point in her life Jane Clarkson had wanted to save the world. She had attended law school, listened to the professors and truly believed that laws were made to rid society of evil men and women. She hadn't been working in the outside world for any length of time before she realised that she had not chosen a Christian crusade, only a job. Being in the right didn't always have anything to do with a verdict. Sometimes a silver tongue and a lot of persuasion helped to win the day.

The court they had been in this morning was situated right out in a country village near the town of Uckfield. As it happened, Jane had friends who owned a tea room in the area, and before she had ushered Derrick and Delia into her car she had made a phone call. The result was that a very nice light lunch was ready for them when they arrived, and almost before they were seated, coffee and hot milk had appeared on their table.

Meanwhile, back at court, five lunches had been delivered from the local pub.

ene Gillingham started the ball rolling
.inking out loud. 'What could be more
.y than the woman who gave birth to
.ur child turning up after six years and
.uddenly deciding it's time for her to be the
child's mother?'

Judge Rickworth had washed his meal
down with half a pint of milk stout. Suddenly, without quite knowing why, he said,
'This case brings to my mind the legend of
King Solomon. In that case there were two
women who claimed they were both the
mother of one baby. After much deliber-
ation, the King suggested cutting the infant
in half with a sword, in order to discover
which parent would relinquish her claim on
the child rather than see it harmed. Text-
book wisdom, eh! Problem solved, and no
blood shed. But that was just fiction. In the
real world, the case we are considering
today, we have to ask ourselves: are both
parents worthy? Or did the woman who has
instigated these proceedings give up her
rights on the day she abandoned the baby?'

A profound silence followed the judge's
words. It was broken by Russell Harwood.

'This case is an utter mess. It should never
have been allowed to come to court. If only
the adults could have been persuaded to act
reasonably and with compassion, maybe a
swift settlement could have been reached.'

'I think you have just spoken for each and

every one of us,' Laurence McDona.
quietly, and his fellow panel members
hear the sincerity in his voice as he .
tinued. 'What can one possibly say to
woman who after all this time has decide
she wants her previous decision to be
reversed?'

Again a thoughtful silence until Edna Carrington felt she had to add her comments.
'Whichever way one looks at this situation,
we must pay a great tribute to Mrs Underwood. From the notes we have read, we
learn that she simply saw a newborn baby
who had been deserted by her mother. She
plainly took that baby to her heart and for
the past six years has loved her as her own.
Not only seeing to the child's needs, but
letting her know she is wanted every minute
of every day through sickness and health.'

One would have had to have a heart of
stone not to be moved by that declaration.

It was a minute or two before the judge
reminded them of Jane Clarkson's request.

Laurence McDonald replied, 'It wouldn't
be the first time that the court has listened
to evidence from a private detective, and I
can bear witness that Discretion Foremost
has proved in the past to be a reputable
establishment.' He then suggested that they
take a vote on the matter.

All five persons in the room raised their
hand.

Clarkson had deliberately returned to court early to have a preview of the terial Anthony Wilbourne was going to ve her.

Luckily he had anticipated this and had written the information down in detail. As he handed her his notes he said, 'And before you ask, Miss Clarkson, yes, I can substantiate every single piece of evidence with written proof.'

They shook hands and smiled at each other.

'Good luck,' Anthony murmured.

'If God is on our side, we shan't need any luck,' Jane replied with another smile.

At five minutes past two, one could have heard a pin drop as Chloe Warburg came forward to stand once again in the witness box. Jane spread her hands across the top of the long wooden rail that was fixed in front of the bench, then looked up at Chloe and started to speak.

'Let me get this straight, Miss Warburg. You voluntarily relinquished custody of your daughter only hours after she was born, and now, six years later, you want to take her to Belgium to live with you and your new husband.'

Chloe nodded. 'You've got it in one,' she replied cheekily.

'Thank you, Miss Warburg – and ( [...]
from these papers I have in my han[...]
that is not your legal name. You cer[...]
have had a colourful past. Have you t[...]
married before?'

'Yes, but that has nothing to do with you[...]

'You are quite right, it hasn't, but I am sure
it will benefit the court to hear that you were
married at the age of seventeen to a very
elderly gentleman who apparently promised
to leave you his large fortune. Sadly, after the
wedding your husband only lived for five
months. He died leaving no will, but his five
children and numerous grandchildren very
quickly settled his affairs. In other words,
they came to an agreement with you.'

Jane Clarkson took note of the shocked
expression on Chloe Warburg's face, but she
pressed on.

'At the age of twenty you underwent an
abortion. Will you please tell the court
whether you had married again by then, and
why you saw fit to abort that pregnancy.'

'No, I will not,' Chloe said forcefully.

Jane let the silence that followed hang for
a moment, and when the judge did not insist that Chloe answer the question, she
carried on.

'When you were twenty-two years old, you
were fined and served a prison sentence for
attacking a male client.'

Chloe remained silent and Jane looked up

In her heart she felt sadness for this ⸺an. Why the hell had she ever degraded ⸺elf by bringing this vicious case to court? ⸺ ask you once again, Miss Warburg, in ⸺espect of the baby you abandoned at birth, why the change of heart?'

Chloe looked as though she was about to panic. In desperation she blurted out, 'Because I have had an operation and can no longer have children. I want the baby I gave birth to.'

Jane sighed softly. 'The baby you gave birth to is now a little girl who goes to school. You would take this child to live in a different country, where she wouldn't even be able to understand the language, where every single person she met would be a stranger. Please, Miss Warburg, explain to the court how, after all this time, you have reached the conclusion that you are the best person to care for this child. Is it not true that the woman she knows as her mother has been there for her from the day you walked away and left her? And as for her father, he not only took on all financial responsibility for her from day one, he also loves her dearly, as he has every right to do as her natural father.'

Chloe felt she was losing the battle, and it showed as she leant forward and raised her voice. 'Look here, you don't understand. I have not had an easy life. I thought I was doing the best for the baby when I left her.

Now my chances have improved. My ⬚
is a wealthy man and he agrees he w⬚
any amount of money just as long as yc⬚
me have my baby back.'

'When you say "back", Miss Warbur⬚
what exactly are you referring to? You hav⬚
admitted you left your baby when she was a
day old. Have you ever had her in your care
from that day to this?'

'No. Now please, all of you stop torment-
ing me and let me try and make it up to my
daughter.'

Jane Clarkson glanced down for a moment,
then looked up at the judge. 'No further
questions, your honour,' she told him.

The judge stood up. 'My colleagues and I
need to refer to our notes and then we shall
make our ruling. There will be a recess of
roughly twenty minutes; please do not leave
your seats.'

Derrick and Delia were holding hands,
both staring at the ceiling.

'What do you think?' Derrick asked.

Dee turned to face him. 'Darling, I can't
think straight, and I certainly can't draw
conclusions. We'll have to wait and see.'

Twenty minutes dragged by, then on the
very dot the five officials were back on the
bench. The courtroom was so quiet Dee
could hear herself breathing. Derrick was
clutching her hand so tightly it hurt.

Judge Rickworth put his glasses on and

.o speak.

as a panel are in complete agreement
t the outcome we have arrived at regard-
this sad case. The evidence has clearly
own that although Miss Chloe Warburg is
ne natural mother of Ann Underwood, she
abandoned the child just twenty-four hours
after she was born and made no attempt
whatsoever to contact her afterwards. It is
also clear that Ann Underwood has been
given a good loving upbringing by her father
and his wife and has enjoyed the affection
and care she has received from a large
extended family.

'On that evidence we are agreed that the
child should and must be allowed to remain
with the only parents she has ever known.
However...'

Dee held her breath for so long she almost
choked, and she was not the only one!

'We debated long and hard about Miss
Warburg's rights. Over the coming years it
will be a hard task for Ann's parents to answer their daughter's questions. Because, as
she grows up, questions there surely will be.
Our decision is that when Ann reaches the
age of sixteen, she should be made fully
aware of who her birth mother was. By then
she will be able to make her own decisions,
and the future will be up to her.'

Inside Delia's head just the one word was
resounding: Yes, yes, yes. She wanted to

shout out, *What do we do now? Where* little girl? *When will we be able to get her*

'Are you all right?' Derrick asked soft.

Delia blinked, and she came back to h. 'Oh … yes.' Slowly a smile spread over h face. 'Yes!' she said again.

Jane Clarkson told them that Ann was waiting in the judge's chambers. She was also warned that they'd have to cope with the frenzy of the press.

She was right. As they stepped into the corridor, they were met with sheer hysteria: flash bulbs and confusion from reporters and congratulations being yelled from all quarters. Anthony Wilbourne was giving them the thumbs-up sign and the elegantly dressed Miss Baldwin was there too, smiling and waving at them. Over the top of many heads they spied Martin and Michael, both of them pumping their fists in the air.

Someone opened the door to the office, and Derrick and Delia virtually burst into the room.

Derrick was watching Delia. He couldn't take the first step; he felt it should be her privilege.

Delia blinked away her tears and stared at the little girl standing so quietly with her back to the window. She was dressed in a dark coat that reached almost to her ankles and a white woolly hat pulled down over her ears, hiding her lovely curly hair. They had

so close to losing her, and now their
s were overflowing with thanks. Delia
ed at Derrick, lost for words.

'Should you pick her up?' she asked.

'Let's go one each side of her,' he suggested.

'Hello, darling,' said Dee. 'We're going to
take you home now.'

There was no reply, but Ann looked at
both of her parents, then reached out and
took hold of their hands.

Outside in the corridor, the masses had
thinned out. When they saw their parents,
Michael and Martin gave a whoop of joy and
without hesitation covered the distance
between them. Michael got there first and
swept Ann up into his arms, hugging her
tightly before handing her over to Martin,
who in turn also kissed her, hugged her and
swung her around. As he put her down on
her feet it was obvious that Ann was crying,
but when Michael took a big white handkerchief from his pocket with the intention
of wiping her little face, she pushed his hand
away, looked up at both of her brothers and
laughed. Really laughed out loud.

It was the happiest sound her parents had
heard for many a long day.

The telephone was ringing as they came into
the house. Martin answered the call to find it

was Laraine on the line. When ⸻
into the lounge he said to his ⸻
done as you suggested, Dad. Lar⸻
that the family won't come round ⸻
give our Ann time to get used to the i⸻
she really is home. She reckons that ⸻
Mum and our Ann will be on the local
news this evening. Anyway, Michael and I a⸻
going to push off now We'll see you
tomorrow.'

So far Ann had still not uttered one word,
but there was nothing wrong with her hearing. Climbing out of the deep armchair in
which she had been sitting, she walked across
the floor and stood in front of her brothers.
As they had done previously, they each in
turn swept her up into their brawny arms and
held her close, assuring her that they would
be coming back to see her again in the morning. It was obvious she didn't want them to
leave.

With their going, the house seemed very
quiet. Derrick picked Ann up and sat her on
his lap before saying, 'Sweetheart, Mummy
and I have a really lovely surprise for you,
but I have to go out for a short while to fetch
this special present.'

Immediately Ann grasped hold of his
shirtsleeve and shook her head from side to
side.

'I shall only be gone a little while. Mummy
will give you a nice bath and you can put

pretty nightdresses on, and
back we'll have a lovely tea and
see what you think of your present.'
the next half-hour Delia felt as if every
she had ever uttered had been an-
ed. Lifting that little body into the warm
py bath water, giving her rubber toys to
splash about with, pouring shampoo on to
her own hands and running her fingers
through that thick curly hair, and then lifting
her out, smothered in a huge warm bath
towel, were all things she had dreaded she
might never again have the opportunity to
do.

Although it was early September, the boys
had lit a fire in the lounge for their parents
and Ann to come home to, and Derrick's
heart missed a beat as he opened the door
and looked into the room to see his beautiful
daughter curled up in her mother's lap. In
his own arms he was carrying a fluffy Cairn
terrier that was just twelve weeks old. He put
the puppy down, taking away the blanket it
had been wrapped in, and immediately the
tiny dog sniffed and then licked Ann's feet.
The little girl was beaming as she stroked the
puppy, and she was chuckling and making
all sorts of gurgling sounds.

'Before we have our tea, I thought we
should play a little game, although it won't
really be a game because this will be for real,'

Derrick said, looking straight into his small daughter's eyes as if forcing her to take notice. He turned his head until he was facing his wife. Delia was smiling, even though her eyes were full of tears.

'My proper name is Derrick Underwood. Mummy, what's yours?' Derrick asked very quietly.

Delia didn't hesitate; she guessed what Derrick was aiming to do.

'My proper name is Delia Underwood.'

Derrick picked up the puppy and, holding him with both hands, put his own nose close to that of the dog. In a funny voice he asked, 'Little puppy, what's your name?'

The puppy yapped twice, and Derrick laughed.

'There you are,' he said to Ann. 'Puppy has stated that his proper name is Fergus Underwood, and now he wants to know yours.'

There was a pause, but only a very slight one, before Ann said softly, 'My proper name is Ann Underwood.' And now the tears were rolling down Delia's cheeks.

Much later that night, after both Derrick and Delia had checked on Ann at least half a dozen times, they lay together in such happy silence they were afraid to break it. Eventually it was Delia who spoke.

'Why do really wonderful days have to come to an end?' she sighed softly.

'So that even more wonderful things can take place,' Derrick told her gently.

'What could be more wonderful than having Ann back home?' she queried.

'A birthday party for our six-year-old this coming weekend. A house-warming party when John and Jodie move into Swan House. A wedding when Alan and Laraine find the right home. Do you want me to go on, or can you not think of one happy event to add to the list?'

'I can think of a whole bunch of them, now you come to mention it,' Delia said, raising herself up on her elbows so that she could see the grin on her husband's face.

'Right-o, let's hear 'em.'

'All right,' Dee said, giggling. 'Try these for size. Reg and Lenny, Adele and Annabel and our boys will all get married, and each family will produce more cousins, nieces and nephews, and best of all, grandchildren. Jodie will fully recover, and she and John will move into Swan House and find real happiness second time around. Alan will finally agree to sell his house, and Laraine will make sure that he learns to live a little and smile properly. Will that do for starters?'

'I rather fancy it will!' Derrick said, beaming, as he gathered his wife into his arms, then under his breath he whispered, 'And may the Lord have mercy on us all.'

The publishers hope that this book has given you enjoyable reading. Large Print Books are especially designed to be as easy to see and hold as possible. If you wish a complete list of our books please ask at your local library or write directly to:

**Magna Large Print Books**
Magna House, Long Preston,
Skipton, North Yorkshire.
BD23 4ND

This Large Print Book, for people
who cannot read normal print,
is published under the auspices of

## THE ULVERSCROFT FOUNDATION

The publishers hope that this book has given you enjoyable reading. Large Print Books are especially designed to be as easy to see and hold as possible. If you wish a complete list of our books please ask at your local library or write directly to:

**Magna Large Print Books**
Magna House, Long Preston,
Skipton, North Yorkshire.
BD23 4ND

This Large Print Book, for people
who cannot read normal print,
is published under the auspices of

## THE ULVERSCROFT FOUNDATION